WHITE HEAT

Book Two
The Perfect Fire Trilogy

K. M. Grant

Walker & Company
New York

First published in the United Kingdom in 2008 by Quercus Publishing, Plc.
Published in the United States of America in 2009 by Walker Publishing Company, Inc.
Visit Walker & Company's Web site at www.bloomsburyteens.com

For information about permission to reproduce selections from this book, write to
Permissions, Walker & Company, 175 Fifth Avenue, New York, New York 10010

Library of Congress Cataloging-in-Publication Data
Grant, K. M. (Katie M.)
White heat / K.M. Grant.
p.   cm.—(Perfect fire trilogy; bk. 2)
Summary: As the conflict in Languedoc, also called Occitan, intensifies, Raimon, having
escaped the pyre, suppresses his longing to find his beloved Yolanda and, together with
Parsifal, carries the Blue Flame to the mountains where it serves to rally loyal Occitanians
to organize against the formidable French forces set to invade their beloved country.
ISBN-13: 978-0-8027-9695-0 · ISBN-10: 0-8027-9695-8
[1. Knights and knighthood—Fiction. 2. Albigenses—Fiction. 3. Languedoc (France)—
History—13th century—Fiction. 4. France—History—Louis IX, 1226–1270—Fiction.
5. Inquisition—Fiction. 6. Middle Ages—Fiction.] I. Title.
PZ7.G7667755Whi 2009   [Fic]—dc22   2008046984

Book design by Nicole Gastonguay
Typeset by Westchester Book Composition
Printed in the U.S.A. by Quebecor World Fairfield
2 4 6 8 10 9 7 5 3 1

For those who fall in love in troubled times

WHITE HEAT

Prologue

A SECOND GREETING

Is it this time already? I have slept too long! Excuse me while I get my bearings. There now, let me see. Yes, thank goodness. I'm in much the same shape as I was when I went to sleep. A few boulders have fallen, the vines have spread, and with their eternal dripping persistence several rivers have worn new paths for themselves. But that's only to be expected. Let me shake myself. I love to feel the tickle of a thousand sloughed snake skins. How they glitter on my crags. See! One has caught the eye of an ibex. He lowers his head and the curved shadow of his horns disturbs a viper nursing her young. I feel her slither back inside her cave even though she'd like to bask in the sun. It must be August.

Now I'm properly awake. At what point in my story did I, the Amouroix, a small county in the larger Occitan resting under the northern side of the Pyrenean mountains, leave you? I think it was when Yolanda—no, that's not the way to do it. While I dozed, you have been busy with other things. We must catch up properly.

I have already told you how the Blue Flame of the Occitan, the Flame that held the essence of the Occitan soul within itself, was brought home in the care of Parsifal, an old and unsuccessful knight, and how it showed itself in my hills when Occitania was under attack not just from the French King Louis but also from within. It was to you that I revealed, hanging my head with shame, that when the Flame returned, instead of finding an Occitan united against her enemies, it found her divided into Catholics and Cathars, each struggling against the other instead of against their real enemy. It's strange to think what fools men were for God in those days. I mean, how can you hate in the name of the God of Love? Yet hate they did, with Catholic inquisitors lighting pyres to consume the living, and Cathar high priests, those they called perfecti, creeping about like shadows. Not that the Cathars feared death. On the contrary. To the perfecti, death was preferable to life since they chose to believe that all the beauties of this world were lures set by the devil. Each of these, Catholic inquisitor and Cathar heretic, wanted the Flame because possessing it would show that the Occitan was theirs alone.

As I take up my tale again, may I ask you something? Why is it that people of your time think that those who lived long ago did not love each other with the passion you so brazenly display? Please don't be affronted if I tell you how very wrong you are. Take Raimon, for example. He knew about love. At fifteen, he had already been swept up in its unsettling and all-consuming rush. For him, Yolanda was the starry future even amid the troubles of his present, and his troubles were not small. His mother, father, and sister had all fallen under the spell of one particular perfectus known as the White Wolf. In thrall to this man's implacable will, his mother had starved and his father and sister had fled. And Yolanda's family, the family of the girl for whom Raimon would have laid down his life, as she would have done for him, could not—or would not—come to his aid. Her family were Catholics, you see, and when her inquisitor uncle was murdered, her brother, Aimery, count of my lands since his father's death, found Raimon a convenient scapegoat and condemned him to burn on a pyre.

Aimery did not see the Occitan's future as Raimon did. He saw only that whoever had the Flame, Catholic or Cathar, it would not be theirs for long because King Louis of France wanted it. And what King Louis wanted, he had the power to get. Already the king's impatience against his troublesome southern neighbor was growing. Soon he would come as conqueror, taking the Flame and with it the Occitan's independence. In a year or two at most, so Aimery reckoned, the Occitan would be no more.

He did not view this as a disaster. Rather, Aimery saw a fine opportunity for his own advancement and mine too. He would not wait for me, the Amouroix, to be vanquished like the rest of the Occitanian counties. Instead, before a drop of Amouroix blood was spilled, he would willingly give me, and himself as my lord, into the king's service. What was more, he would marry Yolanda off to Sir Hugh des Arcis, a French knight of high degree who had the ear and confidence of the king. With Sir Hugh des Arcis as his brother-in-law, Aimery would be safe when the French armies finally rolled in, and my lands would escape the scourge of a war of conquest. And Aimery also had something else in mind, something that would surely cement his place as one of King Louis's newest but most loyal subjects: the king would receive the Blue Flame from Aimery himself. That would be the moment when King Louis would know he had won.

But things had not gone quite Aimery's way. Raimon had been saved from the pyre and now had the Flame in his possession. Moreover, though the boy's heart told him to follow Yolanda north to Paris and reclaim her from Sir Hugh, it also told him that I, the Amouroix, and the whole Occitan, needed him. So he made his choice. With all the courage he could muster and Sir Parsifal at his side, he held the Flame high, turned south, and stood tall for the Occitan and for freedom.

1

Aimery's Château

So come with me now to August 1242, as Aimery stood at the topmost window of his château, gazing out to the fires on the hilltop some way beyond. His ears were filled with the howling of a dog but his eyes had fixed with particular intensity on the small prick of blue on the edge of the far hill. The Flame was taunting him from its lofty eminence, like a splendid future just out of reach. The dog howled and howled.

A servant interrupted the howling. "Alain is back from the hillside, sir."

Aimery stirred. "Will that damnable hound never stop?"

The servant grimaced. "Brees is missing his mistress."

"It was quite wrong of Sir Hugh to leave him behind. He should have let Yolanda take the animal to Paris. A dog could hardly have upset the marriage plans. If he doesn't shut up of his own accord, I'll make him." Aimery took one more look at the prick of blue and then hurried to the great hall. Despite the dozens of flambeaux and torches that lit every corner of the painted vault and despite the men sprawled about, the air was full of a brittle restlessness. Though the new count tried his best to pretend the atmosphere was no different from when his father was alive—the fire was still bright with flaming logs and the usual stench of cooked meat pervaded every corner—even he felt that the beating heart of the place was missing. There were no troubadours singing dawn songs to parting lovers, no knights joshing each other over favors from ladies, no servants tapping their feet to an unfinished rhythm. There was no easy laughter, nobody feasting except to appease their hunger, and above all, no Yolanda spinning over the rushes. Yet Aimery stiffened his spine. What did an atmosphere matter? New times were coming. Soon, Aimery thought, the Blue Flame would be safely in Paris, his sister would be Lady des Arcis, and Castelneuf would exchange the restless vibrancy of the south for the more settled sophistication of the royal court of the north.

It says something for him, perhaps, that though he had never been a sentimental man and had no intention of succumbing now, he still couldn't shake off an unwanted and unexpected tendril of regret as he looked about him. He couldn't deny that there had been good times here, some of which, being older, he could probably remember better than his sister. For instance, he could actually remember the day the two squabbling troubadours, Gui and Guerau, arrived, as unlikely a pairing as a stork and a bull. He recalled when his mother, as a gentle joke, had set up a Court of Love and how he had sat as a page at the feet of a blushing knight on trial for stealing another knight's amorous verses. Aimery had thought it very silly but it was impossible to forget. His thoughts made him uncomfortable and he was glad to see his squire. "Alain. What news?" Brees's howling was still audible, even in here.

Alain was splashing his face in a barrel and now he wiped the drops off with a rough cloth. "We're nearly through the rock, Sir Aimery," he said. "Another couple of weeks, three at most, and we should be able to storm the camp. The men have worked well even in the heat of the day and Raimon's men have only managed to pick off a few. It's a real shame getting through that rock's the only way to carve out enough room to launch a proper attack. Until the rock's gone, those camped up above find it far too easy to use us as target practice."

"Never mind. It sounds as though we shan't have to worry about that much longer." Aimery sat down in a new highbacked oak chair he had ordered for himself. It had curved arms intricately decorated with figures from both mythology and the Bible and he was very pleased with it.

Alain coughed. "There is one bit of bad news."

"Oh?"

"The armorer has gone over to Raimon, and four more of your knights."

Annoyed, Aimery gripped a pair of carved angels' heads until they bruised the palms of his hands. "Idiots. Why, with our victory so near?" It was a question to which he expected no answer. He bit his lower lip hard and then loosened his fingers. "Oh well, what does it matter who joins Raimon Belot now? When we take the Flame he'll be just a weaver again, like his father, without even a loom to his name." He reached out and dug Alain in the ribs. "Weavers should stick to making clothes, not try their hand at strategy and warfare, eh! As for the knights"—he grimaced because, despite his words, their defection did hurt—"when I hand the Blue Flame over to the King of France, I'll still have enough good men about me. If others want to go to the devil with Raimon, let them." A shadow crossed his face. "Just so long as we get the Flame before Count

Raymond of Toulouse arrives. He's another fool, still trying to unite the Occitan behind him. Why doesn't everybody understand that it's really far better to give in to the king gracefully?"

He stood and paced about. "It's so frustrating that Count Raymond's still my overlord. I really don't see why I owe him any allegiance at all now." He spiked some meat from a table onto his dagger as though he were spiking Count Raymond. He waved it about, then ate it and made a face. Mother of all Saints, where did his steward find such wretched cooks? A globule of grease dripped down his chin and he seized Alain's proffered towel without thanks. "Go back to the hillside and tell the knights and all the Castelneuf men that I'll stand for no slacking until they've cracked the overhang. If they don't get the Flame from the weaver before Raymond appears they'll get no pay." He spat. How could meat smell of old fish? "Once the Flame's with the king of France, Count Raymond will be nothing to us. Go at once. You can eat later. I'll have the cooks keep something for you. That should be a treat."

He walked with his squire out of the hall and stopped at the top of the château's outside steps, looking about with some satisfaction. His home was no longer the ramshackle affair it had been in his father's day. The steps on which he was standing were smooth and even and the courtyards had lost their weeds so that the newly naked stones blushed ochre and russet. He had had a loft built above the stables and filled it with carrier pigeons. Never again would Castelneuf be out of touch. Aimery thought that Yolanda would not recognize the place if she returned and then thought it would be better if she never did.

As if he sensed Aimery was thinking of his beloved mistress,

Brees's howls increased in volume. Three pigeons flew off in fright as Aimery finally lost his temper. "I'm coming for you, Brees! I'm coming for you!" he yelled. Unheeding, Brees howled even louder and inside the kennels the hounds began to howl in a sympathetic chorus until the whole place resonated. Aimery ran down the steps and across the cobbles. Seizing a whip from the armory, he threw open the kennel door. When he was finished, there was blood on the straw.

Much later on, when Aimery was long back in the hall, with much scuffling and nipping six dogboys, those orphaned or simple-minded children dumped in the kennels to be brought up as hounds themselves, and the huntsman crept outside. When they got near the gate, they hesitated and then returned to the kennels. While the huntsman kept a lookout, the dogboys used each other as human steps to climb over the barrier and tumble into the stall in which Brees, his howls now reduced to whimpers, was confined. One dogboy licked his nose. Another bit through his rope. On four legs and two, they set about shoveling his ungainly weight over the wooden partition and then scrabbled over after him. He lay panting for a moment before finally crawling into the open where the huntsman regarded him with the pity all huntsmen reserve for dogs with neither breeding nor beauty. "You may be useless but I don't see why you should be thrashed," the huntsman said before turning with tears in his eyes to bid farewell once again to the hounds he was leaving behind. They were dearer than children to him but they needed their comforts, particularly Farvel, the hound he loved best. "Good-bye, my lovelies," he whispered, recognizing each individual sniffle, each sigh. "God keep you." They cocked their ears as his easy, swinging steps receded, and some whimpered.

The huntsman blocked his ears as he neatly bypassed the porter and, keeping his curious human pack at his heels and Brees by his side, slipped through the open postern door. Once outside, he shook himself, saw the Flame flickering in the distance, and set his course toward it.

2

Siege

Raimon was sitting with his back against a weatherworn boulder staring at a bone-breaker vulture riding the current high above him. Beside him, the Blue Flame burned fitfully in its little carved box, the oil in its silver holder a dark glimmer. The boy's slick of black hair was speckled with dust and his skin, drawn tightly over the bones of his face, gave him a look much older than his years. He couldn't take his eyes off the vulture as it glided around and around on its invisible roundabout, and when it plunged he followed it until it dropped out of sight. A hare perhaps, he thought. It was impossible not to be envious.

He stretched, then tensed as he recognized Parsifal's heavy tread. At once he forgot the vulture. Pray God this was the news they had been waiting for. The old knight appeared around the corner of the boulder, glanced at the Flame, and then held out a parchment. His hands, always so much whiter than the rest of him, were hardly white now. Like everybody else, he was filthy with grime that was too deep to wash out even had there been enough water for bathing. Over the course of the siege—for that was what their entrapment by Aimery's men on this untidy, precipitous mass had turned into—dirt had embedded itself into his skin as sand beds into a sponge. As a matter of fact, Parsifal was glad of it because he was beginning to sicken and did not wish anybody to notice. I noticed, of course, because I felt his faltering tread, but his secret was safe with me.

Raimon did not unroll the parchment at once. He just gripped it. "He's coming?"

Parsifal nodded. "He's coming."

Raimon sat down again, and his shoulders sagged with relief. "Thank God for that. We can't hold out much longer. Have you seen the damage the soldiers have done to the overhang just today? They've built a heavier machine. It took eight oxen to get it here." He unrolled the parchment and read it quickly. "It says to be patient, that he's on his way. Let's hope he hurries." He closed his eyes. Count Raymond of Toulouse was coming. Soon, perhaps, it would be over.

It had seemed such a good idea, when he had returned here with the Flame, to set up camp on this small but lofty hilltop plateau, roughly a mile as the crow flies from the Castelneuf château's own lumpy prominence. Its height and width made it a good place to camp and from it, the Flame could be seen for miles. Those first nights, as the Flame had shone through the dark, Raimon had been almost intoxicated just by the taste of the air. He was the champion of the whole Occitan. He had found his destiny. He had stood tall, certain that he could hear the very stones singing out with one voice. Under his leadership and with the Flame as a living, burning standard, we, the counties that made up the Occitan, would not bow to the King of France. We would remain free as God had made us. As for the differences between Catholic and Cathar, with the Flame shining out those differences would simply dissolve.

It had not been long, however, before this vision began to cloud. Instead of asking "what can I do for the Occitan" or exclaiming about the Flame, those who crept up to the camp, women and children among them, were more concerned with whose side the Flame had chosen. "Is it a Cathar Flame or a Catholic Flame?" they asked, and when Raimon said, sometimes shouted, "The Flame's not Cathar or Catholic, it's the Flame of the Occitan," though he saw people nodding, he could tell that they were not convinced. "When you've decided, you just tell us," they said. "We don't mind which we should be, but we know God must be one or the other and we just want to be on the right side of him."

It was very hard for Raimon, this stubborn refusal of those who had come to the Flame to understand what the Flame was about, and it was made harder because he now knew that the plateau itself was a disaster. Certainly, the rocky prominences bulging out over three steep sides and the untidy, crowded ridges that pitted the fourth made the place impossible for an army to storm. They made it impossible too for an army to surround it completely. Nevertheless, over the past two, nearly three, months, Raimon and his followers had found themselves too trapped to escape, partly because Aimery had spread his men in clever clumps and partly because the physical condition of some of Raimon's followers meant that they would have either to be carried (impracticable given the terrain) or abandoned, which Raimon would not countenance. And now that Aimery had decided to blast away one of the great defensive overhangs, they were in very real danger.

When he sat with Parsifal, berating himself for being so stupid, Parsifal comforted him. Had he hidden the Flame it would have been wasted, and had he set up camp by the river, Aimery would have been on them in no time. He also stressed that Raimon should see the plateau's good points, one of which was that however clever Aimery was at positioning his soldiers, people could still steal through the ragged lines. They were not beaten yet. Raimon disagreed with none of this but it did not alter the fact that they were, in effect, under siege and that if help did not come soon, all would most certainly be lost.

And for Raimon there was something even worse, something he could not admit even to Parsifal. He was bored. Despite the constant dangers from enemy bombardments and stray arrows, despite the Flame, despite everything, what nearly crippled him was the absolute, unspeakable dullness of it all. Though every day Parsifal made him practice his swordcraft and told him of his own father's sword, Unbent, and of the day he had actually managed to lift it, Raimon wanted a real fight, wanted to hear his enemies crying for mercy, not the soft drone of stories. Yet all there was to do was to stand about, releasing one arrow at a time as Aimery's siege engines blasted at the rock, and wait. Ah, the waiting. This was not just intolerable to Raimon, it was a curse because it was during the waiting that he began to understand the extraordinary nature of absence.

Yolanda, of course. It was her absence that made the possibility of her presence everywhere. Every shaft of light or dark was filled with her hair or her face, every breeze was filled with her scent, every shadow with her shadow. Sometimes he would whip around, not hoping but actually expecting to see her. Even now, as he held Count Raymond's missive in his hands, she was pressing against his side, her head seeking shade under his shoulder. He could hear her voice too, just as he could hear poor Brees, and feel her, just as he could feel the dog's rough hair and that wet tongue on his cheek.

He stopped breathing. The wet tongue should vanish now, just like Yolanda's voice, yet it still licked. He opened his eyes a crack. The tongue stopped. Raimon blinked and found his face reflected in two eyes of old gold, with a walnut nose very close to his own. "Oh, oh!" he cried and leaped up. "Yolanda!" But of course she wasn't here. It was just her faithful hound.

He sank down, threw his arms around Brees's neck, and buried his head in the matted fur. The dog's tail punched the ground. Raimon was not his mistress but he was a good second choice. Brees began to give Raimon's hair a good wash and Raimon smiled for the first time in very many days.

When at last he told the dog to put his tongue away, he found himself at the center of a small circle. The Castelneuf huntsman, standing, and the dogboys, mostly squatting, were all looking at him expectantly. All of them were scratched and bleeding from the climb. The huntsman gestured around. "A small and useless pack," he said. "We came up through the ridges. I don't think Count Aimery's soldiers even knew we were there."

Raimon's heart swelled. For the huntsman to have come, leaving his hounds behind, touched him most particularly. "Not useless," he said, extricating himself from under Brees. "You can't imagine how welcome you are here, Master Huntsman."

The dogboys sniffed. "The Occitan won't forget you," Raimon said, shaking hands with each in turn. "Do you have names?" They looked baffled by the question.

"They don't, to speak of," the huntsman said. "They just answer to dogboy." He regarded their happy wriggling with contemptuous affection. "I'm glad to be here, although it nearly broke my heart to leave Farvel. Never had a bloodhound like him. But he wouldn't do up here. Bloodhounds need their comforts, unlike this lot. They'd survive just about anywhere." The dogboys clustered around, but now they were looking at the Flame. One put out a brown-stained hand, scorched himself, and jumped back with a tiny yelp. The huntsman called them to order and after trying and failing to find some shade from the sun, he sat and they sat around him, all tangled up together.

Raimon observed them. "He didn't ask whether I was a Cathar or a Catholic," he said to Parsifal.

"He didn't," Parsifal replied. "That means, including Gui and Guerau, there's five true Occitanians up here, and that's not counting the dogboys."

"A knight, two troubadours, a weaver, a child, a huntsman, and half a dozen dogboys," Raimon said. "That's twelve, counting everybody." He shook his head and then busied himself with Brees, murmuring to him, petting him, pulling burrs from his coat, and scratching the top of his tousled head. After a while, he spoke again. "Do you think she's all right?"

Parsifal followed the boy's thoughts perfectly. "She's safer where she is," he said. "Yolanda loves you. You know that. And she'll be faithful. She'll always be Yolanda of Amouroix, not Yolanda des Arcis. I don't believe they can force a marriage on her."

"Do you think she knows I'm still alive?"

"You sent a message, didn't you? And anyway, even if she

doesn't know, she's not going to change." He spoke very stoutly.

Raimon tried to look comforted, for Parsifal's sake. "Yes, you're right. As you say, they can't force her and she'd never give her consent to be married." He knitted his fingers together. "You're sure there has to be consent?"

"I'm sure."

"And meanwhile I have you, and the Flame, and Brees, and the huntsman. And four new knights yesterday, although they didn't seem very sure they wanted to be here."

"The climb had been harder than they thought, that's all. It's very hot and one was caught in the leg by an arrow," Parsifal said gently.

Raimon tried to sound cheerful. "And Count Raymond's coming. When he arrives, everything will be different." He jingled the seal on the parchment. There it was, quite unmistakable: the sickle moon, the star, the seated count with his unsheathed sword across his lap, holding the three-towered castle.

"Cador deserves extra rations tonight," he said, referring to the nimble eight-year-old who had swung like a monkey over the rocks to retrieve Count Raymond's message. The boy had been almost the first to arrive on the plateau. Sent as a page to a knight who had been killed by a band of outlaws, he had had a lucky escape, seen the Flame, and climbed toward it. From the moment he arrived he had adopted Raimon as his knight, paying no attention when his chosen master briskly pointed out that he had no use for a page and that Cador was the one with the knightly blood. Cador had listened, then taken Raimon's rough sword and polished it with more care than usual. He had knelt as he handed it back. That was his answer.

Raimon looked for Cador now but could not see him.

"Don't promise what you can't deliver," Parsifal warned, then bit his lip. He had meant to keep this to himself.

Raimon understood at once. "Are stocks so low?"

"It's getting harder and harder to find much that we can really eat. Aimery has all the corn barns under guard and the cattle and sheep have been driven away. We're still getting birds with arrows and slingshots but unless they fall very close now it's hard to pick them up without being killed ourselves."

"And how long before Aimery breaks through?"

Parsifal hesitated, wavering between optimism and a downright lie. He opted for a hopeful truth. "A fortnight, or thereabouts."

"Count Raymond can't be far." Raimon waved the letter but his look was suddenly frank and full of fear. "We can trust him, can't we, Sir Parsifal?"

"Just Parsifal, please," said the knight automatically, as he always did, for he did not think himself worthy of the knightly title. "We have little choice. We must trust him. He's the official leader of the Occitan and his letter sounds genuine."

"I suppose so. It's just that he should have come earlier."

Parsifal touched Raimon's shoulder. "He'll be here, and he'll be grateful to you for guarding the Flame. I think he understands that you have God's true blessing."

Raimon flushed. "I couldn't have done anything without you." He grasped the old man's hand. "You saved my life. I'd rather have your blessing than God's."

A spasm crossed the old knight's face. He found Raimon's stubborn and often angry dislike of God, a dislike that often bordered on blasphemy, intensely troubling. To him, God was as unjudgable and necessary as breathing or eating.

"Sir Parsifal," Raimon said.

"Parsifal, please."

"What happens if we are wrong?"

Parsifal frowned. "What, you think Count Raymond might turn traitor like Aimery?"

"No, at least—," Raimon's voice was uncertain. He made it more certain. "No. I think he'll lead us to victory. That's what he says."

"Then you should stop worrying. Now let's eat. Rabbit stew?" They moved over to the cauldron, which the old knight kept on the boil even in the glaring heat. Both looked at the hardened ends of bones and the greenish meat hanging off in stringy spikes.

"Perhaps not right now," Raimon said.

"I'll try it on Cador," Parsifal decided. "That boy will eat anything."

Raimon grimaced. It had come to something when Cador would have to eat rotten rabbit. He looked at the Flame a little balefully, remembering the dawn when its light had flooded the whole Castelneuf valley. He had danced for it then with wild abandon and his dance had not been for the Flame; at that moment, he had *been* the Flame. He wanted the Flame not to sit quietly but to make him feel like that again.

Parsifal had seen his look. "The Flame does what the Flame does," he said. "It's still burning. That must be enough for the time being."

Raimon took this for a rebuke and without another word he went to divide up his own rations so Cador would have something to take away the taste of green rabbit. As he pulled apart a heel of dry bread, taking care to catch every crumb, he called for Brees and sat, his stomach cramping, unable to keep himself from wondering what Yolanda was eating in Paris.

3

The City

Though Raimon's message had gotten through to Paris and even found Hugh's house, Yolanda had not received it. You may wonder how I know what happened to Yolanda, for she was half prisoner, half guest, many hundreds of miles from my boundaries. I know because she was part of me and she carried me with her. No place worth anything abandons those torn from it. I know, then, that as Raimon sweated under that bleak August sun, Yolanda was standing in the large, imposing doorway of a house overflowing with food, arguing with a white-faced beggar girl whose hair, peeping out from under a shawl, was a violent shade of crimson. "No thank you," Yolanda was saying for the tenth time.

"Tomorrow?" Poverty made the beggar girl determined and she jammed a dirty foot in the door. Though Yolanda could have squashed her foot in a second, the beggar girl did not think she would do that. This lady was not like some of the other Parisian wives, who would let her in, allow her to spread out all her wares, and even try them on before rejecting everything and depositing her back into the mud, often clipping her heels in the door jamb. This lady, well, hardly a lady for she was no older than the beggar herself, was quiet and withdrawn and she hadn't made any remark, rude or otherwise, about the crimson hair. This irritated the beggar. She used the dye purposefully to cause remark. But then she decided that Yolanda's lack of reaction was because she was foreign. From the few words she had spoken, she seemed to have an accent like merchants from the south. Still, even southern girls liked clothes. "Go on, mistress," she coaxed, holding out a little cap of gold and pearls. Then she looked at Yolanda's hair. A cap would never fit over such an unruly mess. She swapped it for a veil of silver gauze. "You'd look so pretty for your husband."

"I don't have a husband."

"Oh, now, don't tease." The girl pushed her foot a little farther in. "You're Lady des Arcis, or as good as, mistress. Living in Sir Hugh's house and all. Come on, just buy one thing. If you buy even one thing, my master will be so pleased he might let me eat tonight. You've plenty of money."

"But I don't want anything. If you want to eat, go to the kitchens. The cook will feed you."

The girl did not withdraw her foot at once. "Will he feed my dog?"

"Oh!" A tiny flicker. "You have a dog?"

The girl whistled loudly. A gangling, almost hairless creature, all ribs and ears, hopped uncertainly from around the corner, not sure whether to jump up or cringe. "She's called Ugly," the girl said with some pride, "because she is."

Ugly looked warily at Yolanda, then sat down, her nerves setting her skin aquiver. "She don't like doors," the beggar said, "since a lady trapped her tail." She wanted to lean down and make Ugly get up to show Yolanda the kink that would never be straightened. Perhaps that would move her to buy something; rich ladies were funny like that. But she couldn't make Ugly stand without giving Yolanda the chance to shut the door, so she remained still.

Yolanda opened the door a little wider and crouched. "Ugly," she said softly and the dog's tail gave a jerk. She had no flesh on her bones at all. Yolanda moved right out and patted her. "I've got—I had a dog," she said to the beggar.

"Oh? What kind?"

At once, Yolanda wished she hadn't said anything. She didn't want to cry and she couldn't even say Brees's name without her eyes filling up. "Just a dog," she said. She would have withdrawn back into the house except the beggar girl had slipped behind her and was now standing in her way, her basket of caps and veils held like a shield. Her eyes were green slits in her unnaturally chalky skin. "What kind of dog?" she repeated, sensing a chink in Yolanda's armor.

"I want to go back in."

The beggar half moved to the side. She didn't want to make Yolanda angry because angry people were never generous. Ugly pushed against Yolanda's leg and raised her pointed nose. Then she sat down on her haunches and put out a paw, as the girl had cunningly taught her to do. "Go to the kitchens," Yolanda said quickly and then closed the door more firmly than she meant to. Through the thickness of the wood she heard the beggar shouting about heartless hussies and then scolding the dog because there was nobody else to scold. Yolanda was sorry for both beggar and dog but she didn't open the door again.

Instead, she trailed up the stairs and sat on a bench near

the window of this tall house whose stones shone as if lit from the inside. Although she had been offered every beautiful thing to wear, to eat, and to look at, the only thing she seemed to want was this bench. Anybody catching a glimpse of her through the thick-paned window glass would have imagined she was waiting for something or somebody, which in a way she was; she was waiting for Raimon's ghost.

She had expected it all during the long, blank journey from Castelneuf northward during which she had spoken not a word as the mile-posts, like cruel fingers, marked out the distance she had traveled from her home. She had expected it when she called out his name in the night. She had expected it to form itself in the smoke from the fire in Sir Hugh's hall. But she was still waiting, and waiting was so exhausting. She closed her eyes and leaned her head against the stones as her grief drilled a deeper and deeper hole in her heart. Surely, she thought, one day this drill would come clean out the other side and then her heart would die and the pain would cease. Sometimes she longed for that moment, at others dreaded it, for then she might forget Raimon and Brees and me, the Amouroix, and her life would be like a room without a candle. She had not known it was possible to feel so desolate.

The window glass was rough and ill-fitting and a needle of a breeze wriggled through, bringing all the multifarious noises of the street, noises that never stopped, day or night. Paris was a long way from home, and not just in miles. The city creaked and groaned and rumbled, and even at midnight everybody preferred shouting to speaking. Yolanda could not understand now how she had ever imagined, as she once had, that Paris might be glamorous. It was bedlam, and not even just on the streets. Far above her head the ponderous church bells tolled against each other, great balls of sound swinging in an airy tide. How she hated the bells. They made her see things she didn't want to see. *Clang,* and Raimon was on the bridge. *Clong,* and he was being tied to the stake. *Clang, clong, clang.* She buried her face in her hands, aching for Brees to share her misery.

The breeze pestered her hair until finally she lifted her head and her face opened up a little. Was this Raimon's spirit, blown on a wind through the high mountain passes? She heard hoofbeats. Was that the old packhorse with the floppy ears they used to ride together? Involuntarily, she twisted her hands as though twisting them around Raimon's waist. She heard the gush of water and splayed her fingers. Surely that splash was from the millstone below the river bridge! She heard a voice and opened her mouth to answer. It was Raimon! It was! He was teasing her. "Come in! Come in! It's freezing! Come and be an ice maiden!" She heard barking. "Brees," she breathed. "Oh, I'm home. Somehow I'm home." She put out her arms. And here Raimon was, he had caught her! But even before she opened her eyes, she was backing away. That softness under her fingers. That scent of holy incense. Raimon never wore velvet. He never went to church. Her face closed.

"I'm glad to see that you're at last wearing the blue silk mantle I chose for you," said Sir Hugh des Arcis. "It's very becoming."

Yolanda pressed against the hardness of the bench as the man who was shortly to be her husband regarded her with his characteristic half-smile. How she hated that smile. In his own house he seemed bigger than he had when he arrived as a guest of Aimery's at Castelneuf. The face she had once likened to the face of a hero in a tapestry now seemed coarse, and his manner, once so perfect, contrived. He was a knight-jailer not a knight-errant. She could not bear to look at him.

He let her go. He could read everything in her face, and if he had changed for her, so had she for him. The joining together of my southern lands to his northern county of Arcis could have been such a starry affair. He would never forget his astonishment at Yolanda's unfettered, almost mythic dance the first evening he had spent at Castelneuf. Some people were obsessed by the Blue Flame of the Occitan, but for him the magical essence of the place was distilled in the oddly luminous quality Yolanda carried with her. This quality should have made their match brilliant. Yet now it was dulled and his southern sorceress reduced to the ordinary. When he saw her by the window, he felt as though he'd trampled on a fairy tale.

Yet, if he was honest, his whole southern adventure had long lost the taste of a fairy tale. Yolanda was not the only one who couldn't get the picture of Raimon on a pyre out of her mind even though Hugh had an advantage. You see, he knew, from the scrappy piece of parchment he had intercepted from a nervous messenger, that Raimon was not dead. It was why he kept Yolanda more confined than had been his original intention. That boy. He had read the note many times. Its starkness made it oddly moving, more of a love letter in its way than Hugh had ever managed, for all his schooling in rhetoric. And yet, he told himself, the kind of love those two had, or thought they had, would never last. At fourteen and fifteen, what did they really know about anything? On the other hand, the love he offered to Yolanda was adult and solid and appropriate, just the kind of love any sensible girl looked for in a marriage. In time, even she could be happy to be Lady des Arcis, a position offering more than comfortable security for herself and any children she might have. He tapped his fingers against his belt. Why, then, did he not just destroy Raimon's letter? He told himself he kept it to copy its style. He knew too that this was not true. Though he could scarcely admit it even to himself, he actually kept Raimon's letter because it carried with it a certain purity that he found enviable.

He could feel the parchment now, as he looked into the courtyard and saw Ugly. "What's that animal doing hanging about?" He spotted the girl. "And what's the watchman doing, letting beggars inside the gate?" He stared harder. "What an extraordinary color she is. That hair. It can't be natural." He turned back to Yolanda. Raimon's letter crackled. He ignored it. "I'll tell the watchman to turn her out. You have to be careful in Paris, you know, particularly at the moment. Just last night more buildings were sabotaged to try and make them collapse and kill perfectly ordinary people going about their daily work. Nobody can rest easy until this monstrous campaign of terror is brought to an end." His voice hardened. "Such saboteurs are too cowardly for open battle. Not men enough to withstand a charge by the king's knights."

Yolanda suspected he was belittling her countrymen who, so some declared, were the culprits. She said nothing.

Hugh crossed his arms and changed the subject. "Is there anything you want?" She had her eyes fixed on the silk embroidered emblem of the des Arcis fist in the middle of his chest. "You know you can have anything. A new horse, perhaps? There's to be an auction of all the property of a young knight who died of the pox this morning. I know you've Galahad and Bors, but they're old and hardly lookers."

"I don't want any other horses."

Outside, Ugly had continued to bark. She set off Hugh's dogs housed in kennels behind. Hugh clicked his tongue against his teeth. "For goodness' sake—" He made for the door.

"Leave them alone!"

He turned back. Yolanda was standing, holding her hands in front of her. "I told the girl to go to the kitchens and get something to eat. They'll be gone soon and your precious dogs won't be annoyed anymore."

Hugh walked back to the window and peered out. "Oh dear," he said. "I think she's been unlucky."

"What do you mean?"

"The cook has sent her packing."

"But I promised her—"

Hugh raised his eyebrows. "If you want the girl and her dog to eat, I think you'll have to tell the cook yourself."

Yolanda saw at once that she had fallen into a trap of her own making. To Hugh's frustration, she had spoken to none of the servants in the three weeks she had been there. They scrubbed the journey off her as though she were a deaf mute. Only when they tried to wash her hair had she objected and objected so violently that they left it for fear she might harm herself. Nor had she wanted to eat. Eating seemed heartless to her, a failing. But if she wanted the beggar girl to eat she would have to exert herself.

The dog barked again, and now came the voice of the beggar, not whining but furiously astonished. "But she *said*, the girl with the hair *said*. At least give me a bone for the dog. Look at you all! Fat as butter! You can spare it, you lardy gluttons."

The voice of the cook rose up after. "Don't you tell me what

I can spare, you heathen guttersnipe. Now, get your white face and your carrot hair out of here and that monstrous animal after you. Shoo! Shoo!"

"Shoo! Shoo!" echoed the pantry boys, "Ug-ly, Ug-ly."

Hugh frowned.

"Stop them," said Yolanda in a low voice.

"My dear girl, that's your job. I've got my steward to see." Hugh strode out.

Yolanda stood for some time, rocking on her feet, her hands half-covering her ears. The chanting in the yard rose until finally she heard a clanking, a small shriek, and a long yelp. Then she sprang to the stairs, hurrying down two at a time, but even so, by the time she reached the yard the gate was slamming shut. The porter grinned nastily. The beggar girl and Ugly were gone.

"Open the gate," she ordered as the flesh cook, banging together two frying pans, flounced back to the kitchen, the pantry boys doing a fine imitation behind his back.

The porter fiddled with his key.

"Hurry up."

A few of the other servants had ceased in their chores and were looking curiously at her. Some hadn't seen her before, only heard about this foreign creature who sat at the window and never spoke.

"Open the postern at once, on Sir Hugh's orders." She summoned up a kind of desperate imperiousness. "On Sir Hugh's orders, porter." A Hugh-shaped shadow moved around high above. "Do you want him to come down himself?"

The porter slowly put the key in the lock. Sir Hugh had told him to keep the place tightly guarded, but he hadn't specifically given orders about the girl. He hesitated. At once Yolanda wrenched the key, pushed the gate open, and was out.

The geography of Paris was completely unfamiliar to her. She paid no attention when she arrived and had been nowhere since then. Looking right and left, she could not see the beggar girl. All she could see were more people, carts, flocks, horses, and mules in this one street than in the whole of Castelneuf. Pushed from all sides, she was forced to move along. Nobody would wait, not even for a second. Shoved in one direction by one group, then dropped and shoved a different way by another, she fought for a few minutes, then allowed herself to be swept along in the tide, straining for a glimpse amid the throng.

Hugh had described Paris as a city of stone, but Yolanda found it to be a city of wood, indeed, a forest. Not only on the big streets but down the squalid lanes sprang lines and lines of thin scaffolding poles. Woven into trellises, stacked in bundles, laced together in neat vertical, horizontal, or diagonal lines, the poles cast a baffling crisscross of quivering laddered shade as they shook under the weight of men hauling stones to platforms on which there was a veritable frenzy of trimming, molding, and hammering. Yolanda had seen building before but nothing on such a scale. Palaces, court, halls, and houses, many much larger than Hugh's home, grew like animals with the flesh inside the skeleton. Who could live in such a city as this, with everything competing to be taller, grander, brasher? She passed shops too, some shuttered as if sleeping, but all ready to burst like overstuffed cushions. A cunning jeweler was polishing worthless pebbles until they shone like precious stones. A fat lady squatted like an enormous duck, her skirts covering a dozen golden birdcages. From a high window, ribbons trickled like slippery eels, one sou for fifty, and everywhere women were frantically lining up as if for the last loaf of bread.

Eventually, buffeted and bruised, Yolanda found herself on a bridge where she clutched the parapet and stood for a moment, trying to get her bearings. The girl could be anywhere. Underneath her feet the watermills vibrated. She leaned over, desperate for some fresher air. There she found a river not clear and free, but thick and slow, with the prows of the broad barges forging through floating animal filth. She gagged at the smell. The oarsmen didn't seem to notice it. They winked and made rude signs. Yolanda hurriedly drew back.

Over the bridge, though it seemed impossible, the crowds grew even thicker until she felt quite sick in the crush, but she was urged on by the thought of the beggar girl's empty stomach and the dog. It seemed increasingly unlikely that she'd find them. She pressed her palms together.

Then quite unexpectedly the crush grew less and she was in a large square, at the back of which was such a vast hedgehog of scaffolding that it dwarfed everything she had seen so far. Even unfinished, what was being built there dominated the sky, a bound Leviathan waiting to break free. On each flank men swarmed over two squat towers and in the middle, from a multitude of niches and holes, an infinity of biblical figures peered out like an army of disapproving maiden aunts. It seemed to Yolanda, as she stumbled forward, that the king was trying to build a mountain in his city. She wanted to laugh at the stupidity. My mountains were free. Then she wanted to cry for sheer homesickness.

However, she forced herself to concentrate and began to search more systematically for the girl and the dog, tripping over chickens and children. In minutes, her shoes were sucked off in the mud and she moaned at the sheer misery of it all. In Paris the dirt itself was dirty! And the stench! How could people breathe? It wasn't long before her concern for the beggar dissolved. This was vile. Why had she come out?

Near to the scaffolding was a pile of builders' wood neatly sawn into even timbers and she collapsed onto it gratefully, her hair falling in a grainy curtain over her eyes. She breathed in its scent and told herself that it still smelled of me. It wasn't true and she let it swing away. After three weeks in Paris, even her hair was horrible.

Then, an outcry. At first Yolanda took no notice, thinking it was just some city squabble, but the noise swelled as the shadows above her began to crinkle and wave. Somebody seized her. "Come away, you fool! Quick! Move! Move, you donkey."

But she didn't move quickly enough so her savior shoved her under a trestle table and fled. She twisted her head and saw that the scaffolding on the left tower was swaying; the poles, so carefully knitted together, were unraveling and splitting away individually with men still clinging to them like stick insects. From the high platforms at the top of the tower, the stones began to topple off and crash, thumping and bouncing into the mud with huge ragged splashes. Some landed on the top of the table, cracking it. It began to buckle. How strange the survival instinct is. Yolanda could have sworn that she didn't care if she lived or died, but she was quick enough to pull her legs from under the table just before it crumpled completely. Spreading her hands uselessly over her head to protect herself, she ran.

She saw Ugly's skinny tail before she saw the beggar girl. The dog was cowering in the worst possible place, with stones raining down all around her. Yolanda thought people were screaming at the dog and didn't realize that they were actually screaming at her to leave Ugly and save herself. It never occurred to Yolanda to do so. Dodging and ducking, she gathered the dog into her arms and headed for the safety of the porch. No sooner were they under cover than there was a sharp sound. Then, like a great gasp, the scaffolding finally cast off all its moorings and, with slow grace, arched over and down, hesitated, swung, hesitated again, shook off the clinging men, and then folded rather than crashed to the ground, where it settled into the mud like a pile of old bones settling into a grave.

There was one second's appalled silence before the shrieking began in earnest. Pushing through the porch, priests ran to administer the last rites to wretches too injured to move, while barrowmen tipped out their goods and ran to shovel up the bodies. As people surged forward, a thousand thieving hands were quickly scrabbling for valuables that the dead could not take with them and the injured would not notice were missing. Yolanda clutched the whimpering dog. She could see the girl thieving away with the best of them, stuffing things not only into her basket of wares but also into voluminous sleeves that didn't match. She had lost her shawl and her hair now sprang from her head in a halo of blood-colored spirals.

Intently she was pulling off rings and belts, rummaging in pouches, and tugging at shoes. When one corpse was stripped, she moved on to the next. It was at the third that she got into a fight with another scavenger, a limping boy, shockingly bald and even skinnier than herself. The girl used everything she had, bony knees, ragged nails, teeth, and elbows, even the blinding effect of her hair, but the boy had a hawklike grip she could not match. Nor did he waste his breath cursing. He just held grimly and silently onto the girl's basket and refused to let go. She might still have succeeded through sheer brutishness had she not been hampered by the length of her sleeves and their fullness. She also made the mistake of trying to wrap her legs around his, tipping them both over. The boy landed on top and at once chopped her wrist. Her fingers opened. In a second, he and the basket were gone. All her work had been for nothing.

Yolanda thought the girl might scream or throw a tantrum, but she did nothing of the sort. She did not even grimace. She simply got up, settled her sleeves, checking that what she had stowed away in them was still there. Then she brushed herself off, raised her palms like a priest, and began to rotate very slowly, all the while reciting some incantation. Though Yolanda could understand none of the words, she could tell the girl was drawing down some demonic vengeance on the bald boy. Mesmerized, she crept forward and then jumped when the girl suddenly opened her eyes terrifyingly wide, saw her dog, and snapped her fingers. "Give her back." Her order was peremptory and dismissive, as though Yolanda were another thief.

Yolanda, backing away, jolted out a response. "You left her to die in the stones."

The girl curled her lip. "That's my business." Bruises were already dappling her cheek and a green eye was beginning to close. Altogether, she was a very peculiar kind of mess.

"Come back to the house," Yolanda said. "I'll make sure they give you food this time."

The girl darted forward and tried to pull Ugly from Yolanda's arms but Yolanda wouldn't let go. Eventually the girl stood back, aggressively swinging a skirt that Yolanda could now see was a patchwork of stuff cleverly sewn together.

"Come with me." Yolanda was wary, for the girl was strong.

"And be treated like a joke again? Just give me the dog."

"I won't."

"Give her."

"No."

The girl seemed more uncertain now. Her eyes sought the dog, but then, although her lower lip was trembling, she straightened up and flung her arms out. "Oh, I don't care for her anyway. She's just a nuisance. Have her." With that she ran off and was lost again in the crowd.

Yolanda shouted. "No, no, I don't want her. I just want to—," she stopped. Ugly was straining in her arms. Then she flopped and her eyes took on the resigned look of one who expects nothing and usually gets it. Unable to abandon her, Yolanda began the long walk back to Hugh's house, with the dog lying in her arms like a small dead deer.

Where before there had been just bustle, the collapse of the scaffolding had introduced a palpable air of menace. Surging around the mourners, the crowds were looking for someone to blame for what they believed, without any proof, was an act of deliberate sabotage. Festering enmities erupted into fights. People at once took sides. "Kill the traitors!" she heard some shout, though no traitors could possibly be identified. But then they were looking at her, with her tanned skin, her rat-tail hair and unfashionable clothes. "I heard her speak! She speaks with the accent of the Cathar devils!" She tried to push her way past them, but Ugly's legs flapped and people caught at them. Without the dog she might escape, but with her she stood no chance. She was whirled around, and Ugly began to whimper.

Then she saw flashes of silver and hooves striking sparks on the cobbles. Now the crowd started shrieking as half a dozen des Arcis knights began to beat heads and shoulders with the flat of their swords and use their horses as battering rams. It was impossible for Hugh, who was at their head, to swing Yolanda up behind him with Ugly in her arms, so he leaped down and had his men clear a passage through which they could hurry unmolested.

She did not want to be pleased to see him, but she could hardly deny it. Yet she wouldn't—couldn't—thank him.

When he spoke to her, his tone was cool. "These damnable troublemakers should be strung up from the city walls. There'll be a riot now." He propelled her off the main street and into a lane. The horses' rumps made a barricade behind them and eventually any pursuers who were left lost enthusiasm and trailed away. Only then did he sheathe his sword and look down at her. "What have you got there?"

She held Ugly close. "A dog. The one you saw earlier."

A twinge, that's all it was, of discomfort crossed Hugh's face. He had offered her several pretty greyhounds as substitutes for Brees but she had refused them all and this dog, this hideous dog, was not at all what he had in mind for Lady des Arcis.

"She's called Ugly," Yolanda said, echoing the beggar girl with some defiance, "because she is."

"Cruel but apt," Hugh said. They walked the rest of the way in silence and when they reached the gate, she left Hugh berating the porter for letting her out. In the future, Yolanda was to leave only when accompanied by Hugh or one of his household knights. If he came home and found her gone, the porter and his family would be out in the gutter. "Order more men if you need them," he said, "just don't let there be any mistakes."

In the small hall at the bottom of the house, Yolanda laid the dog on a blanket and threw logs onto the fire. Even at the height of a sunny day the house had a dampness to it. The logs smoked and wouldn't catch.

Malnourishment had eaten away at everything that made Ugly a dog rather than just a bag of apologetic bones and two cringing eyes. When Hugh came in he inspected her, and had Yolanda not been there, he would have knocked her on the head. Yet he said nothing when Yolanda summoned the steward and ordered herbs and liquid spices. If the girl was the dog's apothecary, he told himself, it would give her something to do. He saw her bend over Ugly with a conspicuous tenderness from which he was quite specifically excluded. With many of the women he had known, the tenderness would have been part of a flirtation. With Yolanda, it was like a door slamming. He didn't like that.

Three of his knights were waiting impatiently, two clutching breastplates and all with sword belts on. He went to them.

"It's getting worse," one said. "The cathedral itself. I mean, where will it stop?"

"Who are they blaming this time, Amalric?" Hugh asked.

"The Cathar heretics again. Who else? They creep in, fray the ropes, and then are long gone by the time the scaffolding goes. But Notre Dame!" The pockmarks on his face gave him a look of permanent disdain, but the disdain was real enough now.

"Yes, but let's not forget that the king has other enemies besides the Cathars," Hugh said carefully, "and anyway, it's always said that such people don't believe in killing. They won't even eat meat, for goodness' sake. Perhaps it was the Muslims. There are many of them here in Paris and they hear the king speak all the time about crusade. Henri, what do you think?"

A short, swarthy man with a fuzz of gray hair on his chin and scalp answered. "The people are saying it's the Cathars and really, who cares whether it is or not? The king's offensive in the south is pretty sluggish at the moment. If we can pin this terror on the heretics in the Occitan, it'll put some pep into the soldiers' steps." The other two knights nodded. Henri had a way of putting things.

"And don't forget," Amalric said, for he didn't like to be outdone, "it was the Cathars who killed the inquisitors at Avignonet. That boy, what was his name?"

Hugh tried to interrupt but he was too late.

"Raimon Belot," Henri said.

Hugh ushered them out the door and up the stairs but their conversation came echoing down.

"That's it, Raimon Belot. Well, he admitted to being a Cathar at his trial, didn't he, and he was a murderer."

"He said he'd attended his mother when she was consoled by a Cathar at her death."

"So? He's a Cathar then."

Other words were muffled.

Henri's voice was clear again. "I'd forgotten Mistress Yolanda comes from the south," he said, and his tone was ironic. He hadn't forgotten. Not for one second. "I suppose you'll be keeping an eye on her."

"She's not a Cathar, she's a Catholic," Hugh's voice echoed back.

"Yes, but she's a southerner, Hugh. You said yourself, before you went down to—what's the name of the place?"

"The Amouroix."

"That's it. You said before you went that you'd heard that all Occitanians would do anything to keep us out. No offense to her, but they're all untrustworthy. Are you sure her brother hasn't sold you a spy? Aimery of Amouroix is hardly known as a man of integrity. She looks innocent enough but—"

"Be careful what you say, Henri." Hugh's voice was clipped.

"I'm only—"

"Leave her to me. I'll deal with her." Their voices were fainter. The upstairs door was finally shut.

Yolanda could hardly tend to Ugly, her hands trembled so much. How dare they! She ground the herbs hard as if crushing the king, Hugh, his henchmen, and even the beggar girl into a pulp. The sour smell caught the back of her throat. She had ground the stuff until it was unusable. She wiped the mess onto a rag and chucked it onto the fire, where it burst into flames at once, flaring pink and green. For one terrible moment she wondered if she would throw herself on too, and die like Raimon. She crept closer to the flames and placed one foot on the firestones. A log creaked and settled. A spark landed on her shoe. She watched without breathing as the leather resisted and then began to melt. The log settled again and fiery fingers reached for her. She stretched out her own hand. Perhaps Raimon was in the fire. Perhaps these were his fingers. She began to hear his voice again, as it had been during their last conversation. He said he'd seen the Blue Flame, that a man they had jokingly called the Knight Magician had it. He had told her to believe it, to live for it, but it was too hard without him beside her. "Show me," she whispered. "If it's true, show me." She leaned right into the blaze.

It was instinct, not decision, that had her leaping back, flinging off her burning shoe, her skin sticky with fright and her skirt smoking. She seized Ugly and crushed her so tightly against her ribs that the poor dog couldn't even yelp. She knew she looked mad. She felt mad. The flames collapsed back into smolder. As she kicked away the mortar and pestle she was sure she caught a glimpse of something. She dropped Ugly. There it was! There! Surely this was something? Surely at last it was a sign! She opened her mouth and her heart to what turned out to be nothing but a cloud of weightless, ill-scented ash.

Hours later, Hugh came down for her. She was curled up next to the dog, her face streaked with blackened tears. Hugh had never seen a sight so forlorn. He bent down to pick her up. Her eyelids fluttered but she didn't wake. She was utterly spent. He carried her up the stairs, calling for servants to see to her. Then he came down again for Ugly, picking her up with some distaste. He glanced at the outside door, even moved toward it, then hesitated and finally walked upstairs again to deposit her on the end of Yolanda's bed. The dog put out a paw. Hugh ignored it.

4

Laila

The next morning, Hugh summoned Yolanda to his council chamber. They sat in silence for a moment or two, then he said, "We must set a date for our wedding." Hugh did not have to be near her to sense her every muscle tensing, but he would not be deterred. "I'm going away in a month and everything must be settled before I leave. We will be married in three weeks and when I've gone, Amalric will see you to your new home in Champagne. Paris is no place for you at the moment." He still did not look at her. "Do you have anything to say?"

He thought she might sound frightened, but instead she just sounded weary, as if repeating lines she had been given. "I shan't give my consent."

"I'm afraid that doesn't matter. Quite apart from the fact that we were betrothed quite openly in Castelneuf—at your birthday party, if you remember—the law in Paris is different from the laws in the south. The Masters here decree that we have no need even of witnesses. I'd prefer your consent, of course, but I don't need it." Now he did hear her gasp and it gave him a strange feeling, half pleasure that he could exert his will and half sorrow that he had to. "And remember, Yolanda, if we don't marry, the Amouroix will suffer. That's the contract I made with Aimery. Now, we both have preparations to make. I'm going to send you Paris's best seamstresses. Order whatever you like." He glanced at her now. "At least look respectable. You don't want to let the Amouroix down, do you? And I expect certain standards as my wife. Clean hair, for one."

"You're going back to the Occitan." It was a statement, not a question.

"I'm not going to lie to you. Yes, I'm going back. I shall see your brother first at Castelneuf, then go on to Carcassonne. You remember that I've been made seneschal?"

"You're taking an army?"

He hesitated. "But not to destroy the Amouroix. I'm leading the king's army to deal once and for all with Count Raymond of Toulouse. He's gathered quite an army himself. This is the last battle for the Occitan and frankly, the quicker this business is over, the better for everybody."

She sat for one more second, then got up. "Take me with you."

"I can't," he said, stopping himself from smiling at the naivety of her request. "That wouldn't do at all."

"Please. I want to be married from Castelneuf."

"You know perfectly well that's not possible." His voice was brisk.

"I thought you were so grand that if you chose, you could make anything possible."

"I don't choose, then." He waited, dreading that she would beg. He did not wish to see that. But she didn't. His voice was cajoling. "You've a new life ahead of you, Yolanda. You belong here now."

"The Flame—"

"The Flame's gone. You must try and forget all that."

She threw her head back with all the defiance she could muster. "You think I'll forget? How little you know me, Sir Hugh."

"I'm hoping to get to know you much better," Hugh said, trying to inject a lightness to the conversation.

The look she gave him was quite startling, as if he had suddenly come face-to-face with an animal he was about to kill. "You'll never know me," she said. She looked dried out, her thin face no longer pretty, just haggard. It was not what he wanted.

The next morning seamstresses appeared, dozens of them, all clutching different colored bolts of silk and crepe. They brandished scissors, rough patterns, and clashing opinions. Yolanda stood as though in a dream as they set to, measuring, winding, cutting, and stitching. She never addressed them and they never addressed her, so busy were they arguing with each other.

"Blue, I think. Blue, or perhaps green?"

"No, not green. Are you blind? She can't wear green, at least not *that* green." She found plum velvet slung over her shoulders, then ripped away and replaced with rust. "Rust! What are you thinking? Keep up! Keep up! You're so behind the times. Rust was last year's fashion. She needs yellow silk shot with silver. That's what they're all wanting today." Around and around the women went, propelling her one to the other, in one color or another, until she felt quite dizzy. Finally, after one woman produced delicate doeskin shoes decorated with tiny star stitches, the merry-go-round came to an end and Yolanda stood like the dunce in the playground.

"Can I ask you," said Berthe, who had appointed herself chief among them, "is it a tradition among your kind of people not to wash your hair?" No answer. "Heavens above, girl, just look at yourself. You're going to be Lady des Arcis not queen of the dung heap."

Yolanda suddenly made a statement. "I want a cap of gold and pearls," she said. The women shook with laughter. "You'll never get a cap on such a tangle."

"That's what I want," she said, "and I've seen one. A girl was here yesterday. A redheaded girl. That's her dog."

Berthe snorted. "Don't be silly now. We can provide something much nicer than an old cap."

"I don't want what you can provide," said Yolanda flatly. "Sir Hugh said I was to have what I liked. I like the cap, and the redheaded girl must bring it herself."

Berthe argued some more but Yolanda was adamant. Without the cap, she'd send them all packing. She was involved in the argument before she'd really thought about it, but what she wanted, quite suddenly, was the beggar. She didn't want the girl for herself: she seemed rude and unpleasant. But she would be somebody of Yolanda's own, somebody not sent to her by Hugh, and she didn't know anybody else. Raimon's ghost had not come, the Flame had sent no sign, and if the Knight Magician was real, he was not to be found here.

"Find her. Get her," Yolanda said, and in an effort to stop herself from sounding like a whining child, she found that she had quite by mistake adopted the tone of the mistress of the house.

It was late afternoon and the room was afloat with snippets and threads when the girl arrived. She was speaking very loudly, shouting really, half fearful, half boasting, and the servants who had located her with a great deal of irritation and trouble were fed up. She hadn't walked one willing step or uttered one word that wasn't a violent complaint. Just before she was ushered into Yolanda's presence there was a scuffle, a scream, and a loud crash. "If you've smashed that, I'll make sure you die of leprosy, you see if I don't." The girl's language was richly peppered with words Yolanda had never heard. Ugly was scrabbling and howling.

When the girl did appear, she was clutching to her flat and bony chest a highly ornate casket about the size of a cat's coffin. It was this that had fallen, for the seamstresses had tried to remove it from her and the girl was having none of that. Berthe still had ahold of the casket and the girl was growling and yowling in turn.

Yolanda seized the casket herself and banged it on the table as loudly as she could. "Be quiet! Quiet, all of you!" The girl seized the casket back.

Ugly carried on howling.

Berthe was rocking, her fingers theatrically in her ears. "In the name of the Virgin, shut that dog up!"

"Don't look at me," the girl retorted, cracking the bones in her shoulders. "She's nothing to do with me. She belongs to the lady."

Yolanda picked the dog up and held her out. The girl whipped the casket under one arm and roughly smacked Ugly on the jowl with her free hand. "That's enough of that," she said. The dog was silent at once.

Shocked at such a display of wanton cruelty, Yolanda reversed until both she and Ugly were out of reach. This had been a stupid idea. This creature would be no friend to her. She was an alien being from a different world. Nevertheless, now that she was here, Yolanda must find something to say. She saw those two green orbs flicker toward the thread and ribbons and said the first thing that came into her head. "Can you sew?"

The girl's eyes at once turned sly. "I can do many things. It's only girls like you who can afford to do nothing."

"You insolent brat!" Berthe raised her foot, ready to kick. "You've no right even to speak. I know her sort, mistress. She's a wrong'un. Look at her! She comes here quite shameless, without even covering her hair. Her sort have no respect, none at all."

The girl seemed amused. Quite casually she began the same incantation she had chanted in the square in front of Notre Dame.

The women shrieked and threw their skirts over their heads. The girl seemed extremely pleased.

Yolanda stamped her foot. She didn't want to keep the girl and be made to look a fool, yet she didn't want to send her away and somehow side with Berthe. Oh, why had she started this? "Look," she said, "I asked if you would sew for me. Can't you reply?"

"Why? You've enough seamstresses here already to make clothes to last your whole life."

"I'm offering you a job. Do you want it or not?" Yolanda wrapped Ugly up in a blanket and put her down. At once, the dog strained toward her former mistress. The girl ignored this for a while but Ugly was pitiful and persistent. At last she burst out, "Pick her up again, won't you, lady? She's your dog."

"If you sew for me, you can afford to keep her."

"But she won't be mine forever so I'd rather she wasn't mine at all. Pick her up."

"No." Yolanda kept her voice steady. "If you sew for me, you can live here, and Ugly too. There'll be plenty to eat. Now pick her up."

Ugly wailed. The girl looked as though she might bite her. The dog stopped whining, shook off the blanket, and extended a paw. The girl broke and bent down. "Shhh, shhh, you silly animal. I'm here."

At once Ugly began to wag her tail and Yolanda began to breathe again. She opened her mouth but the girl spoke first. "When do I start?"

Yolanda gave a half-smile, then frowned. Half-smiles belonged to Hugh. "You can start today. But before you do, we'd better know your name."

The girl looked at her, weighing her up. "Laila Hajar Mais Bilqis Shehan. It says so—look—on the casket."

The seamstresses began to laugh and the girl flicked them a frosted glare. "And why not?" she asked. "My father is a man of magic and my mother the daughter of a queen."

"A heathen magician! Well I never!" Berthe was loudly scornful because magic made her nervous. "Well, tell me this, your highness. What royalty has hair the color of a butcher's floor?" Her boldness encouraged the other seamstresses to giggle.

Laila interrupted, drawing herself up to the peak of a skinny height that contrasted sharply and favorably with Berthe's pudding spread. She tossed her hair until it crackled around her face. "Scoff if you like, but compared to my ancestors, your queen is a puddle of milk, and sour milk at that."

Berthe lumbered forward, her many jowls quivering. "How

dare you insult our queen. You're not too big to flog, you know. We shouldn't allow any of your sort here except as the lowest form of slave. I've got an idea! If your father's a magician, get him to magic you back where you belong—with the circus vermin."

There was rude laughter from the other women.

Laila was very quick. Darting at Berthe, she flicked up a hand and appeared to pull a black pebble from the seamstress's ear. This she threw into the air and swallowed. Then she coughed and one, two, three pebbles flew out, all different colors. She caught these in a deft juggle, and in a moment they went from four to five then back to four, then three, then two, and finally the girl was tossing the original black pebble like a shiny eyeball from hand to hand. The women backed away. Red hair, green eyes, and skills from the devil. The word "witch" hung about unspoken.

Yolanda interrupted before anybody could say it aloud. "For goodness' sake. I don't care if your father's the Holy Roman Emperor or Merlin the Magician, I just want you to sew my clothes."

"You can't employ beggars off the street." Berthe planted herself like an earthy mound in front of Yolanda. "And Sir Hugh des Arcis won't allow such a monstrosity in his house. He's very particular."

Yolanda slid past her and opened the door. "Out," she said.

The girl gathered herself, Ugly, and her casket together.

"No, not you. You." Yolanda gestured toward the seamstresses.

The girl crowed and, dumping Ugly, produced an egg from beneath Berthe's chin, cracked it, and a black beetle crawled out.

That was the end. The women didn't even gather up their

cloth, but crossing themselves and imploring God and the Holy Saints to protect them, they rushed out of the room and out of the house. Only Berthe hovered, filling up the doorway. This job would feed her children. Her tone was more conciliatory, almost wheedling. "See here, mistress, God will punish you for keeping such a girl. You don't want to go to hell, do you? Or want Sir Hugh to suffer? I know girls like this. They should be burned."

Laila shot Yolanda a glance and met one in return. It was a tiny connection of horror.

Yolanda was coldly regal. "Good-bye."

Berthe began to expostulate. Her little boy had the fever. None of her six girls had husbands. Laila ran at her, growling and snapping, and soon the fat woman and the skinny waif were barking and jabbing like a couple of jackals. As soon as Berthe took a step back, Laila pulled the heavy door and attempted to squash her. "She said 'out.' Didn't you hear?"

"You've cast a spell over her."

"Yes, and I'll cast one over you too."

"Lady des Arcis! You're never going to let her get away with this."

Only when Yolanda didn't respond did Berthe recognize defeat. "I'll send a bill for that cloth, you see if I don't, mistress, and it'll be a lot. And for those shoes, may they pinch all your toes. And I'll tell Sir Hugh you've damned him and his household to hell, don't you think I won't." She thumped the door and yelled as she negotiated the stairs and was still yelling long after she reached the street.

Yolanda waited until there was peace again. "Now you can tell me," she said. "Why do you paint your skin?"

Laila's hand shot up to her head, where a perfect circle of coffee-colored scalp was visible because of a small whorl in her hair. She was all defiance. "Because I like to."

"Is your hair painted too?"

"What does it matter to you?"

"It doesn't."

"Good."

They blinked, each unsure what they were to each other. Were they mistress and servant? Were they friends? Did they care?

"You'll sleep in the house," Yolanda told her.

"In your chamber?"

"I suppose so."

"With Ugly?"

"Is that what you'd like?" Yolanda suddenly felt very tired.

Laila stood as she imagined a girl with queenly and magical parentage should stand. "She and I will try it out and see if we like it," she said grandly.

"And should I call you Laila?"

"I've told you, my name is Laila Hajar Mais Bilqis Shehan. That's what I like to be called." Her dogged pride was almost admirable.

"All right then, I'm Yolanda Eloise Berengaria Dulcia d'Amouroix-in-Occitan."

Quite unfazed, the girl repeated the name and nodded.

"Good. Well, Laila Hajar Mais Bilqis Shehan, you can just call me Yolanda."

The girl did not shorten her own name in response. "I'm hungry," she said instead, "and my favorite food is smoked goat's liver. What's yours?"

Yolanda chose not to answer and the girl grinned. No matter. She would stay here for a while and get what she could out of it. She began to hum and was still humming when the cook, on Yolanda's orders, sent up more smoked goat's liver than even Laila could stuff into her stomach.

That night, as she lay comfortably sleepless, she worked out exactly how much the hangings around Yolanda's bed were worth. "My goodness, a king's ransom," she said to Ugly and sighed with pleasure as she turned her attention to the curtains. A king's ransom there too. Rich people certainly knew how to live. She stretched up her arms to her own personal deity. "Make Berthe as miserable as I am happy," she whispered and then blew out the candle and stared into the dark like a cat on the prowl.

5

Consolation

Bear with me now, for we are going to leave Yolanda for a moment to find Raimon again, moving forward to October, two months after the huntsman arrived on the plateau. Count Raymond had made no appearance and many in the ragtag army were beginning to say he never would. People had begun to sicken and one of the dogboys had died. There were many days when there was no food at all.

From the passage of time, however, you can see that Raimon had had some luck. The progress Aimery's men were making on the protective overhang had been badly hampered when overconfidence saw the siege machine slip and topple, dragging the oxen with it. Nobody could save it and it took time to build another. After that, there had been an outbreak of pox in the town and nobody moved from home except to tend the crops and animals.

Disheartened at first, Aimery had sat sullenly in his hall, but then adopted a new tactic. Though his full-scale assault was delayed, he could still cause Raimon a good deal of trouble. He called for his cheekiest archer and instructed him to lodge himself in a small col and pepper Raimon's followers liberally with barbs and darts every day. This caused few deaths but the injuries and irritation generated by such constant sniping meant that in the evenings, after the archer had gone home, Raimon could not rest. Instead he had to use all the energy he could muster to rally his fading troops. He appealed to them in the name of the Flame, but, although his words were well chosen, with the heat pressing during the day, the occasional frost at night, and the now permanent gnawing of hunger, the fractious crowd was full of resentment. They had rallied to the Flame with considerable danger to life and limb, bringing what worldly goods they could carry and now, though it burned night and day like a small blue star, it was doing nothing for them in return. When Raimon attempted to explain that the Flame was not a servant to be ordered about or a box of miracles, they tried to understand, but the rumbling in their stomachs got in the way. They had come to the Flame. Why were they now being punished instead of rewarded? They began to mutter that it was because Raimon had still not decided whether the Flame was a Cathar Flame or a Catholic Flame. That was the trouble. They were sure of it.

Adding to their torments, the spring water that gushed liberally and unstoppably from a crevice during the early months of the year had dwindled to a trickle. Aimery's battering had somehow disrupted the flow. For nearly a week now, Cador had barely filled a leather bucket and the makeshift cisterns that Raimon had drilled out of the rock were dry. Parsifal thanked God they had no horses, except that the carcasses would have been useful to eat. When Cador gave him his water ration, the old knight would pretend to sip it but secretly poured it into Raimon's cup because he knew the boy had poured most of his into Cador's. He longed for the snow to arrive, but it was not time for snow yet, and if the siege was still going by the time it fell, it would bring its own horrors.

Today Raimon was whittling catapults with Brees lying too close for comfort under a relentlessly cheerful midday sun. The scars from Aimery's beating were long healed and, encouraged by Cador, the dog often tried to bound around as he used to. But hunger and thirst had at last defeated him and today he was prone, his mouth lolling open, a magnet for the insects that buzzed in and out, sometimes singly, sometimes in swarms. They were quite safe. Brees couldn't even raise the energy to snap at them, something that filled Raimon with guilt. He should find a way to send Brees back to the château. If he didn't, the dog would probably die.

Cador was pinging Raimon's slings with great enthusiasm. There were plenty of stones and though the missiles couldn't kill, dispatched from above they were a small counterbalance to the cheeky archer. Cador loved the sound of his stones hitting breastplates or, best of all, noseguards, and every evening he brought Parsifal a careful tally. When the tally reached a hundred, Parsifal had promised to teach him how to fight with a sword.

The old knight was sitting by the Flame, watching Raimon and Cador, his arms stretched out to catch a bit of breeze. He was not thinking about Brees or catapults. Thirsty beyond measure, flies feasting on his sticky eyes and an unnamed sickness eating away at him, he was wondering why he had never felt so blessed. Though it pleased him to ask the question, he already knew the answer. Lonely for most of his life, he was not lonely now. The Flame had brought him his own little family. It was a reward he had never imagined, and it was certainly not the one his father had in mind when, all those years ago, he had brought the Flame back from Jerusalem and entrusted it to his son. Sir Bertrand had imagined Parsifal holding the Flame aloft in victory. But Parsifal, though he had regrets, could not at this moment feel that everything had gone amiss.

"What can Count Raymond be doing?"

Raimon's voice gave the old knight a shock. He had little time to disguise the effort of pulling himself upright. "I don't know what's delaying him," he said. "Perhaps he'll come today."

"I hope so," Raimon replied grimly. "Come. Look."

They slithered down a narrow gully, raising their heads tentatively over the edge. They could see the archer's niche below, and also that the mottled overhang now had a great cleft through its middle. Aimery's chipping was, finally, in its last stages. Any day now, the stone would topple. Already those scraping away underneath were risking their lives, and occasionally one would call out, suspending work as the stone groaned and splintered. Back at Castelneuf, Aimery's troops would be preparing to attack.

"What shall we do?" Raimon's lips cracked as he spoke and his tongue was so parched he couldn't even lick them. "I'd rather blow the Flame out than have Aimery get hold of it."

Parsifal shifted position, trying to brace his legs. "What makes you think that you could blow it out? It's survived this long and remained lit. But even supposing you could, do you really want to?"

"Of course not." Raimon regretted snapping, but he was so tense and so thirsty.

"You could take it and find Count Raymond yourself."

Raimon's cheeks tightened. This was an argument they'd had before. "I can't go and leave all these people. They came because of me and we can't all get away, particularly now. Some can barely walk. I've got to stay."

Parsifal hesitated. But if age didn't bring frankness, what was the point of it? "Have you ever thought, Raimon, that if Count Raymond doesn't arrive in time we might concede defeat?"

Raimon was astonished. "Concede defeat? Why, not for a second, not for a single second. How could you suggest such a thing? Concede defeat? To Aimery?"

"If we concede and Aimery does not have to come and get us, it may bring mercy."

"We are not looking for Aimery's mercy," said Raimon flatly.

"There are women and children here."

Raimon's face darkened. "No concessions."

"Not under any circumstances?"

Raimon looked at Parsifal with some pain. "How can you of all people even think of such a thing? It would be a complete betrayal of the Flame just to hand it over to him."

"I wonder whether it's an equal betrayal to litter this hilltop with Occitanian corpses."

"If you are afraid of death, Sir Parsifal," said Raimon with the stiff and angry courtesy he sometimes adopted when he found Parsifal disappointing, "you had better throw yourself at Aimery's feet. I shan't stop you."

They climbed back to the camp in silence.

The following morning, after a night when the whole country had been still as a painting, the vultures began to circle in greater numbers, several actually landing on the cracked crag and sitting stolidly, like greedy boys hoping for sweetmeats.

Meanwhile, the children in Raimon's camp were crying with desolate persistence, their fathers beating on the empty cooking pots in a tragic attempt to offer some foolish distraction. Raimon never ceased to be amazed at the patience of these fathers. Didn't the children understand that they were doing their best?

An hour later, when every minute had become purgatory, the *clink, clink* chorus of Aimery's hammers chipped away not only at the rock but at Raimon's very core. Where, oh where was Count Raymond? He went to the Flame, but though its very presence could still make his heart jump, it seemed just a flame in a box.

He turned his back on it and gave Parsifal a look, part defensive, part apologetic. "I'm going to get everybody together," he said. Parsifal nodded, wisely not making any remark. *That boy feels the whole weight of the Occitan on his shoulders,* he thought. *It's too much.*

When everybody was congregated, Raimon returned to Parsifal, helped him up, and then brought the Flame to a central place in the gathering. He looked around at all the faces, hair gluey with sweat and cheeks sunken from want, some nursing injuries, some nursing illness, before he spoke. A number of the gathering were strangers to him, for it was not only people from Castelneuf who had answered the Flame's call, and some had their faces wrapped against the flies and the rank smell of human sewage. However, he could see the comely Beatrice, Yolanda's friend, who should have been married, and the armorer, the woodman, and Gui and Guerau, who propped each other up, not singing now, nor quarreling as was their wont. Their silence was somehow the worst silence of all.

Raimon stood near the Flame. "I've called us together

because time is running out," he said. He wanted to touch the Flame's box, but felt such a gesture would make him appear in childish need of support. "Count Aimery's men are almost through the crag and we must accept that if Count Raymond of Toulouse doesn't appear by noon tomorrow, we have two options." He looked squarely at Parsifal and then around the bedraggled crowd. "Concede defeat"—he almost choked on the words—"or fight."

"Concede defeat?" The phrase echoed back to him laced with the same incredulity he had expressed to Parsifal, and something more. Was it derision? He couldn't bear that. "Defeat?" The word was repeated again and again, rising in a wail. "Defeat? But we have the Flame. It's going to save us. You promised."

There was general hubbub. Raimon raised his hand. "I know what I said and I know we have the Flame, but look at us!" He took a deep breath. "If we send down to Aimery, he will show mercy. If we remain up here, well—you see how it will be."

Starvation and a kind of blindness generated a warped rationality. Everyone began to talk at once. "The Flame saved you from the pyre at the last minute and it'll do the same for us. Surely it owes us that? All we've got to do is discover whether it's a Cathar Flame or a Catholic. We've told you that before." They surged forward. Gui and Guerau came and stood by Raimon, fearing for his safety as the hubbub increased.

"Please listen," Raimon begged. "We've run out of food and water. Aimery's men are almost upon us. Don't you see? We've got to make some kind of decision."

"Yes. How often must we tell you? Cathar or Catholic. You have the Flame, so we thought you had the answer."

"No," Raimon said, trying to keep his voice steady. "Don't you see, that's not what the Flame's about."

But they just shouted louder and louder and it was clear that they would not be convinced, whatever he said. When the hubbub reached as much of a roar as starving and parched people can manage, one of the shrouded figures unfolded and Raimon suddenly found his sister, Adela, standing in front of him. He started as though he'd seen a ghost. He was vaguely aware that his father, Sicart, had joined him but he had no idea she was here. She barely looked at him as she took his place.

"Good people," she said in a voice hard as a winter's night, "you are right. Of course we must make a decision."

She threw off her shawl completely. "Raimon doesn't own the Flame. We own it too." Her eyes bored through them. "And if he won't make a decision, perhaps we can. The Flame is the Flame of the Cathars. It always was and it always will be. How do we know? Because Count Aimery is our enemy and Count Aimery is a Catholic. It's as clear as daylight."

Raimon tried to block her. "Don't listen to her, any of you." He had to fight to be heard now. "Count Aimery may be a Catholic but that's not why he's our enemy. He's our enemy because he's trying to sell us to King Louis. Christ in Heaven! There are Catholics here among us, so how can what Adela says be true? The Flame has come to show us how these differences will destroy us. It has not come to make the differences worse." He walked around the circle, forcing people to take notice. "Fellow Occitanians! If we choose to fight Count Aimery, it must be as Occitanians, not as Cathars. This is not a war about religion, it's a war about keeping the Occitan free. You must understand that! You must!"

Adela pushed him aside. "My brother has no business to speak for either the Occitan or the Flame," she declared in ringing and resolute tones. "No true Occitanian would suggest giving in to a Catholic like Count Aimery unless he had some secret reason for doing so." She halted quite suddenly and looked Raimon full in the face. "Does Yolanda still have you dangling on a string, Raimon? Married or not, those Catholic ladies are shameless!"

Raimon staggered as though she had struck him.

She turned back to the crowd. "Think for yourselves," she urged. "You're not fools. You know as well as I do that it's Catholicism that's ruined us all. What is it but Catholicism that's turned Count Aimery from an Occitanian into a traitor who sells his sister and his lands to the king of France?"

A young knight began to argue. "You're wrong!" he cried. "Some of us are loyal even though we are Catholics!"

Adela looked at him pityingly. "Perhaps that was once possible," she said, "but not now." The crowd muttered after her, "No, not now."

"The truth is that Catholics must always side with King Louis," Adela declared, and now everybody was listening. "Because that's what the pope in Rome orders you to do." The knight fell silent. "I don't blame you," Adela continued, still pitying. "I mean, you're only doing as you're told. But now that you must choose between being an Occitanian and a Catholic, perhaps you'll see how unfortunate such obedience is."

The knight opened his mouth to try again, but Adela spoke over him. "And how can there be any doubt where God's sympathy lies? Look at the king with his court and his treasure chests. Compare his life of luxury with the lives of those Cathars dedicated to their country and to God's service. Have you ever met a Cathar more interested in treasure on earth than treasure in heaven?" She spoke with complete certainty because her belief was completely certain, and her certainty, amid all the other uncertainties, was infectious. By the time she was throwing open her arms like a biblical prophetess, most of the crowd, including many Catholics, found themselves ready and willing to suspend all doubt and fall into them. In their moment of need, this was the kind of talk they wanted.

She gathered herself up for one final blast. "The very idea of surrender is abhorrent, good friends," she cried. "Of course we shall all die, but what does that matter? It's what God wants, all part of his plan. Raimon may not be willing to see it, but this is exactly what the Flame's about. We are to make the final sacrifice together and our deaths will be a great Occitanian victory. 'Here perished the Cathars, who were the real Occitanians,' people will say, and our sacrifice will be their inspiration, so that after we're dead, others will follow where we led. I say to you, let Count Aimery come and take the Flame. It will do him no good! He may have the box, but everybody will know that the Flame is really ours, bought and paid for with Cather blood." She was like a woman possessed.

"Adela! For God's sake!" Raimon did not dare touch her, for she seemed untouchable.

"Yes, for God's sake, Raimon, that's exactly right! This world is evil and imperfect but we can be perfect Cathars, perfect Occitanians who will die perfect deaths and spend eternity in perfect comfort and perfect peace. It's the will of God that we should all be perfect like him and reject the world as he did. Do you have it in you to be a perfect Occitanian, Raimon? Do you?" She glowed as though, even in the midst of their current horrors, she could feel the comfort and peace already.

All around, Raimon could see people lapping up the heady

image of being a perfect martyr and, along with it, the whole Cathar dream. He had no tools with which to fight such an enemy. "If the Blue Flame wants us to die as Cathars," went up the shout, "then that's what we must do."

There were a few who slipped away, but Raimon didn't see them. He was transfixed by the sight of Adela playing the swaying crowd as a snake plays a rabbit. "There are children here," he cried at last. "Do you want them to die too?" It made no difference. She offered him only the glazed smile of the fanatic.

But something about her smile made him inhale sharply. He stood on a rock and smashed two helmets together. "Listen to me!" The surprise of the clang gave him a moment. "Listen for just a second! Even if you believe what Adela is telling you, you can't die a perfect death. For that you need to receive the Cathar consolation from a perfectus. If you die without it, your sacrifice will be in vain because you won't be perfect in any way. You'll just be fools who died for a fantasy."

He felt the crowd momentarily sway back toward him. A fantasy? They didn't want to die for that. His heart rose, but only until a voice, smooth as silk, came from under another muslin shroud. "How lucky, then, that I am here and ready," and pulling off his scarf, a man stepped forward. At once Adela, with proud subservience, placed herself firmly at his side.

Raimon's hand flew to his sword. "You!" He felt as though he'd fallen into a pit.

"For those who don't know me," the man said, usurping both Raimon's authority and Adela's quite effortlessly, "my name is Prades Rives, known to some of you as the White Wolf, and I'm the Cathar perfectus who, in God's service, consoled Felippa

Belot, the mother of Adela and Raimon, before she died. She's in heaven now, and I am here and at your service."

"No!" Raimon knew he was shouting and that shouting was not the right way to deal with such a creature as this but he couldn't help himself. "This man's at nobody's service but his own. And he didn't comfort my mother, he killed her." He could tell that the crowd, now gawking at the White Wolf, was barely listening. What had Raimon offered them? Defeat. What was this perfectus offering? A ticket to paradise.

Raimon launched one last appeal. "Please," he begged, "please listen to me. This man believes all worldly things come from the devil. Even the food we eat. He will offer you consolation, yes, but afterward he'll forbid you to eat ever again. You think you'll die as heroes? Well, you won't. You'll die as pathetic skeletons, too weak even to stand."

"And what, pray, are they now?" The White Wolf gave a lean grin. "Where is the food that I will forbid them?" It was a direct hit to which, though the White Wolf waited politely, Raimon had no reply.

The perfectus effortlessly took up where Adela had left off, smiling easily at each person, drawing them into his confidence. "My dear friends. My good friends. We must all die, and as Adela says, we in this place should count ourselves lucky that we can die for God and the Occitan at the same time. Few are granted such special grace. It is one of the joys of our faith."

As a last, desperate ploy, Raimon seized the Flame and held it above his head, hoping that the White Wolf might try to snatch it and that somehow this might jerk people out of the virtual hypnosis into which they had fallen. But the White Wolf was too wise for that and anyway, it was not necessary. As

Adela had said, he did not need to hold the Flame to possess it. Through her words and his own, it was his already.

The White Wolf wasted no more time talking. Instead he sat at once and began his consolations, watching with evident pleasure as those he touched and murmured over were rendered almost drunk with excitement at their transformation into perfecti and, with only slight prompting, volunteered enthusiastically for the fast to the death known as the "endura." Why not? There was no food anyway, and if it helped them to achieve heaven more speedily, it was surely a blessing.

When it came to the turn of Yolanda's friend Beatrice, the girl who should by now have been married, Raimon tried physically to restrain her. She shook him off and clutched her little sisters to her. She would believe in the White Wolf and her sisters too. Why not? What else did they have? Raimon begged harder but the only result was that when she answered the White Wolf's questions, Bea's voice rang out with added conviction. The White Wolf was delightful with the children.

He was also delightful to those coming over from the Catholic faith, fulsomely congratulating them, in God's name, on their bravery. They left his side sobbing, some with guilt at having given up their own faith so easily, others with a confused sense of having been caught up in something they would normally have shunned, and others still who nervously knew they were doing wrong but wanted to follow the crowd. Soon, however, they forgot their fears and their reasons. Here on this plateau, the White Wolf held them in the palm of his hand.

Occasionally the perfectus looked over at Raimon, but not with triumph. Rather, he seemed filled with regretful sympathy, especially when Raimon's father, Sicart, knelt and bowed his head. Parsifal and the few other dissenters, like Gui and Guerau, the White Wolf ignored. Cador he tried to lure in, stretching out in friendship. The little boy spat into the dust as his father had once done when he'd spotted a white crow. This was a tiny source of gladness to Raimon. He wished he'd done it himself. "We'll fight as Occitanians under the Flame and we'll win," Cador declared. "Isn't that right, Raimon? And then your Yolanda will return and we'll all live at Castelneuf."

"Cador," Raimon held him tightly, "if we fight Aimery, we won't win."

The little boy frowned to prevent a tremor spreading, then he gathered himself together. "In that case, I'm going to stand by the Flame with my catapult," he said. "That's a fine way to go, isn't it, defending the Flame of the Occitan? Will you stand there with me, Sir Parsifal, and if I draw blood from one of Count Aimery's men, will you let me have a go with your sword?"

"I'd be honored to stand with you, my boy. If you draw blood, not only can you hold my sword, you can have it."

Cador seemed very excited by that.

Dawn broke shortly after the consolations were over. Raimon sat with Brees's head on his lap and the Flame beside him. The dog's eyes had faded to dirty copper, his tongue to gristle gray. Cador lay against his scrawny flank. All their mouths were white with salt and their chests occasionally rattled. There was little other noise, for the excitement of the consolations had dulled. It felt as though everybody was waiting, although nobody knew quite what for.

"Take the Flame and go." Parsifal crouched down beside Raimon, then his legs gave way altogether. "You could get out of here with Cador. You've nothing to stay for now."

Raimon looked at Parsifal and shook his head. "I'm going nowhere without you."

"Look, Raimon, I'm no good to you anymore. I've played my part. Now I'm just a burden."

"And you think I'd abandon you in this state? Or the huntsman? Or Gui and Guerau and the dogboys? They wouldn't make it down the hill either."

"But getting the Flame away—"

"Does the Flame stand for forsaking those who've stuck by you?"

"No," said Parsifal, rather humbled.

"Then that's not the way," Raimon said. "Even among all this"—he gave a hopeless gesture at those huddled around the White Wolf—"I know it's not the way."

Parsifal looked at his hands. "How I wish it was," he said.

Raimon gave him the briefest and most painful of smiles and began slowly and rather uselessly to pick bits of dust from Brees's ears. As the light strengthened, he sensed the vultures creeping closer. He could already hear their thin whistles and smell their carrion breath. He shivered, and not just because the air was chilly. He stopped dusting Brees's ears and gazed at the Flame for a long time, blinking as it nodded until at last, from sheer exhaustion, he lay down in the tiny, tear-shaped glow it offered, and slept.

It was the flashing that first alerted them all. A few blinding glints some way off. Raimon, who thought he hadn't been sleeping, stood up and peered northward. There, another glint, and another. He squinted, trying to gauge the distance. Three miles, maybe four? He ran to Parsifal and shook him. "Count Raymond," he said. "Thank God."

The camp rose as the news filtered through and the glints multiplied and multiplied until they were like a distant silver river running sometimes above and sometimes below ground. In an hour, they could see the dust raised by an army of horses' hoofs. In two, they could make out the color of the pennants. But the troop was not making its way to them and the pennants were not the colors of Count Raymond. The troop was headed for Castelneuf and the colors, flying high and quite unmistakable, were the colors of Sir Hugh des Arcis.

6

The Wedding

Now we must go back again to September, and to Paris, where we find that Laila Hajar Mais Bilqis Shehan had not exaggerated when she said she could sew. Her stitching was more than skillful and she had a feel for cloth and style that could not have been taught. She seized on the bolts of silk left behind by the seamstresses, tested them, stretched them over a table, and set to with the scissors, glancing up at Yolanda occasionally to see the slope of her shoulder and the set of her neck. She did not inquire as to why Yolanda took no interest in the clothes or why, when presented with a hooded robe stitched so beautifully that it seemed woven as one piece, she turned away and sat stroking Ugly by the fire. If Yolanda wanted to be silent, why, Laila could be silent too.

When Hugh returned from his business and found the seamstresses fled, he came upstairs to inquire, but once he saw Laila's workmanship he made no complaint. Besides, he had his own preoccupations. The army required to subdue Raymond of Toulouse's rebellion in the Occitan would not raise itself. Nor could it be raised haphazardly. Rather, it must be assembled in a very particular order so no baron would feel slighted or exalted unless that was what Hugh and the king intended. The table in the hall of the tall house gradually filled with lists to which scribes added and subtracted in a constant scratch, scratch, scratch. Money, men, supplies; money, men, supplies. Favors called in. Duty owed. Summons to be enforced.

Not that any man had to be coerced. Everything that went wrong in France, from the rise in the price of meat to a surfeit of wasps, was now ascribed to the Cathars in the Occitan. Knights Hugh scarcely knew offered their services and the services of all the lesser knights in their household. Soon, in Paris at least, all Occitanians, whatever their known religion, were referred to as heretics. It was simpler that way and had the added benefit that heretics merited no mercy.

Hugh posted formal guards outside his house, dozens of them. Until Yolanda bore the des Arcis name, he told her, she was the enemy too and must under no circumstances go out. He seemed sorry. She just watched the pile of wedding clothes grow. Had Hugh cast her into a dungeon and melted down the key she could not have been more trapped. Even without the guards, she was never alone.

In the evenings, when dinner was over, she and Laila would leave the knights to their drink-fueled boasts of old battles and retire to an upper chamber. Yolanda would stare out the window and then into the fire and Laila would sit in the corner and examine the contents of her casket until she got bored and then she'd begin to boast quite as well as the knights. She had conjurer's skills, she announced, that were superior to any warrior's accomplishments. She never let Yolanda see into the box and occasionally something inside it would have her counting or grimacing. She never explained why she did one or the other, only sometimes raised a candle and sighed, glancing at her audience, which sometimes included a few of the inside servants, through carefully darkened eyelashes.

Yolanda, who usually had Ugly on her lap although the dog was too large, did not consciously ignore Laila. She often did not even see her, so intent was she on her own thoughts. She could not marry Hugh, yet here she was, about to be married. She could not countenance the Occitan being destroyed by war, yet the enemy war machine was being gathered all around her. She could not imagine living without Raimon, yet here she was, still alive. She thought these thoughts but she seldom cried. That too seemed beyond her now. Instead, a kind of paralysis had set in.

When the wedding clothes were almost finished, Laila made a coat for Ugly from offcuts of wool. She wrapped it around the dog's ribs, rather more fleshy now, and laughed a high, quicksilver laugh when Ugly nervously twisted to inspect her garment and then whined, uncertain whether this was comfort or torture. The housekeeper sitting with them giggled.

"I'll embroider the des Arcis fist onto the sides and then Ugly can be your bridesmaid," Laila said.

Yolanda started. "You'll do nothing of the sort."

"Of course not. You wouldn't want such a hideous creature at your wedding."

Yolanda removed the coat from the dog and handed it back. Laila took it. In the last two weeks, depending on her mood, Laila's hair had been dark, pale, red, and tawny. Tonight her hair was yellow and her skin had a golden hue. Yolanda had gotten so used to the endlessly changing appearance that she barely even noticed. Not so the housekeeper, to whom

Laila's whims were fascinating. She knew of Laila's sharp tongue but tonight she felt brave. Putting down her embroidery she patted Ugly and asked Laila if she chose the color of her hair in honor of different saints.

Laila exploded with laughter. Saints? She had no time for such things. Nor would you catch her bowing to the dictates of the church bell. What did priests know that she did not? She would bow her head to nobody and nothing except the dictates of her own will. The housekeeper, a devout woman, gave a sharp retort that made Laila laugh even more. "You're a cabbage to believe everything the priest says," Laila told her. "Or perhaps that's an insult to cabbages."

"How dare you?" The housekeeper stood up, hotly affronted. "I was only making conversation."

"Look out! There's a spider up your nose!" Laila launched herself at the woman, who knew from experience what to expect. She gave a shriek and ran out of the room.

Highly delighted, Laila seized Ugly, put the coat on again, and added a hat. The dog slunk over to Yolanda.

Yolanda picked her up and continued to stare into the fire. She'd barely been aware of the altercation and had had no desire to interfere. Laila sat beside her and stretched out her feet to the blaze. "You're an odd one and no mistake," she remarked. "You've got everything here and a smart wedding to look forward to and still you're not satisfied." She was feeling mellow with her stomach full, all the bruises life had inflicted fading, the housekeeper scandalized, and a silver coin in her pocket, given to her by Hugh after she had mended one of his shirts. Yolanda started, then rose. The room, lit by a hundred candles on Hugh's instructions so she should be able to read if she wanted to, was baking. She went to the window and threw it open.

Over the rooftops, from a far tower shone a blue light, and without thinking she pushed the shutters wider and leaned out. Farther and farther she leaned until she would have fallen had Laila not grabbed her from behind. "What are you thinking, mistress?" the girl cried furiously. "If you die, I'll be back out on the street."

Yolanda, who had had a fright too, turned on her. "Do you ever think of anybody but yourself?"

Laila was quite unabashed. " 'Course not. If I don't think of myself, who's going to? I've no Sir Hugh. I've just an ugly dog." Her eyes were unflinching and her hair bounced. "It's all right for you. If you don't like life here, I expect you can always run home to a doting father. Girls like you always have doting fathers."

"I don't have a father at all anymore," said Yolanda. "He's dead, and my mother too." Guilt pinched her conscience. She had said no prayer for her father's soul since she had come to Paris, not one.

Laila did not waste her sympathy. "Lucky you," she said. "My father doesn't know I exist and as for my mother . . . ," she trailed off.

"You said you were the daughter of an infidel princess."

Laila shook her curls as though they were daggers. "And why not? My mother was a princess, sort of. It's what she told people. Perhaps she was of better blood than you, Lady des Arcis."

"I'm *not* Lady des Arcis, and I never will be."

"Then you're a fool," Laila said, with a little tip of the shoulders. "Your man is loaded with money."

"He's not my man."

The girl snorted.

"And who cares about money?"

Laila sat down and began toasting her feet again. "Only somebody who's never felt the skin of her stomach meeting the skin of her back."

"You have him and all his money then. You marry him."

"I would in a moment, if he wanted me. I can't think of anything I'd like more."

They glared at each other. Then Yolanda lurched forward as if a boulder had hit her.

"Laila," she said.

Laila was already standing. Grinning wickedly, she took a piece of cloth and flattened her hair beneath it. Then she lowered her eyes and walked very slowly around the room, imitating the gait Yolanda had adopted in Paris: an older gait, not heavier, but less free, as if hampered by more than her skirts. She began to recite. "I, Yolanda whatever whatever, take thee, rich handsome Sir Hugh—"

Yolanda caught her. "In my dress and under a veil, do you think anybody—"

"Perhaps not until—"

"It was too late."

Laila tossed off her makeshift veil and with it some of her bravado. "I'd be thrown in prison as soon as our trick was discovered."

Yolanda was not giving up that easily. "You're always boasting about your magical skills. Cast a spell on him. There was an old woman at Castelneuf, Nan Roquefort she was called. She gave out love potions. Very basic magic, she said. Anybody could do it. You could feed some to Sir Hugh just before the ceremony and then he'd fall at your feet."

"I don't know if my spells are strong enough for Sir Hugh." For a second, Laila looked frightened.

"It doesn't matter," Yolanda was quickly reassuring. "Hugh won't throw you out because he'll know it's my doing. He may be French but he's not heartless. He'll divorce you."

"Then I'll lose everything."

"No, no. He'll divorce you and pay you lots of money."

"Are you sure?"

"Quite sure. He'll pay for your silence because he won't want to look a fool. And I'll pay you handsomely too."

"Sir Hugh'll be paying twice, then, unless you've money of your own."

"What do you care? It'll still be money." For the first time, Yolanda briefly wondered how much dowry money Aimery had sent. How much was she worth? I would like to know too, for Aimery had sold me along with his sister. Was I, the Amouroix, worth more than a chest of Castelneuf gold?

Laila cared nothing for that. Her feet were tapping. "And what will you do when I'm becoming a lady?"

Yolanda didn't even have to think. "I'll go home. Sir Hugh told me the Blue Flame vanished, but I don't know." She felt her blood begin to flow again. "I'll go home and find the Knight Magician. He might still have it. I should have gone to find him the day I met you. I should have run away then. Why didn't I?" She looked baffled, as though she'd just woken up and found herself in a strange place.

Laila, seeing her transformed like this, was suddenly full of suspicion. "Why should you get a knight magician and me just an ordinary knight? A knight magician can probably just magic more money if he runs out. I'd rather have him than Sir Hugh."

Now it was Yolanda who was laughing. Laila was relieved when she stopped.

Yolanda hugged her arms around her ribs. "Do this for me, Laila Hajar Mais Bilqis Shehan, and you'll be rich and an empress among women and Ugly a queen among dogs."

"Don't be ridiculous. Ugly's mother was a bat and her father a fox. Nobody can overcome such disadvantages." The girl's voice was dismissive but her eyes were speculative. "We could try it, if you really want to. I'll have the money first."

Yolanda leaned out of the window more carefully this time and held her face up to the starred sky. Perhaps Raimon was looking down at her. Her pulse quickened. She was still Yolanda of Amouroix and of course it would be in the Amouroix, not here, that she would find his ghost. Whether she would also find the Knight Magician and the Blue Flame she didn't know, but Raimon's spirit would be under the waterfall and in the meadow, or perhaps on the snowline where she climbed in her ibex-skin boots. "Money?" she said to Laila as her heart began to beat in time with mine again. "Why, you can have as much as you like."

Laila pulled her in and shut the window. "You'll have to cut your hair before the wedding and make it stick up. I'm not doing anything to mine," she said.

"I'd shave my head if it meant that I could go home."

"That is a good idea," Laila agreed. "Your hair stinks." She inspected the dirty hanks that hung down Yolanda's back, holding her nose theatrically. "When it's cleaned and cut, though, can I sell it?"

"Sell it?" Yolanda stared at her.

"Oh yes," Laila said. "There's a real market for other people's hair here. Haven't you noticed? Everybody wants to look like King Arthur's queen Guinevere."

"The women of Paris are disgusting," said Yolanda. "Guinevere would never have worn somebody else's hair."

"At least the women of Paris wash," Laila replied pointedly.

"At home we swim," Yolanda told her, "and the river's so clear you can see your face in it. You couldn't swim in the cesspool they call a river here." She moved back to the fireplace and kicked one of the logs. "And you can hear the birds, not captured birds in cages, but real birds, and the grass is green and not trodden into a mire, and you can walk through town swinging your arms because there's room, and sometimes the barges come and Beatrice and I . . . and Raimon and I . . ."

"Raimon? Tell me." Laila threw on another log and her green eyes blinked. She had learned early that knowledge was power. "Tell me, do," she coaxed. And suddenly, because she was too full to keep it all in any longer, Yolanda did. She spoke for a long time and Laila forgot not a word.

Three days before the wedding, the hairdresser was summoned. He viewed Yolanda's locks with distaste. "Cut it all off," she said.

The man leaped as if the hair had slapped him. "Oh no, absolutely not, mistress. Sir Hugh des Arcis won't like that, wouldn't like that at all. I'll wash it, but I'll not cut it."

"Sir Hugh told me to do as I like," Yolanda said with chilly determination, although now the moment had come she felt quite shaky. "I'd like to cut it off."

"We'll at least have to ask permission." He began to put his implements away. Yolanda grabbed the scissors and chopped off a ragged lump. It fell to the floor with a thud.

"Oh, God in heaven," the man said.

"Yes, indeed," Yolanda said. "That's certainly what Sir Hugh will say if I tell him you thought this cut was all the fashion."

The man muttered and mumbled but he grasped his scissors and by the time he had finished, Yolanda's hair swung well clear of her shoulders.

She had expected to feel relief and excitement, for this was the beginning of her escape. Instead, the lightness was the heavy lightness of loss. How odd, she thought, that in such a time of trouble something as unimportant as hair could mean so much. Yet she couldn't deny that she felt altered, not quite herself, as though her childhood had been sliced from her. The ends tickled her neck as she sat by Ugly and she found herself stroking the dog's bald patches again and again.

"You don't look as bad as I thought you might," Laila said helpfully as she sent for pails of water to wash what remained.

"I don't care anyway," Yolanda said, determined that this would be true. Laila humphed, seized a bucket, and emptied it over her mistress's head.

When his future bride appeared at dinner that night, her hair a bronze halo, Hugh broke off his conversation with Amalric and crumbled his bread into small pieces. He watched her walk the whole length of the hall, first in shadow and then in light. The other knights stopped talking too and shuffled their feet. Perhaps things are different for you. Perhaps you can do what you like with your hair. It grows on your head, after all. But at the time of my tale, for a girl like Yolanda to cut her hair was, in the opinion of some knights, an act of such grave disrespect to a future husband that the consequences were unknowable. Hugh was aware that everyone was watching him as he gripped his goblet and then touched the hilt of his dagger. When Yolanda took her seat, his voice was not quite as it usually was. "Why did you do that, Yolanda?"

"Do what?"

"You know very well what."

"I want to wear a cap of gold and pearls for our wedding and my hair was too long."

Hugh waited what seemed like an age. His knights held their breath. Then, at last, he gave a half-smile. "Is that so." He scrutinized her for another long minute, still crumbling his bread, and then let go of his dagger, turned to his other neighbor, and resumed his conversation. The man coughed, then obliged with more lists and plans. Hugh nodded, but all the while he was looking around his hall and eventually he found Laila Hajar Mais Bilqis Shehan lurking. Today her hair was raven black and her skin blue. When she found him staring at her, she stared right back.

The next day, as if a sudden urgency had swept through the house, preparations for the campaign gave way to preparations for the wedding banquet. Flat carts, their iron wheelrims scraping and jarring, rumbled into the courtyard and disgorged carcasses for trimming and preparing in the kitchens. Butchers and huntsmen offered both the ordinary and the exotic. Barrels of fish were rolled along, some rejected outright by the cook, generating fights that the guards had to referee. Closed baskets of chickens, ducks, and pigeons awaiting slaughter were stacked shoulder high. Flocks of geese, their wings pinned, were driven in. In the end, the yard looked as though all the creatures in the world had descended to offer themselves up for the feast.

And after the animals and fowl came cartloads of freshly braided rushes for the hall and lavender to disguise the stench of the sewage now running freely over the flags. Well appointed as Hugh's house was, the one hundred new servants employed for the wedding together with the knights summoned for the muster had sorely taxed the rudimentary drains he had taken pains to install.

The most heart-stopping event for Yolanda, after the cutting of her hair, was the installation of the new tapestries that the des Arcis household in Champagne had worked and sent down as their wedding present. Unrolled and hooked up, these had Hugh and Yolanda stitched in the yellow and crimson des Arcis colors on magical hunts they had never attended, praying together in churches they had never visited, and eating exquisite picnics under bowers of roses in a domestic bliss Yolanda hoped they would never experience. In every one, she was a beautifully solid maiden with childbearing hips and an adoring smile and Hugh was standing over her, her protector and her lord. The certainty of the tapestries that she really would be Lady des Arcis was like a punch. Laila looked at them too, and smiled.

Then there was the efficiency. Hugh's steward fumbled nothing, forgot nothing, overlooked nothing. If the wedding preparations were any indication as to how northern nobles fought their wars, Yolanda could not help thinking, even with the Blue Flame the south was doomed.

The eve of the wedding came almost before they knew it and Yolanda and Laila were talking in furtive tones, Ugly stretched out between them. Laila, luxuriating in cushions, was pulling the dog's ears while Yolanda sat bolt upright fiddling with the rough ends of her hair. There was a tread on the stairs. Yolanda froze.

"What does he want tonight?" whispered Laila.

Hugh knocked and opened the door. "Leave us," he told Laila.

"Don't," said Yolanda.

Laila looked from one to the other, stretched out each leg, and cocked her head to one side. Hugh was irritated. "Get out, and take the dog with you." Laila pursed her lips and vanished.

Hugh sat on a hard wooden settle, fingering a little parcel wrapped in deerskin. The day had been long. There had been trouble between Amalric and Henri that had almost ended with bloodshed. Then the steward, a fussy man, had detained him for hours with needless details about the horseshoes for the forthcoming journey. There had been more atrocities in the city, and now that he was to be married, he found that Raimon's letter sat like a stone at his belt. He shifted his feet. "I wanted to give you a present before tomorrow," he said.

Yolanda pulled her knees to her chin. "I don't want a present."

"Want one or not, it is customary to have one. Here." He touched his belt then held out the parcel. She did not move to take it.

"Yolanda," he said, "you can spend your life being miserable or you can choose to be happy. I may not be the perfect knight of your Castelneuf troubadours but I think we can be very content together if you will allow it." Her silence was the silence of absolute resistance. His fists clenched without him realizing. "Will you try it? It will be very wearing to live in a state of war at home as well as on campaign."

"I don't want the perfect knight. I don't want to be content. I don't want to marry you."

"I'm afraid you don't have much choice. You seemed content enough in my company at Castelneuf."

She breathed a little faster. "You weren't my enemy at Castelneuf."

Hugh leaned back. "And I'm only your enemy now if that's how you choose to see me."

"You're French and I'm an Occitanian."

"Indeed. But south, north, French, Occitanian, we're all joined together, are we not? We all understand each other. We don't need interpreters. Our boundaries are fluid. Our rivers flow into each other."

"It's easy for you to say that. You're the invader, not the invaded."

"My dear Yolanda, you're forgetting why you're here. The whole point of our marriage is to ensure that nobody invades the Amouroix. Once we are man and wife, no soldier is going to loot Castelneuf." He paused. "And perhaps you should also remember that it was not I, nor any Frenchman, who built the weaver's funeral pyre. It was your brother." He still couldn't quite mention Raimon by name.

"And I'll never forgive him for that. Never."

Hugh shifted. The letter crackled. He spoke faster. "Look. Tonight is a night to look forward, not back. Take this." He held out the parcel again, and when she still didn't move, undid it himself and slowly tipped it so she could see inside. There, in a bed of straw, was a tiny flame of hollowed-out blue glass. In the light of the candle, it shimmered like the sea on a summer's day. It could have been a monstrous parody of the real Flame had not the craftsman blown and chiseled it to almost unimaginable heights of delicate perfection. It was the most beautiful thing Yolanda had ever seen.

"It's come from Venice," Hugh told her, watching her closely. "It's for you to have always." He got up and left the parcel on the settle. "This marriage may not be of your choosing but I shall do my best to be a good husband. Now, I shall come to see you in the morning before you put your veil on, to make sure everything is"—he gave her a look—"in order."

As soon as he had gone, Yolanda rose and picked up the glass flame, fully intending to smash it. How dare Hugh give her such a gift! What did he know of the Flame? But it was like holding a ripple of reflections and she found she couldn't let go. Instead, she strode around the room clutching it, hating Hugh doubly for the courtesy he had shown her and for giving her something she couldn't destroy. He was trying to undermine her hatred for him and that, above all, she found intolerable.

She put the glass flame back in the skin bag and was tossing it onto the windowsill when Laila skipped in, waving a bag of her own. Hugh had given her not just one coin but a whole bulging purse. "You should get married more often," she crowed, "or I should. I'm rich and your Hugh likes me." She shook her purse, loving its weight. "There's plenty more where this came from!"

"Be quiet." Yolanda's nerves were raw. "Hugh's coming up in the morning before we can put on your veil. I'll have to be dressed in the wedding dress."

Laila eyed her up. "You've not changed your mind and decided to marry him yourself after all? I'm not giving you the money back."

"No," said Yolanda. "No, of course not. Nothing like that. But I'm going to have so little time to get away." She steadied herself and motioned to her own parcel. "Look what he brought me." Laila tipped the flame out for herself, exclaiming in a long, whistly breath. "This is like that Flame you told me about. What an odd thing to give you. Venetian, do you think?" She rolled the ornament about. "It must be worth a fortune. If you don't like it, you know, you can always sell it."

Yolanda was shocked. "Not everything has a price."

Laila laughed at her. "Yes it does," she said. "My mother sold me to a silk merchant for ten silver sous and my sister for five because she had a lame leg."

"She didn't!"

"Oh yes she did. And why not? We weren't worth anything to her and we were worth something to him. It was a fair bargain." Under its paint, her face became mischievous although it was hardly the time for mischief. "I expect your mother would have done the same."

"She certainly wouldn't have!" Yolanda exclaimed.

"Oh, don't be so grand. Your brother, Aimery, has sold you for a place at King Louis's court, hasn't he? Everything and everybody can be sold if the price is right." She gave a sideways look. "You'd sell me if it could bring that Raimon back to life."

"I—no. I—"

"Oh, you would," said Laila airily. "And if you wouldn't, it would show that you didn't really love him all that much."

"Raimon would refuse to be bought like that."

"Nonsense," said Laila, waving the glass flame in the air. "To be back with you, I think he'd refuse nothing." It was the first compliment she had ever bestowed and Yolanda didn't challenge it, even though it wasn't true. Laila knew nothing of the honor of love. She knew only survival and calculation. That was the difference between them. "We must try and sleep," Yolanda said.

"Yes indeed." Laila wrapped the flame and trickled the money from her purse into her lap. "Tomorrow is my wedding day." She grinned, and then carefully bit each silver coin with small white teeth to make sure she was not being short-changed with base metal before stuffing the purse and locking it in her box of tricks.

They got up very early and when Hugh came in to see Yolanda she was dressed in blue embroidered silk with silver ribbons and rosettes centered with milky topaz. He looked at her with approval and complimented Laila on her craftsmanship. The instant he was out the door, the girls swapped dresses, and now Laila looked every inch the bride and Yolanda, in a dress of matching color but much plainer, looked every inch the servant. Laila, hair dyed brown today, preened in front of a looking glass and fixed on a veil of gauze so heavily embroidered that her features were quite obscured. Yolanda, her veil equally obscuring but not nearly so ornate, didn't look in the mirror at all, except to make sure that the disguise was working. "You're clear about what's going to happen?"

"Well, it's hardly complicated," said Laila. "We both go to Notre Dame and I go straight to the chapel where Sir Hugh will be waiting. I keep the veil on until we've both made our promises, by which time you'll be gone."

"Yes, that's it." Yolanda tried to sound confident. Surely by the time Hugh realized, she would be through the city gates and have found a lift in a farm cart. September was such a busy month on the roads that it would be easy to disappear. Once she got back to Castelneuf, she would search out the Knight Magician as Raimon had told her to do, and then, and then . . . Only in the troubadours' stories were plans brilliant and filled with purpose. In real life, Yolanda quickly discovered, plans were vague and frightening. The truth was that she didn't know what would happen, either to her or to Laila, when Hugh found out he'd married the wrong girl. She only knew that this was what she had to do. She left the glass flame on her bed.

They were ready far too early and Yolanda paced about in an agony of terrified impatience. "I should leave now," she said. "They'd let me out if they thought I was you."

"I doubt it," said Laila tartly, "and anyway, Sir Hugh's expecting two of us so we'd have to get somebody else to dress up. Do you trust any of the other servants?" Yolanda shook her head.

"Well then," Laila said, admiring herself, "unless you think we can use Ugly, you'll just have to wait."

It was over an hour before they were in the covered cart, by which time Yolanda could hardly speak. Laila, however, was thrilled. "If I saw my mother now, I'd look at her and then drive on past, splashing her with mud. I hope she's very unhappy."

Yolanda was nervously pulling at their veils. "I'm sure she is. We live in unhappy times. Now, are you sure—"

"Oh, stop fussing. I don't think we live in unhappy times at all."

She was still arguing about this when they arrived at Notre Dame. Though Amalric and Henri, friends again now, carved out a passage for them, they had a little trouble getting in at first. The crowds had heard that King Louis might appear and were pressing at the portals. The fallen scaffolding had been replaced on the tower, but fear lingered and from time to time there would be a cry and everybody would leap back. The two girls found themselves hustled about before finally being pitched into the gloom with Amalric and Henri one on each side. It was just as noisy here, however, with a veritable market in full swing in the nave and as much scaffolding and as many people inside as out.

"Where shall I go now?" muttered Laila. "I can't see a thing." She made to push the veil up.

"Don't!" Yolanda pinched Laila's arm and pushed her past the buyers and sellers and through the huddled crones reciting their prayers. As she passed them, she added her own pleas to theirs. "Please, by tonight let me be away from here." Then they were on the far side. Here it was less busy. Two chapels had been fully completed and from one of these flowed warmth and light. Hugh had not yet arrived and there was no sign of the king.

"You should stand here," Amalric said, pushing Laila forward, "and you can wait here." He pushed Yolanda back. Laila hesitated.

"Go on, go on," Yolanda hissed, "and don't forget to say nothing at all until you make your vows. Just kneel down and pretend you're praying. And remember, don't, under any circumstances, raise your veil until you absolutely have to."

"I don't want to kneel down and I won't bow my head to any god." Laila's voice was muffled.

"I'll pay you more."

"How much?"

Yolanda nearly kicked her.

Once Laila was kneeling, Amalric and Henri knelt too. They had no interest in the bride's servant girl so it was quite easy for Yolanda to edge her way out. In a dark corner, she discarded her dress, and in leggings and tunic, with an ugly woolen hat pulled low over her face, she was a nobody. Outside again, she slithered through the crowd and ran as fast as she could toward the bridge. It was hard, always pushing against the direction of the market carts pouring into the city, but she threaded her way with dogged determination. There was safety in the throng. Nevertheless, it took longer than she had hoped to get to the gates and she kept visualizing the scene in the chapel. Would Hugh be kneeling beside Laila now? She hoped the priest would give a lengthy sermon. The gate was wide open. She joined a group of peddlers. She was nearly out. She was out. She was beginning her journey home.

She never saw the horsemen waiting under the city wall. She never saw one of them gesture to the others to wait as she walked purposefully toward a group of drovers headed south. She never saw anything until she was swung off her feet and found her face half an inch from Hugh's.

There was nothing courteous about him. Without a word, he galloped with her back to Notre Dame, scattering people and livestock without apology. When they arrived, he flung her down and himself after her and then marched her, his hand like a cattle prod in the small of her back, into the chapel, not caring who he trampled. Laila was still kneeling and still veiled, still waiting for her husband to be. Only when she heard the commotion, then turned and saw Yolanda, did she spring up.

Hugh pushed the girls together. "Did you think I hadn't guessed?" He ripped the veil from Laila's face. "I am not so stupid, Yolanda. I knew the moment you cut your hair." He snagged his signet ring in the gauze and tore a large hole. "I can forgive many things but I won't be humiliated. We're going to be married here and now whether you like it or not." He towered over her, a pillar of fury. A small crowd gathered. Here was a pretty sight! A bride and her husband quarreling before they were even wed, and in the church too. Their gaze flicked from Yolanda to Laila. Was this man trying to marry two women at once?

Hugh caught them whispering and bellowed at them until most scuttled away. He caught one woman. "You. Come here. Swap their clothes," he ordered.

She balked. "Me? What, swap their clothes here in this sacred place?"

"For God's sake, woman, yes. Here in this sacred place. Hurry up."

The woman did not dare refuse. Bustling Laila and Yolanda into the deepest shadow she could find, she huffed and puffed as she did as she was bidden. Laila complained loudly. "It wasn't my fault," she declared, "and I want my money."

"You'll find your money at the bottom of the Seine," Hugh roared, "and yourself there too if you don't hurry up."

He hardly waited for Yolanda to be decent before he came for her, grinding the scattered topaz pearls beneath his feet and calling to the priest.

The ceremony took almost no time. Hugh took Yolanda's right hand and declared, in bald terms that contained no hint or trace of affection, that he took her, Yolanda Eloise Berengaria Dulcia d'Amouroix-in-Occitan to be his lawful wedded wife.

Then it was her turn. "Repeat after me," said the priest. She was mute. Hugh gripped her arm. "We're waiting."

"I can't."

"Do it."

"I can't." Her voice was shrill. "I can't."

"You can and you will." He gripped her arm harder.

The priest had seen this before. If he had his way, girls would be married before they could speak. Not that it mattered, as he explained to Hugh. "The Masters have made a ruling on this. She doesn't actually have to say the words. I mean, she's been living in your house?"

"Yes."

"And she's been preparing for today? Seamstresses, hairdressers, that kind of thing?"

"Yes."

"Well then. The Masters take that kind of behavior to imply consent, if you see what I mean. Especially if the bride's a little"—he coughed—"foreign. You see, quite often foreign brides don't speak at all. I can perfectly well declare you man and wife together." He made the sign of the cross.

Hugh was not content with this. "You'll say the words," he barked at Yolanda. "I can either be Aimery's brother-in-law or his enemy. Which is it to be?"

Yolanda threw back her head and instead of the words of the marriage ceremony, she looked at the ceiling and sang the only song it seemed right to her to sing. She sang the "Song of the Flame," and sang it so loudly that another crowd began to gather. "*In Occitan there hovers still, The grace of Arthur's table round—*," she broke off. "Is this kind of bullying what passes for grace in Paris, Sir Hugh?" She sang some more. She sang as if she'd never stop.

"That's enough!" Hugh was shouting, almost beside himself. "Do you want me to destroy the Amouroix?"

She kept singing.

He shook her. "You've seen the army under my command, Yolanda. Do you understand that if you don't say yes when the priest addresses you, I'll take it down to your precious Amouroix and then we'll see who's singing." He had her pinned against the wall. She was trembling all over but he was relentless. "Marry me or hear the Amouroix howl."

Her song wound down like a dying musical box. She saw me in flames. She saw the people she loved whipped into submission. She saw the "Song of the Flame" lost forever. Her voice cracked and then petered out completely.

Hugh gestured roughly to the priest. "Ask the question now," he ordered. The priest did so.

"Yes," Yolanda whispered. What else could she do?

At once Hugh leashed his temper and lowered his voice though he was still breathing hard. "We're man and wife, then."

The priest nodded violently. "Man and wife. And what God has joined together, let no man put asunder."

"Amen to that." Hugh pulled out a purse. "The bargain's sealed." He handed the money over. The priest took it and hurried away.

Hugh had one more thing to do. Taking Yolanda's unwilling left hand, he thrust onto the middle finger a gold ring inlaid with rubies. She pulled it off. He thrust it on again, scraping her knuckles. "You'll wear it," he said. "That's part of the contract. I won't tell you again."

Then they were out of the chapel and back at the house amid the cheering and feasting. So much color, so much revelry.

Yolanda saw none of it. She felt as though she had been crushed under a rock.

For Hugh too the adrenaline of the day drained away as quickly as wine from a barrel. His wife sat at the head of his table like one of the condemned calculating the moment of her final execution. It should not have been like this. Still, he'd done what had to be done and claimed what he had contracted to claim. And he'd keep his side of the bargain. I, the Amouroix, would be safe. He'd make sure of that.

It was not too long before he gave permission for Yolanda to leave the room and as she walked between the tables, he toasted her. "Lady des Arcis," he said. She heard her new name echo around the assembled company; she heard it echoed by the servants; and she heard it echo through the very stones as it followed her the whole way up the stairs like the toll of Raimon's funeral bell.

7

The Confession

You will know as well as I do that weddings do not end with feasting. At midnight Hugh arrived outside Yolanda's chamber door and did not knock before entering. She was curled up by the window.

Laila was aggressively nervous. "It wasn't my fault. She told me to." He stared beyond her as though she wasn't there. Laila caught his wedding coat. "She's not said a word. Not a word. It's like she's vanished. I think maybe the shock's turned her a bit simple." Hugh pushed her out and Ugly after her.

When the door was locked he set a jug of wine on the table. "I've brought you this," he said, his voice very calm, "because I thought you might need it." He came closer to her. At first he thought she was hardly aware of his presence, but then saw his mistake. Every time he took a step, she pressed her knees closer into her face and wound her gown more tightly around her legs. When he tried to straighten her out, she clamped in tighter and tighter. To take her, as was his right, he would have to use force, and Hugh had never used force for such a thing in his life. After a while, he downed the jug of wine himself, then got up without a word and went back downstairs.

A strange truce manifested itself between man and wife over the next week. Hugh carried on as if all was well between them, bringing presents that found a welcome with Laila at least. She wore the jewels and examined the trinkets, although she was less enthusiastic about the books. Yolanda would look at nothing. Every time he approached her she rolled herself up and at night she made Laila sleep against the door. This was not from fear. Rather, a steely anger of terrifying intensity had taken her over. She felt as though she could stab somebody just by touching them.

Laila thought her behavior quite ridiculous and told her so. "It's over. Done. And in the name of all magicians, don't you know how lucky you are? I've been talking to the servants. This man's wealth is boundless. You be a proper wife to him and just think what power you'll have. He's given you all this stuff even though you bar the bedroom door!" Yolanda visibly shuddered. "Oh, don't be such a ninny. He only wants his rights. It's nothing much, if that's what you're afraid of. Nothing much at all." Laila never let up. "Come now, mistress. Do you really think you're going to do better than Sir Hugh des Arcis? You can't mourn that boy Raimon forever."

Her words made absolute sense to her but no sense at all to Yolanda. Yolanda accepted that Raimon was dead, that her fate was sanctioned by the church and set in as much stone as human affairs can be. She didn't care that her husband was rich. But though she did care very much that her marriage would at least save me, she was also determined that she would never be a real wife. She would resist Hugh if she died in the effort. He had his contract. She had said the word he had asked for. He would get nothing more.

Preparations for war continued. Since Yolanda refused to leave her room, Laila spent a great deal of time at the window, providing a running commentary on the filling of the wagons that would make up the war train. This morning, armor chests, each painted with a knight's colors, were being placed reverently side by side like compact rows of coffins. One priest swung an incense-burning censer over them, another scattered Holy Water with a small stiff brush. She cast a sly glance back at Yolanda. "I've seen the answer to your troubles, mistress," she said. "Onto your knees at once and pray that Sir Hugh's killed. You could be a rich widow before the year's out."

Yolanda started as though Laila had pricked her with a pin.

It was almost time for Hugh to leave. The troops of men-at-arms he had been awaiting from Champagne had arrived, together with crossbowmen, blacksmiths, and carpenters. The siege engineers were waiting outside the city gates. Squires were comparing swords and daggers. Warhorses were shod and in fighting mood. The atmosphere was one of testy exhilaration. They needed to be off. Nevertheless, the steward insisted that the baggage wagons were unpacked once more and then repacked to check that truly nothing had been forgotten. There was another delay when two cooks vanished with four barrels of eels. Then Hugh's huntsman could not decide which hounds and hawks to take. He had been told that there would be no sport on the way down, for they were to move quickly to beat the fast-approaching winter, but he did not believe it. A knight couldn't resist hunting. There must be hounds and hawks. And then there was a natural reluctance to get going, for though to an outsider the whole seething mass looked like the start of an enormous festival, at the back of each mind, from the greatest to the least, was the bleak prospect that the festival would end in a lonely grave on foreign soil.

Hugh took himself upstairs one last time, already dressed for the journey, and this time Yolanda did not escape completely. He caught her and attempted to kiss her, but her lips locked so tight against him that it was colder than kissing a statue. He let her go. "I've tried to be kind to you, Yolanda."

She faced him squarely. He owned her and could do with her what he would, but before he went off to conquer the Occitan, he should be under no misapprehensions. "If things were different, Sir Hugh, perhaps I could feel kindly toward you too. That's the truth. But I don't love you and whatever you've come up here to do, although I can't stop you, you should know that I am not willing and I never will be."

"By God, you just never give up," he said.

"No," she replied. "Occitanians never do. And another thing. You say the Blue Flame has gone from the Occitan, but I think you're lying. I think it will be waiting for you, Sir Hugh, and I think it will beat you."

Hugh had a sudden prickling up the back of his neck, as though somebody was walking over his grave. Without thinking, he spun on his heel and locked the door from the inside. Then he almost ran back to Yolanda and grasped her hands. They were tense enough to break but he did not let go. Down below, there was a riot of sound but in here they were quite alone, for Laila had not hung about. She was skipping about in the courtyard, stealing small things that would fit into her box.

Yolanda didn't breathe as Hugh shuffled her along until he could blow out the candles. Now they stood in the semidark. He could smell the soap in her hair. She could smell the leather of his tunic. Had Yolanda fought him, as Laila undoubtedly would have, the outcome might have been quite different. But she didn't fight, at least not with her fists. Instead, though she knew it would grate, she opened her mouth and sang again, as though if she could just keep singing she could pretend that whatever happened was happening to another. She was hardly aware of choosing a song, but found herself in the middle of one that Gui had taught her about a falcon that loses its love but remains faithful until one day it soars up so high it finds heaven. It was a silly song, really, although the tune was pretty, but she sang it with such intensity in her thin, pure voice that it seemed to cut the air. When it was finished, with unconscious wistfulness, she sang of a knight who took a lady by force and woke to find her dead in the morning. God did not look kindly on this knight. His house and his name sank to nothing and disappeared. She never closed her eyes as she sang, but stared straight ahead.

Perhaps such unsophisticated tunes and sentimental whimsy would have left Hugh unmoved had he never ventured into my lands, had he never been to Castelneuf, never heard Yolanda sing in the château's brilliantly tapestried hall or seen her dance like a rope of smoke. Perhaps he would have been deaf to her song had his first sight of her not been a heedless, utterly abandoned leap into Aimery's arms from the top of the great hall steps. But he had been there, had heard her, had seen her, and had marveled at the sheer uninhibited joy and confidence of that leap. And now, because of all those things and because he could also see in his mind's eye his bones, forgotten and untended in a rough, worm-ridden hole in the ground, her song undid him.

When she finally fell silent there was a long, long pause. In it, Hugh tried to gather himself together again. He had come here as a husband, to make her his wife. That was how he must leave.

But that is not what happened. "When I first agreed with your brother that I would marry you, Yolanda, I didn't imagine anything about you," he said, his voice so low that she had to strain to listen. "The arrangement suited him, suited me, and suited the Amouroix. It was a transaction. Then I met you—" He stopped, and a tremor went through him. He had to wait for it to pass. "Then I met you, and though it was still a transaction, it was not just a piece of paper. You seemed filled with magic. Remember when I called you a sorceress, that first evening at Castelneuf?" He looked straight at her. "I wasn't wrong. You were a kind of sorceress because I found I wanted you, not as part of a contract but for yourself, in my castle at Champagne." He couldn't look at her now. "Do you think me cruel?" She was dumb. "I hope not. I was angry at Notre Dame, very angry. I had hoped so much that— Well, let's just say that I hoped. I'm not angry now. Now I don't know what I am." He went to the window.

The armor wagon was directly below, the chests closed. He felt that prickling again. "I don't think you know about war, Yolanda, or have any notion of the force a king can unleash against those who rise up against him. Thank God you've never seen any of that in Amouroix, though if you had you'd understand better why you're here now." He walked toward her but did not attempt to touch her. She knew he wouldn't, somehow, and did not back away. He gave one of his half-smiles and gazed down into her face. A shifting shadow or perhaps just the arc of her eyebrows or the single chip in her front tooth that gave her mouth such strange distinction finally decided him. "I'm going to give you something that I should have given to you before," he said quietly. He reached into his belt and put a roll of parchment into her hands.

Yolanda took it and held it to a lamp. It was clear that what Hugh had given her was a letter and that though it was addressed to her by name, other hands had already opened it and other eyes read it many times. The writing was completely familiar. It was the same painstaking script as her own and could only have been written by three people: herself, Aimery, or Raimon, because her mother had taught the three of them and they had dutifully copied her style exactly. There was the line block underneath the Y. There was the long tail at the end of the a. Lady Margaret, so careful in many things, had been extravagant with ink. Yolanda began to read. Only halfway down did she begin to realize she had taken in none of the words. She began again. It was hardly long. She stopped, then looked at the signature. It was a cruel hoax. She would read no more.

Hugh, seeing her stop, took the parchment from her and read aloud, repeating the familiar phrases without looking at them. Instead, he kept his eyes on Yolanda, expecting her to grab the parchment. But her hands were grasping each other. He parted them and put the letter into them. "It's not a hoax, Yolanda."

It took her more than a moment to believe him. Then, "How did you get it?" Her voice slipped uncontrollably from low to high.

"It came through a messenger in the pay of Raymond of Toulouse. But I knew already from Aimery. Raimon was saved by the Blue Flame and a peculiar-looking man whom Aimery described as a blackberry bush in human form." That sounded trite and he didn't mean to be trite.

"The Knight Magician," Yolanda breathed.

"The who?"

"It doesn't matter. You knew this and you never told me?" Her voice was now as low as his.

"We had to be married. Remember the contract."

"How long have you known?"

"About three months."

"Three months." She felt a great noise in her ears. "You knew when we had barely set off to come here?" She scrunched the parchment, almost tore it, and then flattened it out again. She had another question, the most vital. "Why do you tell me today?"

Hugh did not want to explain but she would not let him evade her. She came very close. "Tell me, Sir Hugh. You *will* tell me."

He stared into the fire. "I don't want to die with the boy's letter on my conscience. I could just have left it to be opened on my death but sometimes these things go amiss, and today it seemed wrong to hold onto it any longer."

"So just *today* it seemed wrong?" She hardly knew where to put herself. "Where is he?"

Hugh did not pretend not to know. "He's leading a small rebel army that I last heard Aimery had trapped on the top of a hill." He did not soften the truth. He could see no point now. "He has the Flame, so I'm to go and help Aimery bring the siege to an end and make sure the Flame is sent to the king before I move on to subdue Count Raymond and the rebels around Carcassonne."

"Subdue? You mean crush." Yolanda would not allow him to gloss over anything.

His lips tightened. "I don't deny that, but at least there is to be no violence in the Amouroix. When I get there, I'm simply to take the Flame from Raimon and send it to the king. He's impatient to go on a crusade to the Holy Land so he wants this business finished quickly. Once he has the Flame, he thinks the Occitanian spirit will be broken." She made a small noise, like an animal. Hugh's voice was flat now, with no sense of victory. "I know my duty to my king, Yolanda. If Louis wants the Occitan subdued—crushed—as his loyal vassal I'm going to make sure that's what happens."

He imagined she might be weeping or so livid she couldn't speak but when he looked up, he saw something quite unexpected. Yolanda was not really listening anymore. She was reading the note again and as she ran her fingers over the letters, her face, for so long almost a mask, began to blossom before him, bubbling back to some semblance of the face he remembered. He had done her a great wrong and now had given her nothing that would change her situation except the most powerful thing of all: he had given her hope. For these few moments she was untroubled by visions of Raimon besieged on a hill with the most powerful army in Christendom mustering against him. She could only see him alive when for so long she had seen him dead. Now he was moving, speaking, laughing, thinking of her not from some star in the sky but here, on earth, his skin warm and his blood hot.

She folded the parchment. "I'm coming with you."

"What? No."

"I am," she said. "Wives do go on campaign."

"You're going to Champagne."

"Only if you tie me up. Is that how you want your wife to appear? Your prisoner?"

"Yolanda, we're at war. The north against the south. You must understand that. That's why I'm here now. It's why I've given you the note."

"But the Amouroix at least is safe! That's your famous contract, as you never cease to remind me. You cannot forbid me to go there on grounds of danger and I don't ask to go anywhere else."

He made one last attempt. "Don't you know how easily contracts can be broken?"

She gazed at him. "I don't think you are a man to break your promise," she said, challenging him directly, "and you claim that King Louis is more good and virtuous than you are. Is that not true? Will he not honor his word?"

"The king is an honorable man, but as I've told you, he's impatient. Impatient men sometimes act precipitously."

She shook her head. "I'm coming."

He tried a different tack. "You're my wife. I can dispose of you as I wish."

She took his hands, the first time she had done so voluntarily. "Sir Hugh, that's quite true and it's as your wife that I'm asking you. I'll never ask anything else. If you have any feelings for me at all, please don't leave me behind."

You may wonder why Yolanda spoke so calmly. It was not through wisdom. Yolanda didn't possess that kind of wisdom. But she did possess an instinct, and that instinct told her that howling about the past would only get in the way of the future. For now, she must concentrate on what would happen next. That was more important than anything else. She made her request again, pressing Hugh's hands in her own, and when she saw him hesitate, she knew he was lost because, for the first time since Castelneuf, her face was open to him and he couldn't bear to see it close against him again.

In a moment she was calling out the window to Laila and telling her to prepare for the journey. Laila popped something into her sleeves and bounded back upstairs. Infected by the atmosphere, she had already been fuming at the thought that she and Yolanda would be sent to some dreary castle to sit out the winter. She became even more garrulous than usual in her delight. "Will we put Ugly out in the street? I mean, we can't take her with us and once we're at Castelneuf you'll have Brees back and won't have any use for her."

"Of course not. We'll take Ugly too." Laila's casual betrayals never ceased to surprise Yolanda, but she brushed this one off, her heart too full. She addressed Hugh, who was now standing uncertainly by the door. "When do we leave?"

He raised his arms, a visible surrender. "The baggage train files out as soon as I give the order but I and all the knights under my command are required to go to Saint-Denis for the king's blessing. We're to be there by midday. I'll have a cart made ready for your things."

"I shan't need a cart."

"Don't be silly," said Laila, dragging over a large trunk and flinging out the blankets stored inside it. "Your wedding clothes alone are worth a fortune, and look at all these things Sir Hugh has given you." She was quite unabashed, gathering up all the ornaments, jewels, trinkets, and books, and suddenly exclaiming, "Didn't you give her a falcon too? We mustn't forget that. Oh, and the shoes," she muttered. "Six pairs, all of the finest leather. Worth at least ten thousand sous each."

Hugh was on the stairs when Yolanda called him again. She

was haloed in light and had a new gravity about her. Now, for the first time, she looked like a glowing young wife of whom any man might be proud. "You're not going to play a trick and vanish without me." It was a statement, not a question.

"I'm not going to leave without you," he said heavily, "although there may come a time I wish I had. I should have kept silent."

"No," she said. "Your mistake was not to speak before."

He started down the stairs again. "I'll send two men for the chest." Then he stopped. She was still standing above him. "I think, Yolanda, that if you're coming with me, you must also come to Saint-Denis. That's what knights' wives do, and you're still my wife." Her glow made his heart leap right into his throat. "And you must promise to keep wearing the wedding ring."

He thought she might refuse but she did not. Instead she held up her hand and showed him her finger. It seemed to her an easy promise. After all, it was only a ring, a dead thing, and she was no longer dead. Life was tingling through her again, and the feeling was glorious.

8

The Journey

So it was that, as Raimon sweated and starved on his hill-top, Yolanda dressed quickly for the ceremony at Saint-Denis with the help of Laila's dextrous fingers. Waiting in the courtyard, she found a pretty bay pony with black legs and pricked-up ears. Hugh was holding reins of blue-dyed leather. "This mare was for you to ride to Champagne," he said, "but I daresay she'll be as happy to go in a different direction. Her name's Garland."

Yolanda hesitated. "I don't want any more presents."

"I thought she might be more comfortable than Galahad or Bors."

Yolanda stroked the mare's velvet skin and watched it ripple under her fingers. It reminded her of the glass flame. "I can't take her, Sir Hugh. Not now. Not ever. No more gifts."

He gave her his half-smile. "You," he motioned swiftly to Laila. "Yes, you, the heathen beggar to whom I've already given a small fortune." He was determined to appear completely himself again.

Laila drew herself up. "I'll have you remember that my name is Laila Hajar Mais Bilqis Shehan and my father is—"

"Yes, yes. Would you like a pony to add to everything else?"
Her response was instant. "What do you want in return?"

"I don't want anything."

She laughed in his face. "Everybody wants something."

"All right," said Hugh. "I want you to be loyal to your mistress."

"That's all?"

"That's all."

Laila gave Yolanda a scathing glance as she took the pony's reins and sprang on. "I've got myself a bargain." Though it was clear from the way she held the reins that she had seldom, if ever, been on a pony in her life, she looked quite at home.

Yolanda allowed Hugh to help her onto Galahad. Beside Garland he looked heavy and old but she stroked his calloused neck. "Take me home, Galahad," she whispered, but the old horse still waited for Hugh's command before he moved off. That was what he was used to.

They rode the few miles to Saint-Denis in silence, an armed escort on either side. Straw effigies clearly meant to represent strangled Cathars or even Count Raymond of Toulouse had been strung from gibbets. Some of the effigies were charred from being scorched with torches. Yolanda paled and buried her knuckles deep in Galahad's mane. They were soon past, however, and after half an hour found themselves amid the costermongers and vendors crowding the abbey square. As soon as Hugh appeared a roar went up, with women throwing flower petals amid a chorus of "Godspeed, Sir Hugh!" and "Death to all heretics!"

When they saw Yolanda with him, the crowd hesitated and when her southern origins were broadcast, some people hissed.

Hugh clicked his tongue and pressed his horse close to hers. Yolanda hardly noticed. What did these people matter? She would never see them again.

The abbey church glowered in the graying skies. Yolanda walked in and gasped. She had expected to be chilled in the gloom of God's eternal disapproval. Instead she had strayed into paradise. Saint-Denis was ablaze with gilt and gold and sun-bright colors, every statue and pillar a feast of precious rubies and sapphires. From the high altar to the bishops' miters, emeralds and pearls were carefully arranged in patterns of brilliant symmetry while visions of the saints, picked out with studied simplicity in black-bordered stained glass, cast a rainbow of multicolored crescents from their deep, rich glazes. Yolanda's mouth opened as Hugh propelled her through pools of tinted light toward a group of fully armed knights gathered in the apse like shining giants.

Leaving her at the top of the nave, he himself went directly to Amalric and took the shield held out to him. They were just in time. Male voices began to chant from hidden cloisters and the knights standing shoulder to shoulder locked their shields together. The chanting grew louder, and now retinues of hooded monks, each holding a gleaming candlestick, filed into the choir stalls. Yolanda could not make out the words of the chant but she didn't need to. This entire glittering, shimmering palace, together with all it contained, was both a paean of praise for God and a plea, almost a demand, for the success of the warriors going out to fight in his name. Yolanda could hardly breathe. How could God resist?

Standing between the parallel lines of knights were two figures, the taller wearing a dalmatic embroidered with crimson strawberries and holding a twisted shepherd's crook of solid silver. The second man was much younger, younger even than Hugh, and he was dressed in a simple tunic and leggings, much as a peasant might be dressed, except that his leggings were so finely spun you could see the curve of muscle beneath them. At his belt hung an ivory cross and crowning his fair hair was a heavy, unadorned circlet.

Here, at the very heart of this spectacle, was the ogre on whose head Occitanians summoned down all the plagues of Egypt. Here was the fiend who drank blood from his enemies' skulls. Here was the monster against whom Yolanda and Raimon had conducted a thousand imaginary childish battles. Here was the king of France himself. She didn't want to look at him, yet she couldn't look away; and when he raised his face toward the rose window just as the sun broke through, her hand flew to her mouth. Why, he was beautiful! Then he lifted what he was holding and thrust it into the echoing vault.

It was a banner, crimson in color, bound through a series of shining petals to a golden lance, the trailing end split into eight silken flames. Red flames. The whole abbey fell silent, broken only as people fell to their knees, one after the other, whispering, "The oriflamme! The oriflamme!"

This jolted Yolanda. She would not kneel. Of course not! No Occitanian would kneel before the blood-colored symbol of France. Instead, she held herself almost ridiculously upright as the king brandished the banner high over the knights. He began to move slowly toward the nave and stopped at the transept crossing. Here, in a voice of extraordinarily powerful sweetness, he called out Hugh's name. "Behold the banner of France," he cried. "Behold the oriflamme! And behold Sir Hugh des Arcis, the knight in whom I rest all my trust."

Hugh prostrated himself, then rose to his knees and made his oath. "I dedicate myself, with God's help, to the service of my liege lord king Louis. In God's name, and the king's, may I be victorious over all our foes and return here to this place a worthy knight and vassal. To this end I dedicate my life. Pray God for victory in the name of Christ, Saint Denis, and the king!"

"In the name of Christ, Saint Denis, and the king!" The echo was enormous. Then everybody bowed their heads.

Just as she hadn't knelt, so Yolanda didn't bow. Instead she saw how the oriflamme called to these French knights as the Blue Flame called to Occitanians. And she envied them. They were not split between Cathar and Catholic. These silver warriors were joined together as tightly as each link of Hugh's expertly tooled mail.

The king came right up close and at first she kept her eyes firmly to the front. She didn't want to see any more of his youthful glamour. But she couldn't help herself. She turned her head and there he was, standing with his legs slightly apart, the lance of the oriflamme now resting easily on the painted floor, his throat bare, and his fair hair flowing down his cheeks, the very image of the saintly knights of whom Gui and Guerau used to sing. Except, to her relief, he was now so close that she could see that his beauty was not unblemished. Though his face was unlined, worry had already made its mark, denting cheeks that should have been fuller and tensing lips that should have been soft. Fair stubble grazed his chin in uneven bristles. But it was his eyes that caught her most. Though he appeared to be looking straight at her, he did not actually see her because there was no room in his eyes for anything but the fervor of his prayers. Suddenly it was no longer a saintly knight or an angel Yolanda thought he resembled: it was her inquisitor uncle, Girald. Now she understood what Hugh had tried to tell her so many times: that all the brute power of even the largest army was as nothing compared with the implacable resolve of a king who believed himself the chosen instrument of God. Then the service was over, the king gone, and they were on the road toward Orleans, the dust rising in an endless gritty cloud.

It was a joy to her, naturally, riding south where she knew I would welcome her, a joy now seamed with a deep hem of worry, but a joy nevertheless. She would not allow herself to dwell on the king's face or believe that the Blue Flame and the Knight Magician had rescued Raimon for nothing. With every mile that passed she was closer to those she loved, and she would make sure she never left them again.

Yet as the weeks of traveling wore on, she was amazed to find it quite hard to remember she was traveling with the enemy. When the army bivouacked for the night and the men joked, bantering with Laila and feeding Ugly with scraps, she was sometimes lulled into assuming that when they arrived there would be no fighting, that all differences would be resolved over a game of kick ball or in a mock battle like the ones sometimes organized for parties. It was only when she heard the knights shout "Amen" when the priests traveling with them drew down curses on all Occitanians as Cathar heretics that she felt truly threatened.

"You must tell those priests and your knights that not all

Occitanians are Cathars," she told Hugh. "And even if they are, it doesn't make them the spawn of the devil. For goodness' sake, Occitanians are mostly quite ordinary people." With high unease, she stood in her stirrups and looked behind her, suddenly acutely conscious of the sharp spikes of a thousand deadly spears.

"The Amouroix is safe." Hugh straightened his sword. "And Aimery is a Catholic."

"That's not what I mean. I'm not just concerned for the Amouroix and you know it."

"My men must see the enemy in any way that makes their job easier," he said shortly.

"But that's all wrong!"

"It's war." Hugh kicked his horse on.

Yolanda dropped back to ride with Laila. The girl was in her element, flashing heavy-lidded eyes at Hugh's hapless knights. As she intended, they found everything about her, from the odd combinations of skin and hair color to her carelessly bold conversation, both dangerous and thrilling.

Laila shifted Garland to let Yolanda in beside her. They had left Paris way behind and the country was opening up. "Where are all the towns and all the people?" Laila asked. "Is the land here cursed?"

"It's just the country. Lots of it's like this."

"It's not natural," she said. "It's not like this in the Amouroix, is it?"

"Well, I suppose it's quite empty. We do have towns, of course. Ours are more compact than Paris and mostly built up the sides of hills that are much steeper than these."

Laila reined Garland in. "Are you joking?"

"No." Yolanda couldn't help laughing.

"How do you walk if nothing is flat?"

"We don't wear very fancy shoes."

Laila made a face and went back to the soldiers.

But Yolanda pondered on what Hugh had said. If seeing the enemy a certain way made the soldiers' job easier, perhaps she could make their job more difficult. She frowned as an idea began to take shape. Galahad threw up his head as she inadvertently tightened her grip. She let go and stroked him. She wouldn't sermonize. No. Knights hated sermons. How, then? The answer was obvious. She would tell stories. She would show them the Occitan as it really was, paint a picture, make its villages as real as their own villages, its châteaux as real as their own châteaux, and she would start at once.

She fell back again, only this time not to Laila. This time she forced her way into a huddled band of knights riding in silence. She took some time to speak because it was hard to find the right way to begin. She could hardly say, "Now I'm going to tell you what the Occitan's really like." That wouldn't do at all. "It's a pity it's drizzling," she said at last. "I hope the weather clears when we get closer so you can see the autumn colors. They're pretty here, of course, but my mother always used to say that the Occitan produced colors God himself hadn't dreamed of."

"Heretic, was she?" She couldn't see who spoke because nobody looked at her.

"She was French, actually," Yolanda replied. "And she must have traveled this way, just like us. She had the most beautiful hair and she always sewed a swan's feather into my father's cloaks. It had to be a swan's feather." She waited. The rain drizzled on. The horses' bridles jingled. Surely somebody would ask.

Somebody did. "Why a swan's feather, then?"

"Well, once upon a time in the Occitan, there was a knight who was on a journey, much as we are, only there was a violent storm and he was knocked off his horse, quite unconscious, by a lightning bolt. When he came to, he was in a vineyard and there was a girl."

"A princess in disguise? Princesses are always in disguise." There was a ripple of laughter.

"As a matter of fact," said Yolanda, forcing herself to laugh too, "she was not a princess. She was a sylph. We have those in the Occitan. You must watch out for them. If they love you, they can make you happier than you ever dreamed, but if they hate you, well . . ."

She let the silence hang.

"Well what?"

"They'll steal your soul and never give it back and you'll spend the rest of your life searching for it."

The knights seemed to consider this. "And how do you make them love you?" a surly knight asked.

"Yes, how?" asked another, more politely. He couldn't help thinking of Laila.

"You must give them something they want more than anything," Yolanda told them.

"And what might that be?"

"A swan's feather?" the more polite knight guessed.

"Not always a swan's feather," said Yolanda.

"Gold?"

"They want something you value above gold."

"What can you value above gold?" The surly knight leered.

"Something that a lover gives to his beloved," said Yolanda decidedly. "You see, the swan's feather was a private sign of love between my father and my mother, the kind that binds you together tighter than a spring bud and makes your heart happy whatever else is going on." The knights were silent. They knew about that kind of love. The silence became less hostile. Yolanda felt it. "You see, my father would place a swan's feather on my mother's pillow or pin one to her tapestry, and in return she would sew one into his cloak. Lots of Occitanian knights do the same with different things—leaves, flowers, nuts. Actually, we had a friend, Sir Mordac, who liked to give his love birds' eggs . . . until she sat on one he'd left on her chair. It made a very unlovely mess of her dress."

The polite knight chuckled. "I'll bet he was always called Sir Egg after that."

Yolanda flashed a smile. "Quite right," she said.

"But what happened to the knight in the vineyard?" The surly knight was riding beside her now.

And so she began to weave a story, and for the rest of that day and for every day after, from Galahad's steady back she conjured up every myth, every song, every poem from the Occitan that she could remember, every ode or ballad that Gui and Guerau had ever recited or sung, every verse she had heard in snatches at the market in Foix or at her mother's knee. She closed her eyes and became part of the tapestries at Castelneuf. She made the French knights yearn to chase white harts in the snowy mountains. She made them see through the opal eyes of the lynx. She made them feel the dry scaly skins of the lizards, and then, when they shivered, brought them into the scented warmth of the great halls in which peasant and lady danced together, rough hands joined with smooth to celebrate the passing of the seasons. She told too of the Courts of Love that Aimery thought she couldn't remember, and then she spoke of her friends, describing the woodcutter's wife, Blanche, who was the guardian of a secret recipe for restoring sight to the blind; of Pierre the shepherd who had made such a pet of a robin that when it died, he paid for a burial; of Guillaume, who had twice married girls called Guillaumette; of Sir Braillard of Lum whose girth exceeded his height, and of Beatrice and her love of impractical shoes. So vividly did she bring everyone to life that the knights hardly realized that instead of hoping to kill Guillaume, they now rather hoped to meet him; instead of wanting to hang Pierre, they wanted to offer commiserations; and instead of wanting to secure Sir Braillard in chains, they wanted to laugh at him.

Yolanda watched the effect of her words with wide-eyed satisfaction. Yes, she really was fighting for the Occitan, my Yolanda, just as surely as if she wielded a dagger.

Hugh also watched and listened. Unlike the knights, he knew exactly what she was doing and couldn't help applauding. He also saw how cleverly she did not demand all the attention for herself. When the knights wished to tell stories of their own, she listened carefully and always had a funny or sympathetic comment at the end. Some of the men, not just the knights, began to show her injuries incurred by the daily grind and these she treated as best she could, calling on Laila to help her. The war train moved faster, and Hugh knew it was because, though the weather was unkind, spirits were high.

And he was not excluded. Yolanda had no wish to do that

now. She often addressed him and always smiled when she did so. Sometimes she would ride beside him, carrying the falcon he had given her and asking him how to manage it properly. Their conversations became natural and unforced, giving him a kind of pleasure he had never before experienced. Yes, he knew what she was doing, but he did not want it to stop.

One evening, he watched her encourage his trumpeters to try new, syncopated beats, telling them not to worry if they found them hard because there would be an Occitanian—and how carefully she gave that somebody a name and a character—who would be delighted to help them. When they got it right, everybody cheered and other musicians began to play. The music they made was irresistible. Yolanda and Laila flew up and spun like fireflies together, their hair flashing sparks and their shadows filled with womanly secrets. Afterward, unable to help himself, Hugh went to Yolanda's tent. She was his wife. He had a right.

She was silhouetted against the canvas, a blanket of foxfurs draped over her shoulders, her legs bent underneath her, wiping paint from Ugly's face. Laila's nonsense, no doubt. He pulled back the flap. It was clear at once that although her hands were full, she was miles away, and when he raised his lamp, she turned with such a longing in her eyes. He moved forward, his heart burning. The longing vanished before he got halfway across to her, and though she didn't speak, she held Ugly tight. He lowered the lamp and heard his own breathing, heavy and intense, and hers, shallow and alarmed. He didn't raise the lantern again, yet as he backed away he caught her sigh of relief. Such a tiny sound but it hit him hard as a hammer. He never went to her tent again.

Instead, as the great caravan wound its way through country that was swelling and ebbing and through vines of brown, russet, and blue, he found that when he slept, instead of dreaming of victory over the enemy, he dreamed of a time when he would raise the lantern and that longing would not be for Raimon, as he knew it was, but for him. After all, he was the chosen knight of King Louis of France. Surely he could make that happen.

They crossed into the Occitan and when they had traversed the plain below Toulouse, the land began to undulate as if some great animal had stirred deep below. Now, for Yolanda, time seemed to slow. She had almost run out of stories. All she wanted was to get home. They traveled on.

At last, when the clouds cleared, she caught sight of the mountains, already capped with snow. She couldn't have told a story now even had somebody asked, for her cheeks were wet with tears. How she'd missed those peaks, carved out against each other like pieces of slate, gray and black against the sky. The French knights, who had been just as astonished at the vibrancy of the autumn bronzes as she had promised they would be, shuddered and shielded their eyes. How could people live up there, where only eagles would think to build? They drew back from Yolanda. For all her songs and tales, the Occitan was enemy territory.

And Yolanda herself soon realized that whatever she felt, life for her had changed in ways quite beyond her control. She might be the daughter of the late count Berengar of Amouroix returning to the land of her birth and she might be full of Occitanian stories, but she was riding at the head of the war train of her husband, the newly appointed French Seneschal of

Carcassonne, and he had come not as friend but as conqueror. Several times people actually spat at her, which caused Laila to spit back. "I thought you said the place was full of troubadour songsters," she said, eyeing the mountains with a kind of curious panic. "These people spit like pirates."

"They're frightened," said Yolanda defensively, before adding, miserably, "and they think I'm the enemy."

"Imbeciles," said Laila with feeling. Yolanda loved her for that.

At last, after a very early start, they crossed the narrow valley gouged out by the Castelneuf river. Then they were in the meadows and past the graveyards. Only now did Yolanda raise her eyes to the silhouetted château and squint into the sun, searching for Raimon's battered hilltop behind. When she saw the prick of blue she dropped her reins and wrapped her arms so hard around her ribs that she thought they might crack.

Hugh came to her, issuing orders. Once they arrived she must remain in the château. He would not have her watched, he said. He would trust her to obey. She bit her lip and urged Galahad on. Then she strained her ears. Brees! Darling Brees! Surely he should be barking a welcome by now? Her joy began to fade. They rode across the bridge, through the town, and up into the courtyard, now weedless and tidy. Aimery was waiting for them. He was very surprised and not at all pleased to see Yolanda. Surely she should be safely in Champagne, preferably expecting a spring baby? He could not tell at once if she knew Raimon was alive. "Welcome back, Hugh," he said, pulling at his beard. He put his other hand on Galahad's rein. "I didn't expect to see your wife. It is a delicate time here, as you know."

Hugh dropped from his horse without answering. Aimery gave an internal shrug. Yolanda was Hugh's property now, and his problem. Whether she knew about Raimon or not was no matter to him. He handed her down from Galahad and kissed her formally. "And welcome to you too, Lady des Arcis," he said, intoning her new name loudly, half teasing as any brother might, and half deliberately so she wouldn't forget her new allegiance. He would not say welcome home. This was not her home. He was startled when she untwisted the scarf she had bound over her head. "You've cut all your hair off!" It accentuated her features and suddenly reminded him of his mother. He shook himself and twisted his lips into a knowing smile. "Well, there's no accounting for a husband's tastes . . ."

Yolanda tightened her own lips until they were a scarlet thread. "Where's Brees?" she said.

Aimery, with a look, gestured at Raimon's hilltop. "Over there. But don't worry. The siege is at an end." She obviously knew about Raimon, yet she had Hugh's ring on her finger. Good. "We'll be going in to take the surrender as soon as your husband is rested. You can have Brees then. He'll come back with the prisoners."

"Raimon, you mean."

Aimery glanced at Hugh. "Yes. Raimon, among others."

Yolanda called at once to Laila and the girl approached. She had Ugly in her arms. Aimery looked at girl and dog with frank astonishment. "Beauty and the beast!"

"Don't you insult me!" Laila's hair today was gentian.

"Insulting? To be called beauty?" Aimery gave a mock bow and then flipped one of Ugly's ears inside out. "And this creature could hardly object to being called a beast. I can think of much worse." Ugly licked his hand, for which Laila gave her a small smack.

"Don't lick men who call you names," she said.

Aimery laughed loudly.

"Come, Laila," Yolanda said coldly although she felt very hot.

"Where are you going?"

"Up to my chamber."

"Don't be an idiot, Yola." Aimery stopped laughing. "You don't have a chamber here anymore. Luckily, I had the servants prepare the large room for Hugh—you know, the one in the tower with the very leaky roof. It's fixed now and if that's where Hugh goes, I believe you go too." He grinned again and then left to make sure Hugh's soldiers were being given every help. Some were to be billeted in the Castelneuf courtyards and when the last of the war train arrived, it would set up camp near the graveyards by the river bridge.

It was a strange moment for Yolanda. She had been longing to get home, yet now that she was here she couldn't quite grasp it. Castelneuf itself, the place about which she dreamed, was the same yet completely different. So much had been swept away with the weeds and the dirt. Stables, kennels, towers, and patches of garden were familiar yet they greeted her more like children washed and dressed in their best clothes than old friends. The new pigeon loft cast an unfamiliar shadow. The stones of the château, which had always looked as old as the hills from which they had been hewn, now glittered silver and rust where Aimery had had them scrubbed.

She climbed up the steps to the great hall, the same steps from which Hugh had seen her fly into Aimery's arms. She didn't remember that. She only remembered Raimon once using their crumbling unevenness as an excuse to pick her up and hold her tight. Nobody could use them as an excuse now, because the masons had restored them to such smooth, regular perfection that a blind man could have walked down them without fear of tripping. She drifted into the hall and took a flambeau, holding it up to the top of the door. Surely her father's moth-eaten old bear's head would still be there, gazing sightlessly across the room. It was not. Its place had been usurped by the head of another bear, glossy and snarl-toothed, a fine specimen, certainly, but not what she wanted. Somebody caught her arm. Her heart leaped, then sank. It was Hugh.

"Remember what I said, Yolanda, about creeping out of some childhood hole to—to go to Raimon. Promise me."

"There are no holes left. Aimery's stopped them all up." She slotted the flambeau back in an iron holder.

"You know what I mean. You must remain with me for decency's sake, if for no other." He waited. "Yolanda, do you hear me? I'm waiting for your promise." He hated the harsh note he sounded, as if he were her father not her husband. Yet here, in the place of her childhood, she did seem a child again. Even the wedding ring she was twisting did not seem to attach her to him. In some subtle way, she wore it but managed to keep it separate from her, as if it had landed unexpectedly on her finger like an unwelcome blister and she was simply waiting for it to disappear. "Yolanda?"

The face she turned to him was not the face of a child. "I promise," she said, "but I don't promise forever." Their eyes met, equals in this challenge.

Hugh dropped his eyes first. "Ah," he said, with his enigmatic half-smile, "so very little is forever."

"Except love," she said.

"Not even always that," he replied.

"It is for me."

"Ah, Yolanda," he said, and then added, after she had gone, "that's just what I'm afraid of."

9

On the Hill

Half an hour later, Laila was slithering down the hill and out of the town. Yolanda couldn't leave the château, but Hugh had said nothing about anybody else. Laila didn't want to go at first, but Yolanda begged, saying that she couldn't rest until Raimon knew she was here and Brees was returned to her. With great reluctance Laila had given in, and even now she was still unsure. The steepness of the drops amazed and alarmed her. Even making her way down the winding road from the château to the river she couldn't run for fear of falling. Before the bridge she turned left to wind her way around the Castelneuf hill. At least it was impossible to mistake the way, since the track had been widened into a virtual road by Aimery's soldiers and the to-ing and fro-ing of the siege machine. And there was plenty of traffic on it, tired men-at-arms at the end of the night shift who were hungry for breakfast and longing for bed.

At length she began to climb again, first through the trees and then around the outcroppings that sprouted like jagged boils on the face of an ancient man. Never had she had to cope with such shifting and uneven terrain. Aimery's men stood about in desultory groups of a dozen or so and watched her. Now that Hugh had arrived, they knew it was only a matter of hours before Raimon had to surrender. The des Arcis battering rams would not just split the overhanging rock, they would smash it into little pieces. Des Arcis men could also flood the valley floor in far greater numbers than Aimery could manage. The place would be tighter than a noose. So they watched Laila with indulgent interest, their enjoyment increasing as she struggled and swore and her hair almost crackled with the efforts she was making. What a peculiar kind of messenger!

Laila was quite aware of being scrutinized, and heard the soldiers making jokes. When she reached them, though breathless, she spoke with more than her usual imperiousness. "I've been sent by Lady des Arcis to speak to Raimon the Weaver."

"Are you to take his submission? Is he to surrender to you? Pray, do tell us."

"Of course not. I imagine Count Aimery and Sir Hugh will come themselves for that. I just want to speak to Raimon the Weaver and take Brees back. He's my lady's dog."

"Are you sure that's not take the weaver and speak to the dog?" The soldiers chortled and stood in her way. This was as good a way as any of passing the time.

"Let me through," Laila ordered. "It'll be worse for you if you don't."

"Really? What will you do?" A soldier leaned forward and, before she could evade his fingers, chucked her under the chin. Her eyes glinted dangerously. "I'll cast a spell. I can, you know. I've a whole box of spells at Castelneuf."

The men began to laugh loudly although some shifted away. "I doubt you're a match for Nan Roquefort," they jeered. "Is that hair a wig?" One gave it a tweak. "And is that skin a mask?" Another scratched her cheek.

"How dare you! Let me through. I tell you, I've been sent by Lady des Arcis. If you don't believe me, ask somebody back at Castelneuf."

The soldiers conferred. They could see no real reason to stop her. She seemed odd but could scarcely do any harm. They finished conferring and one let out an enormous roar. Laila leaped backward and tripped. The soldiers hooted. With exaggerated courtesy, they helped her up. "You can go, mistress," they said, "if you're skinny enough to get through the crack in the rock, but remember this." They pressed in on her and said in stage whispers, "Those creatures up there, they've had no food for days now and we've heard they've turned"—they paused for effect—"cannibal!"

Laila jumped again. The men's mouths were black-toothed acres of mirth. Her hand itched to slap them but that would give them even more excuse to manhandle her. Her face was almost the color of her hair as she clambered past them and began to squeeze through the cleft.

But her humiliations had not yet ended. As she scraped her elbows and squashed her ribs, a pebble thwacked her head and bounced onto her shoulder. It was sharp and drew blood.

"Demons! Stop that!" she cried. She pulled herself farther up and another stone hit her and then another until she was caught in a veritable storm. She could see why the siege had gone on so long. Just one man could hold off many dozens from such a vantage point. But surely that was all over now.

"Are you insane?" she yelled. The pebbles changed into something softer, but this stank and left stains all over. It was rotten rabbit. "Jesus, Mary, and Joseph," she roared. "What kind of people are you?" She pulled herself onto the plateau and found herself face-to-face with Cador. "What in the name of the Virgin's toes do you think you're doing?"

"I'm making a last stand," the little boy said.

"Didn't you think that I might be a friend?"

"You've come from Castelneuf and you talked to the soldiers, so you must be an enemy." He drew his catapult back again.

His arm was caught from behind. "Cador! You can't fire at a girl." Parsifal shuffled up.

"I'm not sure she is a girl. Look at her hair."

Laila was not going to let that pass. "And I'm not sure you're a boy. Why, you're nothing but a skeleton."

They glowered at each other. Parsifal wiped his eyes. "Who are you? Why have the soldiers let you through?"

She stood tall, shaking bits of rabbit from her dress, determined to demand some respect. "I'm Laila Hajar—oh, never mind," she said. "All you need to know is that I've come from Lady des Arcis to find her dog, Brees, and to give a message to Raimon the Weaver." She was unprepared for his reaction.

"Lady des Arcis?" Parsifal repeated the name. He was as pale as if she had announced a death.

"That's what I said. If you don't know her, I need to see somebody who does."

"Did she use that name?"

"Of course she did, and why not? It's what she's called."

Parsifal took her by the arm and pulled her farther onto the plateau. He couldn't speak.

Laila now found herself in the center of a macabre scene, where the figures appearing and surrounding her were all living but nobody looked quite alive. Some of the figures were half armed but none looked fit to fight. Indeed, it was like being surveyed by a battalion of dirty ghosts. Through them all, scraping with his front paws and dragging his back, for he could no longer support himself on his legs, came Brees. The smell of Yolanda on this girl was so strong that he'd have fought to reach her through his death-throes.

"Brees?" Laila said, and her voice softened a little. "Your mistress certainly didn't exaggerate. I've got a dog called Ugly, but I'm not sure she's as ugly as you." She knelt down and then a shadow blocked the light. She looked up.

Raimon had heard the commotion, and when Brees suddenly grunted and shuddered and began to pant, his own heart had begun to pound. He stumbled after the dog, trying not to run. His disappointment when he saw Laila almost floored him.

He was not alone in his disappointment. Laila could hardly believe that this was the boy whose name Yolanda murmured in her sleep. He hardly looked a hero. He looked as skinny and dirty as everybody else. Nor, glaring at her, was he showing any of the deference Laila thought she deserved.

"Who are you?" It was more of a demand than a question.

"I've already said." She got up.

Parsifal tried to intervene but Laila talked over him. "Look," she said, quite kindly for her, given what she'd endured. "I'm sent by Lady des Arcis to—"

Raimon interrupted. "Lady des Arcis? No—"

"Yes," said Laila, and now she didn't bother to hide her irritation. "Why does everybody keep repeating that?"

Raimon kept his voice as steady as he could. "What would such a person want with me?"

Laila was amazed. "What do you think? She's sent me with

a message and I have to say that this is not the kind of welcome I expected."

Raimon heard himself ask, "By Lady des Arcis, do you mean the girl who was Yolanda of Amouroix?"

"Who else? She's here and she wants her dog back." Laila knew that this was not the way Yolanda wanted her message delivered but these people seemed stupid beyond measure. "She'll take it very ill that I was molested."

"Cador was only trying to protect us. You see how things are." Raimon's voice was hollow as a shell.

"Well then, I'll just take Brees." She put her hand on the dog's head and began to turn.

Brees whined, unsure. Raimon started forward and Parsifal put a cautionary hand on his arm. Raimon shrugged it off. Lady des Arcis. Could it really be? "There was a wedding, then?" He had to ask.

"Naturally there was a wedding and a party and Lady des Arcis went to Saint-Denis to see the king." Laila waited. She would tell him more if he asked but information was too valuable just to give away. She'd already told him more than she might have done.

"Did she send a note?" Raimon found it hard to get the words out.

"No, no note."

His face closed up. Brees whined again. Raimon looked at him. "Brees won't make it back to the château on his feet. Wait here." He went to find the huntsman. Once out of sight he found himself slightly breathless and he bent over, his hands on his knees. Though he had entertained the fact a hundred times that Yolanda might be married, he had never quite believed it. And though he would not believe she had married willingly unless he heard it from her own lips, the fact of the marriage at all, the knowledge that it had actually occurred, that Hugh des Arcis had claimed Yolanda as his wife, had lived with her as his wife these past months, and had paraded her as his wife before the king, made him dizzy. Yet she was at Castelneuf. She had returned. But as Lady des Arcis she might as well be on the moon. It took him some time to straighten up.

The huntsman was cradling a bundle of bones in his arms. Another dogboy's life was eking away. "Go to sleep, my beauty, my pretty, and wake in the thornless hunting grounds where the scent is always high and the buck always running," the huntsman was crooning as best he could through a throat that was parched and flaking. "Sleep now, my lovely. Can you hear the horn of Saint Hubert? Can you hear the wind of heaven? Sleep now. Where you are going every day is full of promise." The other dogboys were snuffling, too weak to cry. And where would the tears come from? Their bodies were completely dried up.

"Get up now and find a barrow," Raimon ordered sharply. "Brees is going back to Castelneuf and all of you with him. It's over."

The huntsman stopped crooning. "We came to fight under the Blue Flame of the Occitan," he said.

"I know," said Raimon, trying to speak more gently. "But there'll be no battle. The White Wolf has seen to that, and even without him, we couldn't fight with us so few and them so many. Sir Hugh des Arcis has brought half of France with him. But I shan't forget that you came here—and the Flame won't either," he added because he knew that's what the huntsman would like to hear. "If you go now, the dogboy may survive. And don't worry for yourself. Count Aimery has no real cause to quarrel with you, and now that Sir Hugh is married"—he tried to keep his voice perfectly even—"to the count's sister, I'm sure he and Lady des Arcis will make sure you are well treated. They'll send men up later to bring the rest of us down." He was relieved to find that if he called Yolanda Lady des Arcis, as if she were somebody he didn't know, he could manage. "Up now, I'll help you." Two barrows were found and the dogboy placed in one and Brees in the other. They pushed past the White Wolf and Adela. Neither said a word.

Cador had not yet finished with Laila. "We have the Blue Flame here, you know," he was saying. "It's older than these hills. It was lit at the time of Christ's death and it's come to save the Occitan. It's the most valuable thing on the whole earth. People would give anything to have it, and we've got it."

"Show me, then."

At once, Cador was wary. Even he realized that the look of the Flame's box was hardly the kind of thing to impress a girl whose hair was the color of hell and grew in corkscrews. "I don't think so." He glanced at Parsifal.

"Oh well. I'll see it quite soon enough anyway, back at the château," Laila said loftily. Parsifal flinched.

Raimon tried to make Cador go with the huntsman but the boy steadfastly refused and Raimon had to give up. They stood together as the little group staggered and slithered to the crag. At first the soldiers only wanted to let Laila through, but then some des Arcis men arrived to see which machine might be best to finally finish off the overhang and once they had made their calculations, they volunteered to escort the sorry procession to the château. A huntsman, five dogboys, one of whom looked unlikely to survive the journey, and a skeletal dog were unlikely to turn into dangerous fugitives, they joked. It was difficult to get them all over the rock, with Brees so ungainly and the dogboys so frail, but once that was accomplished they soon disappeared.

Raimon went straight back to the Flame, took a stick, and began to dig at the earth in front of it with small vicious jabs. He had to do something.

"She may have been forced to submit to the wedding," Parsifal said, standing over him.

"I know that," Raimon said through gritted teeth. "Of course I know that, but it makes little difference. She's married, Sir Parsifal. She's married to a Frenchman." He jabbed the stick so hard that it snapped. He threw it away. "And later today I must hand over the Blue Flame to Aimery. It's hardly a heroic end. I'm just petering out like the spring in the hill."

Parsifal rubbed his chin wearily. "Raymond of Toulouse could still come."

Raimon gave him a look more miserable than withering. "I don't believe he was ever coming, not to us. He's been told that we're all Cathars on this hilltop, Sir Parsifal, and he's frightened of being labeled a Cathar himself. He may be King Louis's enemy but he can't afford to be thought a heretic. That's why he's not here. So the White Wolf has won." He glanced at all the men and women sitting about, some still full of their consolation, others now looking less certain. He picked up the Flame with ironic bravado. "Whether we've been consoled or not, we're all Cathars now."

"Nobody will believe that you're a Cathar."

"Of course they will!" Raimon spoke faster and more wildly. "Why not? That's the romance of the tale, isn't it? How the unassuming Cathars—and nobody looks less assuming than the White Wolf—were given up to the Catholic French king by a traitorous Catholic count and how the Occitan died with them? Nobody's going to remember that, in their own way, the perfecti were just as bad as the inquisitors. And don't try to comfort me by saying that I've still got the Flame. The White Wolf's even managed to claim that for his band of brothers. It's the cleverest touch of all. Don't you see, Sir Parsifal? We're not writing the future of the Occitan, you and I. Nor is Aimery, or even Sir Hugh des Arcis. The White Wolf's doing that. The Cathar martyrs! Loyal Occitanians to the end! You know that's nonsense, and I know it. But who'll remember us? In an age of fanatics nobody bothers to remember the people stuck in the middle." His voice thickened. "This has all been for nothing. I gave up Yolanda for nothing. You came back here for nothing." He looked as though he might dash the Flame to the ground.

Parsifal snatched it from him. He was trembling from head to toe and the Flame seemed to spill out over his hands. "Don't ever think that! Don't ever say it! It's not all over for the Occitan. How could it be, as long as there's even one person who still believes in it?" He summoned up strength he didn't know he had. "Listen to me, my dear boy. I know that fighting against fanatics like the White Wolf—or, for that matter, the Catholic inquisitors—is the hardest fighting of all. In comparison with such fights, a full-scale battle with Aimery, knight against knight, archer against archer, would be a simple affair."

Parsifal felt a fire light in his belly. His illness was consuming him, but he kept going. "But that doesn't mean we have to give up! It's just that we must fight a different way, not with spears or swords, or not with them only, but with words. Though people don't listen, we have to carry on telling them that God is the God of life, not death." His breath was shortening and he could see that Raimon was still glowering, his heart still cracking in two, just like the crag. "Raimon, listen to me. Last night when I urged you to flee with the Flame, you said that you wouldn't abandon those who had remained loyal to the Occitan." He pressed the Flame back into Raimon's hands as he spoke. "And now, if you don't want the Occitan's history to be written by either Cathar perfecti or Catholic inquisitors, you mustn't abandon hope." He gripped Raimon's shoulder. "Look at the Flame, boy. Look at it. Look at it and then talk to me about your life petering out and everything being for nothing. Go on. Look at it."

Parsifal pushed the Flame so close that at first Raimon saw nothing but the filigree box, and when he fixed on the Flame itself he saw reflected in it only resentment and despair. But Parsifal would not let him look away.

It was not easy for Raimon to remain still. He felt weak and hollow and humiliated.

"Breathe slowly," Parsifal said, "breathe slowly and the Flame will breathe with you."

Raimon breathed, and as he breathed, the Flame pulsed as though it might explode, but it did not explode. Instead, it kept itself curled and smooth, its kernel almost vanishing so the blue hovered over the wick like a moonbeam. Raimon focused on the very top of the Flame where it trailed upward and dissolved into smoke, then he followed the smoke as it bent and arched and danced as he had bent and arched and danced the previous spring. He felt himself move, not so much dancing as simply melting into the serrated blue shadows that the box was casting over him. The smoke dwindled and now the Flame drew Raimon into itself, right in, until all he could see were azure and aquamarine cones, each flowing into the other and forming a color too beautiful even to name. For a moment, Raimon was no longer on the plateau. He was suspended in a place where nothing could touch him except the Flame itself, and he surrendered to it.

It was a very long time before Parsifal took the Flame and put it down and longer still before he heard Raimon, with a sigh that shook the very fiber of his being, say, "I wish it could speak, Sir Parsifal. Then it could tell everybody what I don't seem to be able to."

The old knight was fiddling with his belt, making a pouch ready for the Flame. He just wanted to feel it there one last time. "The Flame's like God, Raimon," he said at last. "It sits in silence. But that doesn't mean it doesn't speak. It speaks to you."

"I don't want it just to speak to me. That's what makes everything so hard."

"Hard," Parsifal said, "but not impossible. You must have faith."

Raimon drew in his bottom lip.

"She will come back to you," Parsifal said, "whatever has happened in Paris."

"How can you say such a thing?"

"Because I believe it."

Raimon sat down and the old knight sat next to him. Raimon helped him put the box into the pouch. When it was secure, he leaned back, his head touching Parsifal's shoulder. "Life isn't as the troubadours would have it, is it, Sir Parsifal?" he said.

Parsifal could feel the warmth of the box against his side. He closed his eyes and gave a tired smile. "No," he replied. "No, Raimon, I'm afraid it's not. Not as the troubadours would have it at all."

10

Surrender

By late afternoon it was all over. Two of Hugh's siege engines had been hauled into place by men and oxen. Four well-aimed boulders finished cracking the rock. Half crashed down at once in a storm of stone and dust, the rest a few moments later. When it had settled, Aimery, who had been waiting impatiently in the valley, rode up through the trees as far as his horse could manage and then dismounted and completed the climb on foot, with twenty knights behind him. Hugh was not there and Yolanda had not even asked to come, which had disappointed Aimery because he wanted her to witness firsthand the moment when Raimon had to hand over the Flame. Just before he reached the plateau, Aimery suddenly stopped and thought for a moment or two. "Go back to the château," he ordered his page. "I shan't take the actual surrender of the Flame here. I'll take it in the great hall. But I want trumpets and drums when the Flame comes through the Castelneuf gate, just to let everybody know what's happening. Tell the musicians to be ready."

Raimon, Parsifal, the two troubadours, and Cador were standing shoulder to shoulder in a line. Parsifal, leaning on

Cador for support, took the Flame out of his pouch. He didn't want it to be snatched from him. Those who had been consoled were standing quite separately, huddled behind the White Wolf. He stood quite fearlessly at the front, a shepherd guarding his flock.

Raimon knew, without even looking, that Yolanda was not with Aimery, and he was thankful that their first meeting would not be in such a public place. He looked out beyond the hills, unable to stop himself from scanning the horizon for any sign of Count Raymond. There was none. Then he noted that Aimery, as a deliberate insult, had not even bothered with armor. Thirst plagued him. If only he had some water, his brain would stop scratching his skull and he'd be able to think properly.

This was an almost dreamlike moment for Aimery too. Though he had known for weeks that the Flame would finally be his and though he had seen the prick of blue every night, it was still startling to find himself so close to it. Parsifal got Cador to put the box down on a flat stone so that Aimery would pick it up rather than Raimon having to hand it over. A little thing, perhaps, but it felt significant.

Aimery watched, his mouth suddenly dry. The Flame was smaller and its box shabbier than he expected. From all its years of traveling, many of the filigree holes that had once been so attractive had collapsed into each other and it was scraped all down one side. In a market bazaar, you'd have given nothing for it. Nevertheless, his skin prickled. Keeping his eyes on it, he spoke to Raimon. "You should kneel," he said. "Even kings kneel when they submit."

"I'm not a king," Raimon said. The warmth had gone from

the day and the wind was strengthening, sweeping the grass and whipping clothes against skin in the first real intimation of winter. The Flame flattened right down into the oil.

Aimery couldn't help himself. "Oh, take care! It'll go out!"

Raimon said nothing. The wind dropped. The Flame grew again. Aimery raised his eyebrows and looked around. There were Gui and Guerau, and Raimon's father and sister. He did not recognize the White Wolf, for he had never seen him before. He did recognize others. They looked at their feet. Aimery creased his brow. Something was not quite as he expected up here but he couldn't quite work out what. The White Wolf occasionally smiled. Everybody waited.

"I don't want you to hand over the Flame here," Aimery announced finally. "You'll hand it over in the hall at Castelneuf in front of Sir Hugh and Lady des Arcis." He looked for a spasm to cross Raimon's face and was not disappointed. "Some formality about such an occasion would be in order, don't you think? So. You'll carry it back. Pick it up."

Raimon did. It seemed discourteous to the Flame not to. At once he was flanked on all sides by Aimery's household knights. Other knights had to hand over their weapons to colleagues in order to help Parsifal and many of the others to walk. At last they were assembled in some kind of order, and with Alain holding the Castelneuf standard, they began their descent.

It took three long hours to get down the hill, cross the valley, and climb up through the town because they all went at the pace of the slowest. Trumpets blasted when the Flame finally reached the château gate. Raimon deafened himself to them and blinded himself to the curious crowd. He concentrated only on putting one foot in front of the other.

By the time the prisoners, as we must now call them, were all reassembled in the château's hall, it was dusk and many of those from the hill were in a state of such mortal collapse that they could not even rush to the barrels of water that lined the walls. Instead, they simply lay on the floor. Others plunged their heads into the barrels again and again. The White Wolf stood still as a pillar among them.

Settling himself on the dais in his new chair, his musicians ready behind him, Aimery clicked his tongue at the chaotic spectacle. Laila took one look, shuddered, and went to repaint her face.

Aimery called his steward. It went against all the rules of hospitality that people should starve in the hall, whatever they had done. "Bring food and drink, John," he ordered. "The prisoners should be able to stand at least."

Raimon and Parsifal were together. The sound of splashing water made their tongues stick to the roofs of their mouths but they would not move. The steward approached them with brimming tankards.

"Drink," Aimery shouted at Raimon. "You can't hand the Flame over properly if you can't speak."

Raimon didn't want to take the tankard but now that it was in front of him, his whole being fixed on it. He clutched the Flame so hard the box creaked. Drip, went the water, drip, drip on the top of the box. The Flame hissed. Parsifal gently took the box himself. "Drink," he urged. "Everybody else has drunk. I shall drink. Drink. If you drink, Cador will drink. He's waiting for you." And it was true. The little boy was shaking, his skin shriveling, but he would not drink if Raimon did not.

Raimon took the tankard and almost dropped it. He could not judge the weight. He held it to his lips. The water glanced off them, as it would glance off leather, but when it trickled into the cracks, they ached and stung so that Raimon wanted to groan. "Drink!" Parsifal repeated. Raimon moved his tongue and when it caught the first drop, the relief made tears spring to his eyes. At first he could only sip, and the water was like fire in his throat. Then he couldn't help himself. He was clutching it and pouring the liquid down, choking and spluttering. When the tankard was empty, much of it on the floor, John filled it again and this time Raimon gave it to Cador. The little boy gurgled and hiccuped. Filled again, Raimon gave it to Parsifal, and all three drank and drank. Though their stomachs were sickened, they felt as though they could never drink enough.

The hall was filling up with des Arcis men but still there was no Yolanda. Raimon saw Hugh, though, looking older and more weatherworn than when he had last seen him. Two men-at-arms were holding his standard and it was crossed with Aimery's, the fist over the bear: des Arcis over Amouroix. And there, behind, was the oriflamme. Raimon looked away.

Aimery was growing impatient. "Now, let's get on." He stood. "You"—he gestured to Raimon—"you must come up here holding the Flame high so everybody can see." Parsifal made to follow Raimon but was prevented.

Somehow, having to hold the Flame above his head made everything worse. It seemed hideously undignified, although, as Raimon tried to tell himself, what was dignity at such a moment? Yet it mattered. He lowered the Flame and held it in front of him. Aimery made an angry exclamation that Raimon ignored. A fanfare pealed out.

When he reached Aimery's chair, he was forced by two

knights to kneel and hold the Flame toward him. The fanfare came to its climax. Aimery coughed, and when the last of the peal had died away, he began to speak, quite deliberately drawing out Raimon's anguish. "People of Amouroix," he said, watching Raimon's arms shake. "This is indeed a great moment for us. We may be the smallest of the counties of the Occitan but today we are right at its heart. So now I take the Flame of the Occitan in the name of the Occitan and in the best interests of the Occitan. I take it from those who would harm the Occitan and I vow to use it in the Occitan's best interest." He was pleased with the patriotic tenor of his words and nodded at the musicians, who burst again into a paean of triumph while the drummers beat a sonorous rhythm. He waited until that was over. Raimon's arms were in agony.

The actual moment that Aimery took the Flame from Raimon, it thinned and guttered and Raimon felt a moment of complete panic. What was he doing? He should have done anything rather than this. Above him, he could hear Aimery breathing hard as he reached down. The count was anxious too. He didn't want to spoil the moment through clumsiness. Their fingers brushed against each other. It was then that Raimon felt soiled, soiled as he had never felt on the hillside even though the filth was still on him, soiled as though he might never be clean again.

He did not wait for permission to get up. As Hugh's men applauded, he stumbled back down the steps and wedged himself very tightly against Parsifal, hoping that nobody would see how badly he was trembling.

Aimery hardly noticed he had gone. Here it was, in his hands at last, the Flame of the Occitan. He couldn't stop staring at it and he found, just as Raimon had, that though it was tiny, it drew him in and filled his vision. He wanted to fight against its magnetism but the blue was so intense. He had no idea how long he stood there before he managed to hand it over to Simon Crampcross, the Castelneuf priest, who was beside him, licking his lips.

"The Flame should have a new box," Aimery said quickly, as though that was all he had been thinking about. "This old thing will never do. We'll have a smart reliquary made, studded with jewels." The priest's tongue flickered. "Take it to the chapel," Aimery said and the box disappeared into fat hands that were greedy for the claim to have held it. Aimery watched the Flame go and then turned his attention back to the hall.

The servants were busy pulling out trestle tables and filling them with food: bread, meat, and cheese. However, although the children were begging their mothers and although the mothers were gazing at the food as though it were a vision, Aimery could see very clearly that nobody was actually eating except Gui and Guerau. He called down to Raimon. "Why are these creatures not stuffing themselves? Have you turned perfectus and forbidden them to eat, true Cathar style?" He hadn't seen the White Wolf standing in a corner, his hand held up, forbidding any of his followers to approach.

"I wouldn't wish starvation on anybody. Hang me as a rebel if you want, but I'm no Cathar." Raimon's shoulders slumped. A light had gone out of him.

Aimery clicked his tongue. "Prove it. Eat something yourself."

It was hard to rouse himself. Parsifal whispered to him. Raimon looked up. "The children must eat first. I'll not eat before they've eaten," he said.

Aimery ordered that all the children should be pushed to the front. "The weaver wants you to eat," he said. "Come on then, eat. I'll not have anybody starve in this hall. Eat." But though the children lurched forward, their hunger more acute because they were no longer thirsty, their parents still held them back. They didn't look at Aimery or Raimon. They looked only at the White Wolf. Aimery was a count and a powerful lord. Raimon had led them once, but he had failed them. It was the White Wolf who seemed to hold their immortal souls in his hands. They felt they could not eat without his permission. Nevertheless, the less committed began to fidget. They had volunteered to go without food when the prospect of food was very distant, if not gone for good. It was not so now. Surely he would not stand there, his hand held up, forever?

Aimery had some cheese brought up to him and ate it himself with very obvious enjoyment. The children dribbled and whined. He threw a slab of meat down to one of Beatrice's sisters, but Beatrice caught it and, weeping, dropped it. Though the White Wolf was far from her, she thought she could feel his breath, savage on the back of her neck.

Aimery, deeply suspicious now, put his hands on his hips. "If it's not Raimon who has forbidden you to eat," he said, "somebody else must have." He scrutinized them all. "Could it be that you have an actual perfectus in your midst?"

Adela stepped forward, shaking off her father's pleading arm. "We're all perfecti now," she said in the same voice she had used on the hill. "Well, all except Raimon and his cronies. The rest of us, even those who used to be Catholics, have taken the Cathar consolation. It's in God's name that we refuse your food." She was quite unafraid. Aimery was nothing to her.

"Indeed," Aimery said grimly.

"You see," Adela continued, reaching for her martyr's crown, "we don't need the devil's food when heavenly food awaits us."

There was a general groan. What had seemed like salvation on the top of the hill was turning into torture, pure and simple. Yet the White Wolf still held sway.

Aimery gave an internal shudder. If all these creatures were heretics, the inquisitors would insist that they were all burned. He cared little about the knights and the other men. But children? Mothers? Yolanda's friend Beatrice? He strode off the dais. If there was a perfectus among them, he would find him and put an end to this nonsense. He had not even reached the bottom of the steps when the White Wolf presented himself. "I think you are looking for me," he said.

Aimery ground to a halt. "You." He was the first perfectus Aimery had ever seen and it was disappointing to find that he looked as ordinary as the Flame's box and spoke with perfect civility. "My name is Prades Rives but everybody calls me the White Wolf. It is I who offered all these good people consolation and I'm proud to say that they've all taken it. We don't need your food." He might have been passing a polite time of day.

Aimery put his hands on his hips. "The children don't seem to agree," he said, "or their mothers." Indeed, some of the women had begun to cry and a few of the braver ones even plead openly, if not for themselves, then for their babies. The smell of roast fowl and fresh bread made them all drool. Aimery was disgusted. "Tell them to eat. I order it."

"No."

"For God's sake, man."

"It's for God's sake that they've chosen not to."

"If you tell them they can, they will."

"But I will not tell them."

Aimery was in the hall now, pacing up and down.

The White Wolf stood as though without a care. He seemed to feel no hunger pangs. "You may have the Flame of the Occitan, Count Aimery, but we"—he gestured to his followers— "are the real Occitanians and this is how we choose to show it." His eyes were enormous twin globes in his skull, colorless, but not plagued by any doubts. "You can take the Flame and do whatever you like with it but you'll never possess it, not really. Don't you see?" His laugh was taut as a drumskin. "You counts and kings are still fighting the earthly fight for earthly symbols. You have yet to understand that it's the heavenly fight that counts."

"You and your heavenly fights." Aimery was livid. He was being outsmarted in his own hall and in front of Hugh, who was standing by the door observing. He walked around, his footstep heavy with menace, staring into people's faces. "Do you really accept what this man says? You can't really believe that God will welcome into heaven a lot of starving crows like you. Your White Wolf is a charlatan. The clue is in his nickname." He was suddenly inspired. "Why is he called the White Wolf?" He seized a wretched child. "What do wolves do? Tell me." He shook the child, whose teeth rattled quite audibly.

"Th—they—they eat people."

"And before that?"

"They kill them."

"Exactly. They kill people and then they eat them. That's what this perfectus intends to do." There was muttering. The

White Wolf's smile became a little fixed. Aimery didn't hesitate. "You see, you'll all die before this creature and then he'll eat you. How do you think he's survived so far, except on the flesh of his victims?"

All the children and most of the mothers began to scream. Aimery never let up with his fairy tale. "Clever, isn't it! These perfecti pretend not to eat meat, but it's only certain types of meat they don't eat." More screaming. Aimery let it go for a while, then banged his scabbard on the floor. "In this château you are under my protection," he declared and drew his sword for added effect. "If I see a wolf, do you know what I do?" He swished his sword over his head. "I kill it before it kills me!" He thrust the first child away and seized another, this time the smallest of Beatrice's sisters. Lifting her into the crook of one arm, he called a servant and issued an order. The servant ran out and returned with Simon Crampcross. The priest was holding the Flame as though it were his pet cat.

Aimery picked up some bread and then waved it in the air. "Listen here," he said. "I'm now the Keeper of the Blue Flame of the Occitan and in its name I'm giving this child food. If the White Wolf's god dislikes what I'm doing, he must send the Flame to roar out and reduce the child to burning ashes." Yet more screaming. Aimery waited. "All right, all right, that's enough. If that happens, you can all starve as you please. I'll even turn Cathar myself." He looked with distaste at the little girl's running nose and the sores on her cheeks and then gave her the bread. She barely touched it, so quickly did she cram it into her mouth. Aimery held her toward the Flame. Beatrice was sobbing but the Flame did nothing. Aimery broke off more bread. The child's eyes fixed on it and her small fists shot out. Aimery handed the bread over. She crammed that in too. He held her to the Flame again. Nothing. The crowd murmured. Aimery carried the child aloft like a trophy, crumbs dropping onto his shoulders as she chewed. "That's it," he said. "In the name of the Flame, I order all of you to eat."

Still they hesitated until the children, feeling the grip of their parents relaxing at last, rushed like hounds to the trough. Then they were all at it. In seconds, the White Wolf's authority had been usurped by the authority of meat and gravy and he was left smiling the smile of the abandoned divine. Even Raimon's father, Sicart, stumbled toward a table. Adela alone remained loyal. Aimery supposed there was something admirable about that although he couldn't quite see what.

Raimon's struggle was very hard. To eat Aimery's food, on Aimery's orders, and with Hugh standing by, revolted every fiber of every bone. Yet not to eat would grant the White Wolf a victory and that was worse. He pressed his thumbs into his palms, then walked swiftly to a trestle. He gave bread and cheese to Cador and took some for both himself and Parsifal. Parsifal was paler than ever. "Come," Raimon said gently, "eat." And turning away from Aimery's smirk, he pulled out the soft inside of the bread and put it in his mouth. Like the water, it nearly choked him but the second mouthful was easier. "Eat, Cador," he said. "Let's all eat." The little boy ate.

Parsifal let himself down onto the floor and sat supported by the wall. "Sometimes the heroic deed is the most ordinary," he said. "Isn't that both a disappointment and a relief?" He broke off a sliver of cheese. He was really beyond eating but he would try. "Not rabbit at least," he murmured.

"Not rabbit," Raimon said, but he could not smile.

While others stuffed themselves and groaned aloud, their shrunken stomachs heaving with complaint, Raimon ate slowly. The effort was such that after only a few minutes he felt weaker than he had on the hill. His tongue was furred and sour. His throat seemed to have closed up, and the world too.

He was not left in peace. After about half an hour, four guards came for him and Parsifal, two more for the White Wolf and Adela, and while everybody else lay about in the great hall, they were pushed through the door toward the smaller hall, with the wispy figure of Sicart, clutching a piece of fish, hovering behind until the door was shut in his face.

Raimon almost carried Parsifal and was grateful to do so because he could use the old man as a barrier between himself and Adela. He wanted nothing to do with her. In his mind, they were not brother and sister anymore. At the last moment, Cador, his mouth bulging, had squashed himself against Raimon's side. Raimon tried to make him go back to the great hall but the boy shook his head obstinately. "Where you go, I go," he said and took Parsifal's arm to help shoulder the weight, although there was so pathetically little weight to shoulder.

11

The Challenge

It was in the small hall that Raimon saw Yolanda. She was standing near the fireplace in deep shadow with Brees at her feet. Involuntarily, his lips parted, then closed again. It should have been such a moment, yet he was made to walk straight past, as if she were a stranger. He did, however, notice that her hair was cut short and could not think what it meant. Yolanda didn't move, but Brees gave a throaty grunt, heaved himself up, and planted himself in front of Raimon, beating his tail. Then suddenly Yolanda was in front of him too. He wanted so badly to meet her eye. They could speak without words. But he had one arm hooked tightly under Parsifal and was still being pushed from behind by a guard. All he could do was to touch Brees's head with his spare hand. Her hand rested on top of it for a second. Raimon glanced down and at once saw Hugh's ring. He pulled his hand back and, his cheeks burning, walked on. Yolanda returned to the fire. Her cheeks were burning also.

Aimery had his chair brought through from the great hall and placed against the back wall, facing the fire. He settled himself in it with Hugh on another chair, less ornate than Aimery's, on his right. On his left was a table with a jug of wine and several goblets. The four prisoners were lined up in front of them, guards to the side and behind. With some annoyance, Aimery ordered a bench for Parsifal when he realized the old knight couldn't really stand. He had been going to send Cador away but he provided a useful prop.

He addressed the White Wolf first. "It's easy to deal with you," he said. "You'll have to burn. I shall send for the inquisitors to pass proper sentence. And don't you worry. Everything will be done according to the law, right down to the number of faggots for your pyre. Until then, you'll be my prisoner. I think I shall have you caged and kept where I can see you. In here, perhaps, so Simon Crampcross can give you a sermon every day and I can eat my dinner in front of you every night. Believe me, death won't come soon enough." The White Wolf just smiled.

Aimery turned to Adela. "What a troublesome family you Belots are," he said. "You'll have to recant, you know, or you'll burn too."

Adela threw him a look. "I won't recant."

Aimery tapped his fingers together. "My, my, what devotion. I wonder if the inquisitors will manage to change your mind. They're quite persuasive."

Adela clenched her fists and the White Wolf laid his hand on her arm. "You will be strong," he said to her. "We'll be strong together." She nodded violently but her lips were trembling.

"Take those two away," Aimery said to four of the guards, "and put them in the cellars for now. If they escape, I'll have the entire guard detail flogged." Adela could be heard praising God as she was removed. Raimon didn't look at her.

Aimery glanced up and down Parsifal's ramshackle remains. The old knight was unrecognizable as the blackberry bush figure the count had described to Hugh. "Who on earth are you?"

"I'm just—"

"He's Sir Parsifal de Maurand," Raimon said.

A spider ran across the flags and Aimery crunched it underfoot. "Sir Parsifal de Maurand. Well, I think I'll let the inquisitors deal with you too, although you don't seem up to much." He noted Parsifal's papery skin and the yellow tint in the whites of his eyes. He had seen that tint before. He shook his head. "Take this old man away and find him a pallet to sleep on," he said. "Set a guard outside his room, but I don't think he'll be escaping. Get this boy—what's your name?"

"My name's Cador and I'm—"

"Get this boy to help."

"But I don't want—"

"Go with Sir Parsifal, Cador," Raimon said.

Yolanda moved from the fire. "I'll send Laila with medicines," she said.

Cador objected. "The girl with the painted hair? I don't like her."

"She's clever, though," Yolanda spoke softly. "She might be useful to Sir Parsifal."

Raimon couldn't help turning. Now he saw Yolanda clearly in the firelight. She was dressed in green velvet that had never been trailed through the mud as all her old dresses had been. She was a wife of whom any man would be proud. He turned back to Cador and his voice was suddenly very clipped. "Go on, Cador. Go right now. Sir Parsifal needs you."

The two remaining guards picked Parsifal up and, with

many more objections, Cador followed. The door closed. Now it was just Aimery, Hugh, Yolanda, and Raimon.

There was a long silence. "Well, I don't know, Raimon Belot," said Aimery. "Why can't you just die or vanish?" He stood up and walked around as though Raimon were a horse to be inspected. He halted behind Raimon's back. "As you are really nothing but an escaped criminal, you know, I could have you executed at once," he said, and making his fingers into a noose, he circled Raimon's neck lightly. Raimon tried not even to swallow. Aimery let go and came around to the front. "No, not hanging. We could either try again with the pyre or give the axman something to do. We've a good one here at the moment and he's short of work." He turned around. "What do you think, Hugh?"

Hugh had been scrutinizing Raimon but was now leaning against the wall watching Yolanda. He could see the tension in her shoulders and was remembering how her face had blossomed when he had told her that Raimon was still alive. "I think you should spare him," he said.

Aimery was taken by surprise. "Spare him? Whatever for?"

Hugh could see Yolanda's fingers clasped around Brees's collar. The knuckles were white. "The boy has taken meat and drink, as you ordered. He's a fool, even a dangerous fool, but at least he's no Cathar." He sat down again. "And I suppose that he's been loyal to the Amouroix according to his conscience, and Amouroix blood is not supposed to be spilled unless it's heretic blood. Sparing him will make you look merciful, which is never a bad thing. King Louis likes a merciful man."

Aimery laughed. "Well argued, Sir Hugh. But the murder charge against him, for which he was initially condemned back in June. That still stands, does it not?"

Hugh paused. "Are you quite convinced of that?"

Aimery could not meet Hugh's eyes. "It was—"

"Yes. I think we all know what it was."

Aimery flushed. "But if he's spared what am I to do with him? I can hardly just let him go."

Hugh heard Yolanda take a deep breath. He saw her begin to move toward Raimon. He couldn't bear it. "Send him to the king," he said suddenly. "Send him to the king with the Blue Flame. Let Raimon deliver it." Yolanda stopped in her tracks.

Now both Raimon and Aimery stared.

"For God's sake, Hugh! Raimon the Weaver take the Blue Flame to King Louis?" Aimery rocked on his heels.

"Why not?" Hugh stood again. "If Raimon takes it, the message will be very powerful. The king sets great store by the feelings of ordinary people. Raimon Belot, peasant leader of the rebels, would be the most welcome Occitanian messenger of all."

"But Raimon wouldn't do it." Aimery's voice was rising. "He'd say he would and then run off again and take the Flame with him. That would hardly please the king. And besides—" He hesitated, not wanting Hugh to guess that he was absolutely determined to give the Flame to the king himself, with his own hand. It was to be his crowning achievement; the king would never forget the generous gift given to him by Count Aimery of Amouroix.

Hugh guessed perfectly well. He would not draw attention to Aimery's vanity but nor would he cave in. "We could set a price on failure. We could keep hostages. The boy and that old knight. The thought of them would keep him to his task."

Aimery stood very still. He wanted more than anything to refuse. But Hugh had been given the sign of the oriflamme by the king himself. A suggestion from such a man was almost a command, particularly with more of the French war train arriving every day. Still, he had one last hope. "Did you hear that, Raimon the Weaver?" he asked. "Sir Hugh des Arcis offers you a bargain. You take the Blue Flame to King Louis. We keep your tattered friend and that child and if you fail to deliver it, they die. Of course, the old knight may die anyway. If that happens, I'll find somebody to take his place. Will you hand the Flame to the king yourself?"

Raimon felt a throbbing in his temples. All the time he was aware of Yolanda just out of sight. It was torture to see her and torture not to. He shook his head, trying to clear it. "Of course not. I'll not do your dirty work for you. And anyway, it's a trick. The king would never see me."

"There," said Aimery, with some relief. "He won't do it."

Hugh stepped forward. "Do you care about your country?"

Raimon stared at the floor.

Hugh came closer. "Look," he said, "even without the Cathar heretics, the Occitan couldn't withstand the might of France. You must know that as well as Aimery does. If you take the Flame to King Louis you can play your part in saving the Occitan just as Yolanda has played her part in saving the Amouroix."

Raimon wanted to shout "don't even speak her name" but Hugh had every right. She was his wife. He didn't know what to say. He was deathly tired. "Count Raymond of Toulouse will be here and when he arrives life won't look so easy for you," he blurted out and then, though he tried his best to stop it, his whole body began to slide. Everything was receding: the room, Hugh, Aimery, the feeling of Yolanda behind him, everything. He staggered, then jerked, then staggered again. Hugh caught him. "Sit, sit," he said, and virtually carried him to his own chair. Raimon sat, his head between his knees.

"Leave us for a moment," Hugh said to Aimery.

"I've more to say."

"A moment. Please. Raimon and I have unfinished business." Hugh gave a small gesture toward Yolanda.

"Ah, I see." Aimery gave an ugly smile. "Of course. I'll be outside."

When Aimery had gone, Hugh poured some wine. "Drink this," he said to Raimon. "Afterward you can rest, but not now."

Yolanda ran forward but Hugh stopped her. "Go back to the fire."

She protested but she dared not disobey in case he turned her out. She didn't want to lose sight of Raimon.

Hugh pulled Raimon upright and pushed the wine at him. Raimon didn't want to take it but Hugh was insistent. The wine, sharp and thin, needled its way down his throat.

Hugh waited with a well-disguised sense of helpless unease. Through all the dirt and defeat, how was it possible that this boy, this weaver, still had some of the same starriness about him that Yolanda had when she was happy. Why had it not been stamped out of him? He shook his head and then, because he didn't know what else to do, gave his characteristic half-smile. Raimon misunderstood the smile completely. "If you wish to crow, why not get the others in. I'm sure Count Aimery wouldn't want to miss it." He was croaking and pulling himself up. He didn't like Hugh being above him. He didn't like Yolanda witnessing this. He just wanted to get away.

"I've no wish to crow, only to do business with you." Hugh sat in Aimery's chair so that Raimon could also sit down, which he did, fearing that otherwise he would fall.

"Conquest is not business," Raimon mumbled. It was all he could do to form the words.

"It is, in part. For God's sake, Raimon. You must know why Count Raymond of Toulouse isn't here."

"He's busy elsewhere."

"No. He's hesitating."

"For good reason, no doubt."

"Yes," Hugh said. "He hesitates because he has already made promises to King Louis, made them and broken them, and is now hopelessly compromised whatever he does. I'm afraid he's given your precious Occitan a bad name. Whatever you think of Count Aimery, at least he's been honest in his intentions."

"Honest?" Raimon's voice rasped. "He sold Yolanda and betrayed the Amouroix. That may pass for honest at the French court but it doesn't here—at least it didn't under Count Berengar."

"No," Hugh said more coldly. "Berengar thought it honest to hide in this château and pretend all was well with the world. That doesn't seem to me to be very honest either, or wise. You may not approve of the new count's methods, Raimon, but at least he's not in the business of pretending. He leaves that to Count Raymond."

A great lump rose in Raimon's throat. He swallowed but it just stuck there. He saw Yolanda half get up and then, at Hugh's gesture, remain poised. He put his head in his hands and tried only to think of what Hugh had just said. Count Raymond of Toulouse a traitor? Could it really be true? Raimon felt physically sick. Certainly, the count had been very slow when Raimon had asked for help, but he had sent that note and so many things might have delayed him. He knew Raimon had the Flame. Perhaps he thought they could hold out while he set up defenses elsewhere. He couldn't believe such a man was a traitor.

He wouldn't believe it. Hugh was lying. He felt heat from the fire, yet his feet were freezing.

"Look," said Hugh quickly. He was aware that Yolanda would not be held back from Raimon much longer. "Look. If King Louis were to come here and capture the Flame, he would snuff it out. If Aimery takes it to him, it will be accepted as a trophy. But if you give it to him, well, I don't know, but it seems to me that that would be different. The king is a spiritual man. If the Flame comes from you, who have nothing to gain from giving it, I think he would accept it as a gift, a holy relic, something that he must keep in trust. Would that not be the best outcome of all?"

Raimon could not look up. It was so unexpected, this extraordinary suggestion, that a terrible thought struck him. Had Yolanda put Hugh up to this? Had she changed her loyalties along with her name? It seemed impossible. But then so many impossible things had happened. When he raised his head, he was careful not to look in Yolanda's direction. "I don't believe you," he said to Hugh. "King Louis is not coming here, and if I take the Flame to him he'll just think all Occitanians are cowards to give in so easily."

"You don't know the king," Hugh said. He spread his hands over his knees. "Look, Raimon. Only stupid people believe their enemies to be the kinds of villains created by storytellers to frighten children. King Louis is a man as well as a king, and a good man, or so I believe. But he's also an impatient man and a man who, much like Aimery, knows where his best advantage lies."

Raimon found himself transfixed by Hugh's hands. The idea that those long slender fingers with their squared ends—

capable hands, knight's hands—had touched Yolanda made his stomach churn. He felt beaten, finished. *This is how old men feel,* he thought. He longed to see the Flame. It alone might sustain him. A log splintered. He took another gulp of wine. "Why do you care what happens to the Blue Flame or to the Occitan?" he said. "What's any of this to you?" He felt Hugh shift and suddenly the silence between them vibrated. Ah, here was the nub of the matter.

Hugh opened his mouth. He wanted to talk about practicalities, about how conquered lands fared better if they submitted, about how King Louis didn't really want to be given the Flame by Aimery as if it were a favor, and about how the Occitan could retain something of its integrity if Raimon followed his advice. But in the end he uttered just one word. "Yolanda."

Raimon closed his eyes. So this was it. Yolanda. Everything here revolved around her. Hugh loved her, and what was to say that she didn't love him too? That's what wives were supposed to do.

A voice rang out. "Send me with him." Yolanda couldn't stand by any longer. She ran to Raimon's side, Brees lumbering behind. "Send us together." Raimon tried to rise but she would not let him.

"Yolanda—"

"I'm here, Raimon, I'm here."

A log crumbled and in a twitch of the light, Yolanda's expression reminded Hugh of a doe he had once come across when he had been hunting alone as a boy. The doe had been grazing a patch of meadow and he had approached her downwind, startling her. He expected her to flee at once and had raised the bow to take aim. She held her ground for what seemed like hours, but could only have been seconds, just long enough for Hugh to notice the white dapples on her green-stained muzzle and to see himself reflected in wide dark eyes. He never released the arrow and eventually she bounded away, disturbing the rest of the herd. He had killed nothing at all that day, he remembered, and in the evening he had been as glad as his father had been angry that there was no meat for dinner.

"If Raimon has to hand the Flame to King Louis, I want to be with him," Yolanda was saying. "As Lady des Arcis, I can vouch for him and make sure he gets a fair hearing."

Hugh pushed the image of the doe away. "I must go straight to Carcassonne," he said.

Raimon gripped the chair's arms and levered himself uncertainly to his feet. He could feel Yolanda's shoulder against his. "Nobody is suggesting you come too," he said.

"I could have you flogged for that."

Yolanda moved a fraction away from Raimon. "Don't you trust me?"

"It's not a question of trust."

She moved farther away and stood alone. "Hugh, please," she said. "If this is to be the end of the Occitan, let's try to make it the best end possible." It was the first time she had used his name without his title.

Hugh began to walk about. Why could he not just say no? "Aimery won't like it." He knew it was a poor excuse.

So did Yolanda. She raised her chin. "I am Lady des Arcis," she replied. "What are Aimery's likes and dislikes to me?"

An enormous struggle erupted in Hugh's breast. Yolanda had made a preposterous request. He ought to refuse. Yet, a part of him whispered, if he let her go, might she not also come back to him? After all, hawks did that. If you kept them too tightly leashed, they grew to hate you. If you freed them, they returned. Certainly, if he did not let Yolanda go as she asked, any chance that she might love him would vanish. He knew that. He knew too that it might vanish anyway. She might never look at him in the way he so wanted, never see him as anything more than the man who had married her as part of a contract, and he found he did not want to shackle her to him like that. This thought shocked him. Women, to Hugh, had always been belongings. He had married his first wife because his father had arranged it. Two months after her death, he could not remember her face or how many children they had buried. She had been a fact of his life rather than a living part and he had never dreamed of her as he dreamed of this girl standing before him, demanding that he send her on a journey that could end anywhere.

He walked about for many minutes. Raimon and Yolanda never moved. When Hugh spoke again he kept his voice quite flat, as if the discussion were simply part of the business of war. That was the only way he could continue. "If I do agree, I hope you'll remember that this is not just about the Occitan. That the old man and the boy will die if you don't return."

"Of course," Yolanda said. She took a step back.

Hugh's face darkened. "And I hope that you'll repay my trust by never forgetting, not for a minute, that you're my wife."

Yolanda held up the hand that bore his ring. "As if I could." She was standing next to Raimon now, shoulder to shoulder again. Now Raimon was not the only one who felt a little giddy.

"Don't imagine you'll be alone," Hugh said sharply. "I shall send a dozen men-at-arms with you. The whole country is full of mercenaries and outlaw knights who've nothing to lose and much to gain by murder and kidnap." He came now and stood directly in front of Raimon, and his voice was as hard as it had been in Notre Dame. "I want you to know that if anything—*anything*—happens to Yolanda, you'll get your pyre, and this time there'll be no escape." He began to say something more but Aimery came barging back in.

At once Hugh moved away and sat down. "Raimon has changed his mind," he said, his half-smile back in place. "He'll go to the king." There was a pause. Aimery didn't hide his displeasure. Hugh took a breath. "And Yolanda will go with him, with a guard of my soldiers, and also Yolanda's servant girl, Laila," he added.

Raimon frowned. Too many people. But Yolanda pressed his arm and he said nothing.

Aimery was not so reticent. "What?" One hand plucked his beard, a sure sign his temper was rising. "First it was Raimon and now it's Raimon and Yolanda? Don't be so foolish, Hugh. You can't send them off together with the Flame. It's—it's—it's unseemly as well as—"

"Be careful, Aimery." Hugh's voice was icy. "This is Lady des Arcis you're talking about."

"She may be your wife but she's still my sister."

"And it's as a wife and sister that she's going. As Lady des Arcis and Yolanda of Amouroix, she'll ensure that Raimon gets to see the king."

"But it's still—"

"I thought you wanted to do the best for the Occitan."

"I do, but this—"

"This is a useful arrangement. It means that you can see to the king's business here, and there's business still to do. Count

Raymond, albeit belatedly and in some confusion, is winding his way down toward Castelneuf. You must either persuade him to come over to the king once and for all or lead your men into battle against him."

He spoke easily again, his voice both authoritative and certain, and Aimery felt it better to remain silent, at least for now. Raimon might take the Flame, but Aimery would make sure the king knew exactly where it had come from. As for Yolanda, well, if Hugh wanted to look a fool, Aimery could hardly stop him. He couldn't, however, resist one last dig. "I hope you do better with the king than you did with that crowd on the hill," he said, wagging his finger in Raimon's face. "It wasn't hard to get them to turn away from the White Wolf and eat, was it now? Are you sure you actually tried?"

But Raimon did not hear him. Finally, the last of his strength deserted him and he could remain upright no longer. He slumped and crashed to the floor. Aimery skipped out of the way as Yolanda fell to her knees. "He'll not get farther than the end of the road," Aimery said in a tone of high satisfaction.

"He'll get there," Hugh said and shouted for help. When Raimon had been carried out with Yolanda following, he caught Aimery before he could leave. "Aimery! A moment more. What will you do with the prisoners still in the hall?"

"I'll let them go, except for Sicart. Stupid old man's still wandering around with a fish in his hand and nothing in his belly."

Hugh raised his eyebrows. "But you'll free the others? Even though they've taken the Cathar consolation?"

At once Aimery was on the defensive. "I'm not going soft if that's what you think. It's just that now that they've finished eating, they're all lining up to confess the error of their ways to Simon Crampcross. If the White Wolf, Adela, and Sicart burn, that should be enough. I mean, I imagine King Louis, the merciful *man of the people*"—it was a deliberate gibe and Hugh flushed—"will want to find Castelneuf a thriving place, with a decent number of inhabitants. And don't you worry, Hugh." He drew his sword and flourished it. "I shan't shirk my duty. If Raimon and Yolanda don't give the Flame to the king and come straight back here, I'll execute that decrepit knight and that bony boy myself."

The sword's glitter reminded both Aimery and Hugh that if, in fact, Yolanda and Raimon did run off with the Flame, Parsifal and Cador would not be the only ones to suffer. Hugh currently had the king's complete confidence but if Louis believed he had let him down, that confidence would evaporate in seconds. There would only be one fate for him then. On impulse, Aimery whizzed the sharp edge of the sword past Hugh's ear and when he lowered it, Hugh put out a finger and touched the blade. A small drop of blood trickled down it. Aimery wiped the blood off and the two men left the room in silence.

12

Together

Raimon was taken to a chamber where he was tended with reasonable care. On Aimery's orders, Yolanda was forbidden entry either to his room or to the room where Parsifal and Cador had been billeted together. She gazed at the door but forced herself to be patient. Tomorrow. She just had to wait until tomorrow and it was already late evening so tomorrow was not far away. She found Laila dancing around the château with Ugly in her arms, pouting scarlet lips and poking her persistent nose into nooks where she certainly wasn't wanted. "You should make up traveling bundles for us both," she told her. "We're leaving again."

The girl threw Ugly down with theatrical despair. "Are you people never still?" Yolanda didn't answer, just hugged Brees close, reveling in his musty smell. He had never left his mistress's side, not for a minute, since she had reappeared, and occasionally, as he did now, he caught her sleeve between yellow teeth, a soulful reprimand for having allowed them to be parted. She felt him against her leg as she went to the chapel. It was time for her to see the Blue Flame for herself. But Simon Crampcross was still sitting there and she did not want to speak to him.

It was very late by the time she reluctantly passed the door of her childhood room and went slowly up to the chamber Hugh had been assigned. He had given in to her demand. She would not give the servants cause to mock him behind his back. She dragged one of the furs from the bed, made a nest for Brees and herself by the window, and blew out the candles. When Hugh found her there, her face silvery in the moonlight and her covers awry, he spent some time looking down at her and then, with Brees growling at him, took off his cloak and tucked it around her. He sat for a while, sunk in thought, then went back to the great hall where he found Gui and Guerau, having reclaimed their instruments and softly singing an old lullaby. All his knights were sleeping.

Very early in the morning, before she thought anybody would be stirring, Yolanda got up, started when she found herself folded in Hugh's cloak, and, without a glance at his bed, returned to the chapel. There were guards posted outside and they reassured her that Simon Crampcross was not yet about before nodding her through. As Lady des Arcis and Aimery's sister, they felt they couldn't stop her. She was disconcerted, however, to find the chapel was not empty. Hugh was kneeling in one corner and Aimery in another. She found her own place and knelt down too. Brees flopped to the floor, his paws spread-eagled and his tail creating a billow of dust. He yawned, yet was acutely aware of Yolanda's every movement. You could not have slipped a piece of parchment between his flank and her leg.

The Flame sat between two lit candles, casting odd-shaped gleams in a small circle around itself. Though hardly aware of doing so, Yolanda began to creep closer and Brees crept with her.

When they were close enough, he reared up and put his paws on the altar, sniffed, then dropped down, not liking the heat. Yolanda patted him but remained where she was. She wanted to touch the box, partly for itself and partly because Raimon had done so. Yet it felt presumptuous and unearned. After all, she had done nothing for the Flame. In the end, she just gazed at it, into it, and through it, in awe at its great age. She tried to imagine it being lit by God's fiery breath and as she did so, she whispered:

In Occitan there hovers still
The grace of Arthur's table round.
Bright southern heroes yet fulfill
The quest to which they all are bound.

No foreign pennant taints our skies,
No cold French king snuffs out our name.
Though we may fall, again we'll rise.
No Grail for us, we burn the Flame!

The Flame, the Flame, the Flame of Blue!
Sweet Occitan, it burns for you.

The words had a certain irony now but the Flame still seemed to like them, sending out spiky tongues that caught and swallowed them. She stretched out her fingers and felt, as the Flame hissed and kissed them, the same kind of momentary suspension that Raimon had felt on the plateau. "Oh!" she cried silently. "Oh!" She pressed her fingers to her cheek and then bowed her head. "How will we ever give you up?" The

Flame fluttered. Yolanda could hardly look at it again. She had not thought to feel a traitor herself. As she left, she passed Hugh. He didn't try to detain her. Nevertheless, she kept a sword's length between them, and once out the door she hurried away.

Still feeling the Flame on her cheek, she went to the kennels, where she found the huntsman stirring the porridge trough, quite unable to disguise his joy at being reunited with his hounds. She could see the dogboys larking with the young mastiffs, their faces still gaunt but their spirit returning. Her presence inhibited their pleasure so she left them and climbed up to the top of the château's main keep, beyond the room where equipment was stored in case of siege and on to the battlements. The dawn had fully broken now and a freshening wind was scudding the clouds and clutching at her skirts. She leaned over the drop, trying to settle her thoughts. Raimon, Hugh, the king, the Flame—how jumbled everything was!

She threw her head back so the wind streamed through her hair, then she shook herself. All would be well. It must be.

She leaned over again and was able to see Raimon's hilltop very clearly. The last of the siege was being cleared away and the great gash where the crag had been shone white. Soon there would be nothing apart from the scar and the vast lump of rock at the bottom of the hill to show that anything had ever happened there. Yolanda opened her arms to the wind until it nearly blew her away. Then she came back down and helped Laila pack.

Unsurprisingly, it was actually several days before Raimon had recovered enough to start a journey and Yolanda lived in terror that the day would never actually dawn. But it did. The morning after their third night, she saw Galahad, Bors, and Garland together with twelve others adorned in des Arcis colors and two pack ponies in the courtyard. She went down at once to wait. Laila, her hair an unexpected shade of green, was fussing with her bundle. "No, *not* in the cart, you clumsy clodhopper. I'll have this one strapped to the saddle. What exactly about that don't you understand? Oh, he'll be here soon," she said when she saw Yolanda. Yolanda nodded.

Raimon had no difficulty getting Aimery's permission to see Parsifal and Cador. The count thought it would bring into very sharp focus what would happen if he did not return. Parsifal was lying on his back, his arms crossed over his chest like an entombed crusader knight and his skin, clean now, was the color of an old scroll. It was a happy reunion. Then, quickly, Raimon spoke. "I've come to say good-bye," he said.

"Good-bye?" Cador was astounded. "Nobody's told us anything." The happiness was draining from his face. "We've only just gotten here, and anyway, Sir Parsifal's your knight and I'm your page. You can hardly go without us."

"I've told you before, weavers don't have pages," Raimon said, and kneeling down, he explained with complete frankness what was to happen. "But don't worry, Cador. Please don't worry. After I've delivered the Flame I'll be back for you—you and Sir Parsifal."

The little boy could not take it in. "How can you give the Blue Flame away?" he asked, looking up at Raimon earnestly. Then his face lit up. "Don't give it away. Don't come back here. I was prepared to die before and I still am." He looked over at Parsifal and his face fell again. "The only thing is that he might die before me and I don't know if I'm brave enough to die on my own."

"You're brave enough for anything," Raimon told him, and touched his cheek.

"Do you think so?"

"I know so." He hugged him and then got up and went to Parsifal.

The old knight curled his fingers around Raimon's, to keep him close. "Can you not take the boy?" he asked. "Then you'll have nothing to come back for."

"I'm coming back for both of you," Raimon said, though his eyes were full as he saw the true extent of Parsifal's decline. "Don't give up, Sir Parsifal, please. You've got to stay alive for Cador's sake, and for mine. We need you."

The three words were very sweet to the dying knight. He raised his head a little. "Dear Raimon. You don't need me, not anymore, but I do want you to do something for me."

"Anything."

"When you are able, I want you to go to Chalus Chabrol. You remember? Where my father sacrificed himself for me after I shot the arrow that killed King Richard the Lionheart?"

Raimon nodded.

"Ah," said Parsifal, and a look of pleasure spread over his face. "Do you know, when I told you that—it must have been our very first meeting—I thought you weren't listening."

"I was listening," said Raimon, who now wished he had paid better attention.

Parsifal's voice cracked. "Would you see if you can find my father's sword? Unbent, he called it, and it might still be there. If you find it, I want you to have it and use it. You deserve it as

I never did. It would be fitting for you, as the Flame's new guardian, to have it."

"Your father would want it to be yours."

"I somehow think I shan't be needing it, and my father, like me, would be proud to think of Unbent in your possession."

Raimon found it hard to speak. "I'll get Unbent," he said, "and I'll bring it to you. You can give it to me yourself."

A spark lit in Parsifal's rheumy eyes. "I'd like that," he said, "but it may not be possible. It's in God's hands."

"God!" Raimon whispered.

"Yes, God." The old knight sank back to gather his strength and then took a deep, rattling breath. "Do you remember that once I said that maybe the Flame didn't stand for freedom in the paths of righteousness, as my father told me, but for freedom from the paths of self-righteousness?"

Raimon nodded.

"Well, that's God's freedom as well as the Flame's, Raimon, because that's true freedom. I think that's why God lit the Flame and gave it to the Occitan. He thought we would understand. It was a great gift and a great responsibility and we haven't lived up to the challenge. But you've a chance to put that right. And you will. I know you will, because you understand what freedom really means."

Raimon sat quite still. "But how can I put anything right? Freedom brings so much grief. How can the kind of God you believe in bear it? How can the Flame?"

"Men bring grief, Raimon, not freedom or God. If you look into your heart, do you not see that?"

"I see it with the Flame, but God?"

The old knight raised himself. "Listen to me. If you have

faith in the Flame, you must have faith in the force that lit it. Do you have faith in the Flame? Real faith?"

"But I've got to give it up!" Raimon sprang to his feet and walked swiftly about. Cador watched, wide-eyed and trembling. "I don't know what I believe anymore." He returned to the bed. "The Flame seems like everything, then it feels like nothing. It doesn't make sense." He buried his face in the sheets.

Parsifal stroked his hair. "Everything makes sense if you keep it simple, Raimon. We try and make things so complicated, but if you keep faith, you will see the light on the path."

"Keep faith with what, Sir Parsifal? With the Flame?"

"No, Raimon, not just the Flame, but with all that the Flame means. I think if you keep faith with God, the Flame, and love you can't go too far wrong. Can you do that?"

"I don't know. It's too much."

"No, it's not too much, Raimon, because in the end they are all the same thing."

Raimon held him close. "When I'm dead," the old knight said, "Unbent will help you. Come. Be strong. It's time to go."

Raimon held him closer. There were many things he wanted to say but Parsifal put a finger over his lips. "There's no need to say anything, Raimon. I trust you completely."

Tears streamed down Raimon's face. "I shall think of you every day."

"Yes, do that. But never with guilt, Raimon. Whatever happens, never with guilt. Think of me with joy because here or in heaven, that's how I shall think of you." He could not say any more.

Raimon folded the two pairs of hands, the very old and the

very young, together. "Look after him, Cador." He dropped a kiss on the little boy's head.

"Sir!" Cador's lip was trembling. Raimon stopped. "I know you'll think of Sir Parsifal, but you won't forget me, will you?"

"I'll be back for you."

"Perhaps you will," Cador said, "but that's not what I mean."

Raimon's heart contracted. "I know what you mean," he said. He looked at him directly. "And no, Cador, whether in heaven or on earth, I'll never forget you. If I'm a knight, you're not some lowly page, but a proper squire. Of course I won't forget you."

The little boy stood so straight and true that had Yolanda not been waiting, Raimon would have found it impossible to close the door behind him.

When he got to the courtyard, Laila was already sitting astride Garland. The pony was fretting about the large bundle that Laila had finally managed to get the grooms to tie to her satisfaction and Ugly was at Garland's shoulder, wagging her tail, her tummy bulging with breakfast. This life of movement was a strange one and she was nervous around Brees but there was food in abundance and nobody kicked her. It was heaven enough.

Before Raimon got near, Hugh silently lifted Yolanda onto Galahad. He wanted to say something that his wife would remember, but though he had spent the previous night pacing up and down the hall thinking, he had come up with nothing. And now he could see that even the most beguiling troubadour would not have reached her this morning, for though she was silent, she seemed contained in a song of her own. It occurred to him as he checked the buckle on her reins, her gaze already beyond Castelneuf, that he could still prevent her from going. He toyed with the idea only for a moment then stamped on it hard.

The Flame's appearance caused a momentary silence. It had been set in a robust basket that was spiked into Bors's saddle. Raimon glanced at Yolanda and mounted. He knew that she too was thinking that they would not speak until they could speak alone. He found Aimery gripping his leg. "I wouldn't be doing this if it wasn't for Sir Hugh des Arcis." The count made every word a threat. "We hear that the king is moving south. Head for Toulouse first and get news of him there. Deliver the Flame and be back here by the turn of the year."

"The turn of the year!" exclaimed Yolanda, horrified. "But it's already November. That's not nearly long enough. What if we don't find him? What if we have to go all the way back to Paris?"

"You'll just have to make sure that doesn't happen. The new year should be plenty of time. You're not traveling with an army, for goodness' sake. You can move as fast as you like. Anyhow, that's all the time you've got and if we get word that the king has begun slaughtering Occitanians and burning our towns, we'll know who to blame." He slapped Bors on the rump. "The old knight and the boy had better start praying that you have a good journey."

Raimon never looked back as he urged Bors toward the gate. Yolanda followed, and as she left the courtyard she found Hugh beside her. He touched Galahad's nose and smiled, not a half-smile but a full one, though it was the saddest, most troubled smile Yolanda had ever seen. "Take care," he said, then paused. "I shall miss you." He stood back. She raised her hand. "Good-bye, Hugh."

Galahad and Bors trotted flank to flank through the town, over the bridge and past the graveyards by the river with Brees, still too thin for travel but game anyway, keeping his shaggy head next to Yolanda's stirrup and the Flame, burning brightly. Garland cantered along behind. Only the phalanx of des Arcis troopers revealed that the scene was not as perfect as it seemed—that and an unexpected wall of awkwardness which, though they could now speak reasonably freely, seemed to spring up from nowhere between Raimon and Yolanda. Neither could have said why it appeared. They were together again and for all the bitter circumstances and the awe both felt at the burden they were carrying, the presence of the other should have been the loveliest thing in the world. Yet their speech was hampered for Yolanda by a sudden fear of saying the wrong thing and for Raimon because there were things he both wanted and didn't want to know. The result was that the silence thickened with every passing second. Yolanda chattered to Brees, hoping that just the sound of her voice would crack Raimon's silence, but it didn't. Then Laila barged alongside, her dress a patchwork of floating ribbons. She made a coy reference to the bath she had given Raimon after he collapsed and Raimon quipped back. That thickened the silence further. Yolanda asked how far they could get in a day. Raimon answered, but somehow their old intimacy, the intimacy it had never occurred to either they could lose, completely eluded them. Raimon began to fret.

They passed through the meadows and into the chilly darkness of the woods, then along the forest's ruffled edges, the leaves thick underfoot, until finally rejoining the glassy river. Here they turned due north. A flock of untidy sheep straggled past. The shepherd was hurrying them, for it was really too late to begin the long trek over the mountains to winter pastures in Spain and their bells clanged dully. Brees bared his teeth at them and Ugly looked with frank amazement. Yolanda cautioned them both.

Laila was riding some way ahead now, and singing, which amused a group of swineherds. They called to her. "Sing one for us, ribbon-lady!" She obliged, choosing a song from the streets of Paris that fortunately the swineherds could not understand. They clapped and whistled until they saw the des Arcis pennants. Then they hurried their pigs away. Raimon hated the looks they threw after him. They thought he was French too.

A mile farther on, a boy and a young girl, sent to fetch water, had abandoned their pitchers and were splashing each other, shrieking with laughter. The boy, showing off, turned himself upside down so his legs waved in the air. Quick as a flash, the girl stole the shoes from his feet and they fought, tumbling and choking like puppies. Yolanda took a deep breath. "Do you remember the last time we swam?"

"You didn't swim."

"It was so cold."

"The river won't be much warmer now."

"No."

The path broadened and Laila hung back, forcing herself between them. She prattled on, filling up the silence.

They pushed on as hard as they could until the light faded and the horses stumbled in the gloom. There was great tension between Raimon and Hugh's men as they pitched camp. The troopers made it clear that they would take no orders from an Occitanian, not even about the position of the fire. Yolanda dismounted. One word from her as Lady des Arcis and they would have to obey Raimon. It was hard to remain silent. But she was wiser than she had been when the troubles first began, so she stood in full view of the troopers but said not a word. It had the effect she sought.

Darkness fell and Raimon sat cross-legged with the Flame beside him. Nearby, Laila amused herself by brushing Yolanda's hair. Raimon didn't even know he was staring. One of the soldiers whistled a tune, another beat time smartly on a saddle, yet another drummed two sticks together. Laila didn't want music so she abandoned Yolanda and began to entertain the soldiers with magic tricks. Seductress or witch, she soon had them enthralled.

Raimon let his eyelids close and heard Parsifal's last words echoing in the night breeze. Then he felt a light hand on his shoulder. "Come to the river," Yolanda said.

He didn't know why he hesitated. "What about the Flame?"

"We'll take it with us."

They stepped out of the firelight and at once there was a melting between them, as though the light had been freezing and they needed the dark to warm them. With only a blue gleam as a guide, they ran to where stiff grass gave way to a softer blanket and slid quickly, urgently, heedlessly down the bank, through the tree roots and to the water's edge. On the tiny pebbled shoreline, Yolanda scarcely waited to kick off her shoes and pick up her dress before she waded in. It was cold, very cold. The soles of her feet were numbed even before

Raimon had settled the Flame in the prickles of a bush and, leaving Brees its unwilling guardian, thrown his boots to the right and left and was in the water beside her. The current gushed up the backs of their knees and Yolanda put out her hand. Raimon took it. The silence tightened, but this silence was different. It was no longer thick, it was the silence of the moment before you jump off a cliff. Brees felt it and left his post. He had two feet in the water before Raimon ordered him back and he reversed slowly to his sentinel's place and sat bolt upright.

Still tight as tight, the silence lasted as they pushed their way upriver until the stream widened out into deep shelving pools. Then, as one they made for the bank and pulled off their clothes. Yolanda shivered from top to toe as she stepped out of her felt skirt, but she would not be stopped now. She waded back in and raised her arms like a diver, a cream-colored ghost in her woolen shift. She stretched, flipped over, and was gone. Raimon stripped off his shirt and belt and dived after her. They rose, gasping and treading water. Yolanda disappeared. Raimon sank down too. Beneath the surface, his hands found hers again and their limbs tangled together. Down here, in this different world, a world where there could be no words, even Hugh's ring could cause no awkwardness between them. When they could hold their breath no more, they floated up, still holding on to each other. Raimon eased them both gently to where they could stand and cleared the hair from Yolanda's eyes. "Why did you cut it?" he asked.

"My hair?" With his own slicked back he looked all smoothed out, although she could feel his bones through the skin. "I tried to disguise myself as Laila and run away."

Raimon let go of her hands and circled her neck. She bent back so his hands were trapped and her lips were dark smudges. There was no hesitation now as he took what he thought of as his own and their kiss was as natural and luxurious as the silence had been unexpected and stiff.

They lay on their backs. The cold didn't seem to matter anymore. "Wouldn't it be lovely to be a fish?" Yolanda said. She could no longer remember how or why it had been so difficult to speak before. How silly they had been!

"You'd be a starfish," Raimon said, rolling drops of water on his tongue. The abundance of it was still a miracle to his throat. "I heard a man who'd been to the fair in Pamiers talking about such things once. He said they dropped out of the sky, which seemed nice but unlikely."

"A starfish," she replied dreamily. "Like this." She stretched her legs and arms out and he spread himself out beside her, the water drifting around them both in a circle, now touching, now not. "When did you get my letter?" he asked.

"Hugh gave it to me after we were married."

Then they stopped floating and though there were subjects they both skirted around, they talked and talked as though they could never stop.

It was some time before they made for the bank again. Yolanda was now so cold she could hardly rub herself dry and was glad when Brees bounded down to help. Raimon grabbed his clothes and forged back to take Brees's place by the Flame. Next to the midnight blue of the sky, it was shining whiter than he had ever seen it. With his shirt still only half on, he knelt down and peered into the box. When Yolanda was dressed, she came and knelt too, her shift clammy against her skin and her hair bedraggled. For a minute she was frightened that the silence would descend again. "You look like a water vole, or perhaps an otter," Raimon said quickly. "Or even an otter who's eaten a water vole."

"And you look like one of those wild creatures from the Dark Wood. Do you remember that story?"

"Remember it? I made it up."

"You? Wasn't it me? Yes, definitely me, the summer we adopted that family of frogs."

"Don't you mean ants?"

"Ants? We never adopted ants."

"Didn't we? I was sure it was ants." As they held out memories to each other as gifts of love, he was cutting two thin strips from his belt, each of which he tied in a circle and held into the Flame on the point of his dagger. The Flame drew the strips in, blanketing them, and when Raimon brought them out, the knots had melted and transformed them into crude but solid rings. He dropped them onto the grass to cool, then picked them up. "These rings are forged in the white heat of the Flame," he said. "We can't make any vows for the future, Yolanda. Perhaps we never can. But whatever happens, however this ends, let's never doubt each other."

She did not need to speak. She just took her ring, pressed it against Raimon's heart, and then tucked it into her dress next to her own. He pushed his over the knuckles of the middle finger of his left hand. It left an ashy trail.

They made their way back to the camp, with Brees between them, each plunging a hand into his fur for warmth. He twitched with pleasure. "Do you feel guilty?" Raimon couldn't help asking.

"Guilty for loving you? No."

"Guilty for tonight?"

"No. Never."

"How did that man get you to marry him?"

"I never said the words," she said, "not the real words."

"He forced you!" Raimon flushed with anger.

"Yes, I suppose he did. But afterward he was kind. He seemed sorry. I don't know how to explain." She was relieved when Brees's hackles rose and suddenly Laila was there. It was too early to talk of Hugh.

"Where on earth have you been?" Laila's eyes darted from one to the other. "When I saw the Flame was gone I thought you'd run off together."

"We went for a swim," Yolanda said.

"Oh yes, I'm sure."

Raimon walked faster. Damn the girl, spoiling things, and damn Hugh. He didn't want to think of him as kind. He wanted to hate him and for Yolanda to hate him too. Back in the camp, as he watched Laila fussing over clothes and dressing Yolanda's hair, he felt he was losing her again.

He had to wait until after Laila had gone to bed before Yolanda came to find him and she could see from his face where his thoughts were leading. She took his cheeks between both her hands and now she was not tender. "No doubts about each other, that's what we agreed," she said fiercely. "Did you think that would be easy?" She shook him. "I wear Hugh's ring here"—she pointed to her finger—"because I have to. I wear yours here"—she put her hand on her heart—"because that's where you are. Do you understand?"

Raimon looked over her head in the direction of the water.

"Yes," he said. "Yes, I do understand, but perhaps sometimes I'll just find it hard to believe." She touched her lips and then touched his. "Believe," she said, and wrapping his fur blanket around him, she left him to sleep.

13

In the Clearing

They moved quickly onward the following morning. Raimon and Yolanda rode side by side in quite a different way now, much of the time making wild plans involving somehow duping the king and delivering the Flame to Raymond of Toulouse. Both refused to believe Hugh's warnings about the count's duplicity, choosing instead to believe that he was playing his own clever game. Once he had the Flame and the support of all his vassals, barring Aimery of course, they would take on the king just as Raimon had hoped and the Occitan would be saved. When Yolanda sounded a note of caution, Raimon set his jaw and drove Bors on faster. She did not pursue it. There was no need. Both knew that even if Count Raymond appeared at this very moment, they still had to do what they had to do. Parsifal and Cador could not be forfeit.

Many miles were covered over the next two weeks. Gradually the land flattened from crag to hump and then to plains. They lost all sight of the mountains. The weather worsened, but although the troopers complained, Raimon tried to keep them from seeking hospitality even on the most dismal nights.

Soldiers always talked and what did Hugh's men care about the Flame, or Parsifal and Cador? They were Frenchmen.

Surprisingly, Laila never complained of discomfort. She combated the cold by wearing her clothes in eccentric layers. She would, however, stare at the Flame's box for hours, sometimes giving it a small nudge to make it dance. Yolanda wished she would leave it alone.

"Why does it never go out?" Laila asked Raimon as they were getting ready to set out again, their fifth day on the plain. They were not friends, these two. Raimon didn't trust her and Laila knew it, and she was jealous of him. With Raimon there, Yolanda had no need of her company. The girl felt ignored, particularly since Ugly, more confident now, had also detached herself from her mistress and attached herself firmly to Brees. They ran together, the two ugliest dogs the troopers had ever seen, half aware of being the butt of everybody's jokes but completely uncaring. Laila would have called Ugly back to her but she was frightened she might not come.

"So why doesn't it go out?" She wasn't really interested in the answer. She just wanted to be a pest.

"Because it was lit for the Occitan and Occitanians and we're not finished yet," Raimon replied shortly. He didn't want to explain anything to Laila and he didn't like riding on the plain. It felt unnatural. He would rest easier when the land rose up again.

"I thought it would at least be in a beautiful vessel," Laila observed. "Really, it looks like nothing." She sounded accusatory.

"It doesn't need a fancy container." He was putting it back into the basket, now greasy with Bors's sweat.

Laila pushed back her hair, which was purple today. A trooper was waiting to lift her onto Garland. They loved to do this, taking turns and quarreling for the privilege. She had to admit that made up a bit for Raimon and Yolanda.

They had an uncomfortable morning. The villages through which they traveled were palpably anxious. They had suffered from previous wars between King Louis and the Occitan and now, with trouble simmering again, were rebuilding walls and digging defensive ditches. They'd heard that the new Seneschal of Carcassonne had brought an army with him and wanted to be prepared. Some towns already had archers posted on the walls. Bartering for food was more difficult here but at least nobody seemed interested in anything except getting them to pass on as quickly as possible. They soon discovered why. Not only did Hugh's army threaten, inquisitors were about, sniffing out Cathar heretics and not too fussy about whom they caught in their nets.

By evening, they had twice seen men dressed just like the White Wolf fording rivers and hurrying south, and each time, a mile or so farther on, other groups of men followed, often wearing ill-matched armor that was clearly not their own. "Outlaw knights," said the des Arcis troopers with terrified disgust. "Bandits. What they do if they catch you makes the inquisitors look like pussycats." When they camped that night, Raimon stayed on guard himself.

It was three days later, as they left the plain, that they saw the remains of a pyre. The ashes were cold but the smell lingered, a flat, heavy, sweet aroma that made their gorges rise. The inquisitors had left a crude sign nailed to a broken branch. "Thus, in God's name, perish all heretics. A fire on earth followed by the fires of hell," it read. Charred body parts were not in heaps but scattered where predators had seized them in hope of a strip of flesh. They had been disappointed. Fire had consumed even the marrow of the bones.

Half a mile farther, Ramon pulled up. "You go on," he said, his voice unnaturally brisk. "I'm going to bury what's left. I can't just leave them. It's not right, not even if it was the White Wolf himself who was burned."

Yolanda turned Galahad. "I'll help."

"No," Raimon said. "It's horrible. I'll keep two of the soldiers. Stick to the road and find somewhere to wait for me." He gestured to the troopers. They shook their heads emphatically. This was not part of their duty. In the end, Yolanda lost her temper. "You forget that I am Lady des Arcis," she said. "Do as Raimon bids." She gave Raimon a hard look afterward and touched her hand to her heart. He understood.

Laila and Yolanda rode on, sticking close to one another. Yolanda, silent, knew that Raimon would be reliving his own burning. Laila chattered and it was hard for Yolanda not to slap her. "Why don't you and Raimon just go off together?" the girl repeated and repeated. "It would be so easy. Nobody would ever find you."

"And Parsifal and Cador?"

"We've all got to die sometime."

Yolanda turned on her. "We've made a promise. How could we betray them?"

"Aren't you betraying the Flame by giving it to the king?"

"We're doing the best we can," Yolanda told her with a certain weariness. She was looking back but Raimon and the troopers were still out of sight.

"I don't think I'll ever understand you." Laila tossed her head, half in puzzlement and half with contempt. "You love your country but you're giving it up."

"You don't understand because you're not an Occitanian."

"Thank God," said Laila fervently. "It doesn't seem a very useful thing to be. At least the only thing I can betray is myself and since I'd never do that I'm perfectly safe."

"You could betray Ugly," Yolanda said, paying a little more attention.

Laila glanced over at the dog, padding beside Brees. "I've told you before, I can take her or leave her."

"I know what you told me," Yolanda said, and not wanting to listen to Laila anymore, she pushed Galahad into a canter. "I can hear a stream ahead, we'll stop there." The soldiers obediently followed.

They waited for what seemed like far too long for Raimon and the other two soldiers to reappear. Raimon's hands were filthy, but not wanting to sully the stream, he found a puddle and washed in that. "Mount up," he said, wiping them again and again on the grass as if they could never be clean. "We're moving on."

Very soon they met rather more orderly groups of people, also journeying south, some on foot and some on horseback. From the baggage trains that followed, most did not look as though they had been driven from their houses but were traveling somewhere they had chosen to go. Thinking they might have news of the king, Raimon spoke to an elderly knight.

"We know nothing of the king," the knight told him. His family and armor were in a cart behind him. He looked carefully at the des Arcis colors, which he didn't recognize. "We're just—just—"

His wife intervened. "We're just going on our way. Come on, husband. Don't dally."

When they had disappeared, Raimon grew very agitated. "They're gathering to fight," he said. "Count Raymond must be up here, mustering support. That's what he's been doing, and they're all going down to some rallying point. If they knew we had the Flame and what we are doing with it, God knows what would happen."

"We're doing what we must," Yolanda said.

"We're giving the Flame to the king."

"But we've got to think of Parsifal and Cador, and if King Louis looks after the Flame instead of crushing it, isn't that a good thing?"

"You've been infected by your time in Paris," Raimon told her. "Even if there's no bloodshed, the Occitan will never be the same. It will be subservient."

She blanched but fought back. "Nothing stays the same, and you're only subservient if you choose to be so."

He shook his head. "That's for philosophers, Yolanda. How will you feel when we're surrounded by pyres?"

"The king won't do that, surely."

"He'll burn everybody it pleases the inquisitors to label a heretic," Raimon said shortly. "He'll see that as God's work— and a good way of frightening people."

Yolanda remembered the king's eyes as he had passed her in Saint-Denis and she could not say that Raimon was wrong.

That night, curled up as far away from the troopers as he could get, when sleep came to Raimon it was full of terrors from which he woke raving and sweating. Yolanda was holding his hand, dripping water onto his forehead. "Talk to me," she said. "Tell me."

"I can't."

"Yes, you can."

He was quiet for a moment, then gave a great, shuddering breath.

"That pyre. Oh God, that pyre, Yolanda. Sometimes I wake up in the night because I think I'm still tied to the post. My face felt so cold—can you imagine that? How could it be cold, with the flames leaping?" He rocked, trying to hold himself together. "I thought of you, I tried to think only about you, but in the end, I just wondered whether I'd scream or not." He swallowed. "What would have happened if Sir Parsifal hadn't come for me? Those people today—they had no one to rescue them. They felt that cold and that heat and their flesh shrinking. They smelled themselves roasting and heard themselves screaming. And the pain. Can you imagine it? I can't bear it when Cador treats me like a hero because I wasn't a hero. Parsifal was the hero. He hid both himself and the Flame in the pyre to rescue me. The Flame. Without that and Sir Parsifal—," he caught his breath. She held him. "I've got to go to Chalus and find Sir Parsifal's father's sword. I owe him more than I can ever tell even you. He knows things, explains things."

Yolanda nodded. "One day, when all this is over, we'll go to Chalus."

"But it'll never be over, Yolanda, never."

She drew his head into her lap. "Everything is over in the end," she said and she sat quite still, singing a song her mother used to sing. But even with her hand on his head it was a long time before Raimon slept again.

Nowhere did they hear real news of the king and they could no longer ignore the awful possibility that they might have to go all the way to Paris. If this was so, the time allowed by Aimery would never be enough, not even if they rode all day and night. Nonetheless, Raimon pushed them faster. But some days the rain bogged them down. Then some of the horses lost shoes and had to be reshod. One of the troopers fell ill. Laila made a potion that she said would cure him and it made him so much worse that eventually they had to go to a village and persuade an old woman to take him in. The other troopers insisted that the man could not be left alone or the old woman would murder him and they squabbled about who would stay. But then a peddler told them that the king had crossed the river Loire a week ago and they sped on.

At dawn at the beginning of the fifth week, Raimon was trying to imagine himself actually handing the Flame over, when, in a natural clearing, they stumbled across an entire herd of deer completely hidden in a blanket of mist. Like visions conjured up by Laila's magic, the deer rose in shaggy waves virtually from under their feet. Confused, they tried to run backward, shoving between Galahad and Bors and leaping over Brees, their musky scent thrilling his veins to the exclusion of all else, even Yolanda. In a trice, he was no longer a pet but a single-minded killer intent on blood. He bayed and gave chase and Ugly, suddenly and unexpectedly intoxicated, followed his lead.

The horses shied and crashed into each other. Garland began to run with the deer and Raimon had to gallop after her and seize her reins. Laila was laughing, but she had had a fright. The trooper holding the des Arcis colors dropped them and was off his horse, stamping and swearing, half of him clouded by a wispy pale gray sea through which his legs appeared from time to time as the mist thickened and cleared in turn. In the swirl, it took the company some time to collect themselves back into some kind of order and it was only then that Yolanda realized Brees was missing. She pulled Galahad around in a circle, her eyes straining. "Brees!" she called, then more urgently, "Brees!"

"Ugly's gone too," said Laila.

"We've got to find them." Yolanda was already kicking Galahad into the trees.

"Wait! Stick together!" Raimon cried, as he and Laila set off after her. The troopers followed but the forest was a web of sticky, swallowing creepers. More deer appeared, leaping and twisting and careening off each other. Bors plunged gamely on. Now Raimon could hardly see Galahad. He put up his hand to protect his face then dropped it, feeling madly for the basket in case the Flame had been swept off. It held firm. The first shafts of sunlight, piercing through the naked frosted branches, blinded him. He could hear Yolanda's cry of "Brees! Brees!" but now Galahad had vanished altogether.

Five minutes later, they all fell out of the forest into another clearing, this one in no way natural. The trees had been felled in a circle, the trunks cut into sharpened planks to make a defensive palisade. Inside the palisade, a tented village had been constructed in which were standing a dozen or so rough-looking men, unshaven and dirty and clearly very surprised. Some were seizing armor that hung about on poles and grabbing spears still stained with old blood. Three men were handing out shields whose heraldic devices had been scratched off so that even their original owners would not recognize them. The man in charge of roasting a boar, whose head, with skin attached, was drying on a rack beside it, was holding his knife above his head. For it was in front of him that Brees and Ugly had brought down a stag.

Yolanda, standing in her stirrups, screamed, and Galahad, misunderstanding, launched straight into a gallop, leaped after the dogs, and unseated Yolanda completely. Without a thought, Raimon clapped his heels into Bors's side and he too leaped over the palisade with Garland following suit, Laila clutching wildly at the pony's flying mane and landing back in the saddle only through luck. At once, stag, dogs, and people were jumbled up. Knives were flashing, blood flowing. Raimon, fighting to get to Yolanda, found himself hampered by Ugly, who was hurling herself at him and howling, and by Brees, now confused and vaguely mortified, who was blundering in circles. One of the bandits had been sliced cleanly up the middle by the lethal sweep of the stag's antlers as it flailed in its death-throes. This man alone was silent. Amazed and almost disbelieving at his neat dismemberment, he sank and died without a word. His burly friend jammed a log into Brees's mouth and booted him away as the stag arched, then crumpled.

Yolanda, struggling for Brees, was picked up and held at knifepoint and Raimon knocked almost senseless by the swing of an ax handle. Only Laila escaped violence. She sat aboard Garland, her mouth opened in comic horror. Galahad and Bors, panting and sweating, stood stock still as they had been trained to do.

When the rough men saw the des Arcis troopers, six of them charged on foot toward them, but the troopers showed no inclination to fight. "Bandits!" they cried out, one to the other, and hung back. The trooper with the pennant dropped it again and this time didn't bother to retrieve it. When one turned to bolt, the others willingly joined him. The rough men cheered.

As the chaos and noise gradually died down, Raimon was hauled to his feet and expertly bound. Bruised and battered, he pulled toward Yolanda but could not reach her. The horses were seized. He watched with terror, waiting for the moment the Blue Flame was uncovered. However, the horses were just held, apparently for inspection.

The stockiest of the ruffians, a man who Raimon could see had once had a fine bearing but had allowed himself to run to seed, seemed to be in charge. He was quite a sight, his skin pitted with the scars of old lesions and his speech impaired by the loss of nearly all his top teeth. His companions, a ragbag of displaced nobles and disgruntled journeymen, addressed him as "Sir Faidit" half in mockery and half with the last vestiges of respect. He had a fine sword, this Sir Faidit, which he could still use to no little effect, for he had been a trained mercenary for many years. Without him, this flotsam and jetsam were a bunch of hoodlums. With him, they had some pretensions as a unified fighting force. It was he who made them say prayers every night, as he had been taught to do on crusade, even though when one of their number had fallen and broken his leg, Sir Faidit had simply run him through the heart. "First rule: no baggage," he said, before begging God to have mercy on the dead man's soul.

He scrutinized Raimon. To start with, he was unable to place his class or his position. Yolanda, however, he placed at once, for her ring gave her away as the wife of a nobleman. He would discover which nobleman once he'd had a chance to inspect the ring at close quarters. The nobleman was not Raimon, though.

Of that Faidit was sure. Had this boy been her lord, or indeed anybody's lord, those troopers would not have fled without a qualm. No. This was intriguing. He suspected that Raimon had kidnapped Yolanda and was now holding her for ransom. Yet the girl did not have the look of a hostage about her. Then there was Mistress Purplehead—perhaps a witch.

"So," he said finally. "Your dogs have killed one of the king's stags. You know what the penalty is for that?"

Raimon stared straight ahead. The man struck him, making his mouth bleed. Yolanda flung herself about. "Let us go!"

Sir Faidit walked over to her. "Perhaps I will," he said, "perhaps I won't, but before I decide, I need to know who you are and what your business is. A boy, a girl, and a witch is a strange combination to be rushing about these woods. Were the troopers your guards or your pursuers, or were they just a random bunch of cowards?"

He made a beckoning gesture and Brees, muzzled now as was Ugly, and knowing he'd done wrong, was dragged over. Sir Faidit drew his sword. "The penalty for killing the king's deer is death," he said.

"No!" cried Yolanda. "Don't! Please! I can get money!" She looked wildly around. "Or armor! Or anything! Only, please don't kill my dog."

Sir Faidit touched Brees with the tip of his sword, then moved over to Ugly. "Well, one of them must pay," he said. "That's only fair. Which one is it to be?"

"For pity's sake!" Yolanda was in agony.

"Not for pity's sake, but for the sake of justice," shouted Raimon. "The dogs may have driven the stag in, but your men killed it. Look."

Sir Faidit, taken a little by surprise, followed Raimon's

pointing finger and saw that what he said was perfectly true. The animal had been finished off by a spear in the chest. "Well, aren't you observant," he gibed, but he put his sword away. "We'll deal with the dogs later. Now, what's your name and what's your business? Catholic or Cathar? French or Occitanian?"

"Our names and our business are our own," Raimon said. "Let us go and you'll hear no more from us. We'll say nothing about the stag."

"Indeed," said Sir Faidit drily. "That's mighty kind of you." He glanced over at the horses. "Fine horses, if a bit battle-scarred. I don't reckon they belong to you, though." He pushed Raimon's chin up with his hand and pulled out the sword tucked into Raimon's belt. He curled his lip at its poor quality. "No. The horses are not yours." He threw the sword at one of his followers who caught it and stuck it in his own belt. Then he went to Yolanda, grasped her hand, and inspected her ring closely. "French," he said. "I'm surprised. You have the look of Occitania about you. Catholic, though, I'm guessing, and I don't think this boy is your husband." He turned to the other men. "We may have ourselves an eloping couple here," he said. "Now isn't that just sweet."

He gestured to one of the men to pull Laila off Garland. She had untied her bundle and had it perched in front of her and when the man approached, she leaned down and, quick as a flash, pulled out an oak leaf from his ear. She held it up, as if inspecting it. The man hesitated. She leaned forward again and this time pulled a bright red pebble from his nose. She threw it in the air, clapped her hands, and it vanished. The man backed away.

"A real witch," said Sir Faidit, rubbing his hands.

"Not a witch, a magician," said Laila haughtily.

"Get her off the pony," said Sir Faidit, although he didn't go near her himself.

Laila threw a glance at Raimon, then abandoned her stirrups, for all the world as if she were about to dismount. She hunched, and still clutching her bundle, stood on her saddle and stepped neatly on to Bors. With an inexpert but forceful tug, she pulled his head around and drove her heels into his side. The horse grunted and jerked forward, knocking down the man who held him.

"Go, go!" cried Raimon. Bors heard his voice, felt Laila's sharp fists and heels, and gathered himself together. He was not fast, but he knew what he was doing. Though Sir Faidit's men stood in his way and waved their arms, he galloped back to the palisade and leaped. The spikes scraped down his stomach and hind legs but he was out, and gone. "It was her magic," screamed Sir Faidit's men. "She bewitched us."

Sir Faidit beat his sword. "Keep better hold of the others," he roared. He was more angry about the loss of Bors than Laila. The horse was valuable and although the girl might blab, they could be out of here before she led anybody to them.

Raimon had no idea whether to be relieved or not.

Sir Faidit ordered camp to be struck, but before they had even begun, Laila reappeared outside the palisade. She had painted her eyes and lips crimson, striped red into the purple of her hair, and draped a green silk cloak belonging to Yolanda around herself and over the entire saddle. She looked like an apparition from some sinister myth. Raimon and Yolanda, shackled together, froze. Brees and Ugly, also shackled together, whimpered. Bors whinnied to Galahad.

Faidit's men rushed to the camp's gate, but remembering tales of mysterious and deadly forest creatures, were reluctant to go farther. Even those who had seized bows lowered them. To kill such a creature would need more than wood and steel, and who knew what her vengeance would be? Sir Faidit, safely inside the palisade, stood on a stack of planks and Laila addressed herself entirely to him. "I've come to negotiate," she said. "I have something you want and you have something I want."

"I don't want that horse if that's what you're offering," Sir Faidit said. It was a time-honored tactic of his always to deny what he wanted to begin with. "It'll be even more scarred now."

"I'm not offering you the horse," said Laila. "First let me tell you what I want. I want the ugly dog."

Sir Faidit wondered if it was a trick. "They're both ugly," he said.

"The ugliest one."

Sir Faidit had the dogs dragged to him. "This one?" He pointed to Ugly with his foot.

"Yes, that one. And untie the other. He won't go anywhere without his mistress."

"You don't want her as well?" His voice was mocking.

Laila threw back her head. "What slave wants a mistress back? She's nice enough but I want my dog."

Sir Faidit spread his legs. "And what, pray, will you give me in return?" He eyed Bors again.

Laila didn't even hesitate. "The Blue Flame."

Sir Faidit began to laugh. "The Blue Flame of the Occitan? You have the Blue Flame of the Occitan? You?"

"I have it here. You may not ask how, but if you don't believe me, well," she shrugged and began to pull Bors's rein. "I can find other buyers."

"Wait! Wait!"

She waited.

"But why, if you really have it, would you swap the Blue Flame for this mangy creature? You could get almost any price for it."

"A magician doesn't need money, and I like my dog. I don't want to betray her by leaving her behind." She threw a glance at Yolanda. "But if I can't have her, never mind."

Sir Faidit was still unsure. Bors still seemed the more certain prospect. "Let me see the Flame."

Laila considered, then swept back the cloak, unhooked the basket, and held it up. The sun caught the edge of the Flame's silver holder and Laila swung the basket gently so there was a glitter of blue sparks. Then she opened the basket and showed the box. Some of Sir Faidit's men fell to their knees. "My God," Sir Faidit said.

Laila carefully hooked the basket back on Bors's saddle, making ready to go.

Sir Faidit climbed down from the planks and pushed his way through his men to the gate. "We'll take it," he said.

"Free Ugly and come alone."

The dog was freed. She ran first to Yolanda, who stared at her dumbly, and then, when Laila whistled, raised her head. Sir Faidit caught her, pulled a belt from one of his men, and leashed her. Raimon called out to Laila and was kicked in the stomach for his trouble.

The exchange was effected, a lengthier affair than was expected, for Laila leaned down and whispered for some time in Sir Faidit's ear. He nodded. Then Laila had Ugly in front of her and was gone.

Sir Faidit walked swiftly back into the palisade, holding the basket in front of him. One of his men tried to take it. "Get back," Faidit barked. "Get back." They shrank from him. He took the basket to his tent and then emerged to summon four of the youngest men. "I'm setting you to guard this in shifts," he said, "and if it disappears, or anything happens to it at all, that witch has assured me your noses will fall off and your ears will shrivel. Do you understand? And don't take the box out of the basket. If we do that, the Flame may go out and then it will be worthless. Get it?" They nodded. They didn't really believe Laila was a witch, but they didn't disbelieve it either. "Well then. On guard," Sir Faidit continued, "and the rest of you, let's move. If anybody comes after us they'll find the bird has flown. We must be more careful now that we've some real treasure. Oh, and loose that other dog."

Sir Faidit watched as Brees ran straight to Yolanda as Laila had said he would. It was a little thing, but his confidence rose. Magician or not, that monstrous-looking girl had just presented him with the mightiest piece of good fortune of which an outlaw knight could dream.

14

The Bell Tower

Back in my château of Castelneuf, everybody was waiting. So much of human life is spent thus and so much of the waiting then begets more waiting. But I, the Amouroix, do not wait. What would I be waiting for? Things happen. That's all I know.

Hugh moved on to Carcassonne and waited to hear from the king. If Raimon delivered the Flame, there would surely be no need to unleash his army against the Occitan. Aimery waited too, hoping for a summons from the royal court in recognition of his part in the Flame's transplantation and the offer of a plump French heiress as a wife. Parsifal waited for the release of death. Cador, gaining strength from regular meals, was waiting for a different kind of release; but as the winter completely froze away the lingering tawny glories of autumn, no matter how hard he tried, even his optimistic heart grew dark around the edges. Every day he repeated his belief that Raimon would return. He repeated it to Parsifal and to himself and to anybody else who would listen. He stopped only when he found it was the only thing he could say. Even then, he never stopped trying to believe it.

Raimon had said he would come. He would come. If he could.

It was their only comfort, being together, but it was also torture for Raimon and Yolanda. More than anything else now, more almost than the travesty of the Flame falling into such hands as it had, both were agonizingly conscious that time was passing—too much time. It was hard to keep track of the number of days or weeks of their captivity as there was no pattern even to the hours. They were bundled about, stopping and starting both in light and in darkness. Sometimes they were pushed onto horses, although they were not allowed the reins. Sometimes they were almost smothered under sacking in a cart. Raimon fumed about Laila, imagining her on her way to Paris, where she would doubtless sell Bors for meat and laugh at their expense. What did she care about Parsifal and Cador, or the Occitan? Nor did she care for the Flame, or for Yolanda, since she had bartered the Flame for Ugly. Ugly! Laila cared only for herself.

Yolanda defended her. How could Laila know about love or honor or anything good? Her mother, her "royal-blooded" mother, had sold her and she had no father. Everything she had she had scavenged. Hugh's was the first house in which she'd ever lived. And she was French. Why should she care about the Flame or the Occitan?

It fell to Raimon to comfort Yolanda, though, when Garland disappeared on a miserable day of downpours and fog, taken by one of the men and sold to an abbess. Too high-stepping for a pack pony, she was quite clearly the property of a lady, with no place in a company of outlaw knights. It was feared that she would draw unwelcome attention and Sir Faidit preferred the rhythmic thump of gold coin at his belt to an animal he had to feed but could not use. When Yolanda protested, Sir Faidit listened because he prided himself on his manners. He was even sympathetic. "I'm afraid it's too late," he said, "and the abbey was rich. She'll be well looked after." He smiled slyly. "When you're ransomed, I daresay your husband will buy you another."

"Send to him now. I'll tell you who he is and where he is. Send to him, he'll pay, and then let us go."

Sir Faidit laughed out loud. "I've worked out your husband's name and the weight of his coffers already, thank you, and I'll send when I'm good and ready."

"Why doesn't the Flame help us?" Yolanda railed, just as Raimon had once done to Parsifal.

"The Flame has its own rules."

"I wish I knew what they were."

Having sworn his men to secrecy about their forest encounter, Sir Faidit kept the basket carefully in the chest in which he stored the hodgepodge armor he had stolen from the backs of dead or dying knights, some of whom had been his friends. He had never had anything like the Flame before and hardly dared open the chest for fear of it going out. How Laila had kept it alight on horseback in the first scrum of the morning of the Flame's arrival—he had no recollection of exactly who had been carrying it—he did not know. He knew only that she had whispered that keeping it alight was all part of her magic and that if he let it go out, he would never be able to relight it. He was pretty skeptical of this, but nevertheless did not want to take any risks. So he kept the basket well shielded and, when they traveled, he packed up the cart that carried it with clods of earth so the chest would not be rattled.

The question of what to do with it began to consume him, keeping him awake and ruining his appetite. Soon he could think of nothing else. There were just too many choices and there was nobody in whom he could confide. Should he sell it to Count Raymond of Toulouse? He might pay handsomely for it. But could Raymond also give Sir Faidit back the castles that had once been his grandfather's and make his family great in the land once again? He doubted that. Count Raymond was too frightened of King Louis. Should he then sell it to the king himself? He liked the thought of a king having to negotiate with a bandit. But the king would never do such a thing. Rather, he would send an army of scouts followed by boundless waves of men-at-arms to root him out. Far from the king paying Sir Faidit, Sir Faidit would be likely to pay the king—on the gallows. Perhaps Mistress Purplehead was already selling information about him. Perhaps scouts were already looking. He was certain he would be very hard to find, but he still struck camp earlier and earlier, wanting to keep on the move.

Christmas passed and after escape proved impossible, Raimon tried everything else: anger, reason, and bribery. In the end, he fell to his knees and pleaded. Sir Faidit must let them go and give them the Flame. The lives of an old knight and a little boy were at stake. Surely Sir Faidit didn't want those on his conscience. The bandit leader listened as he had listened to Yolanda. He thought hard about what Raimon was saying. Then he wagged his finger and dismissed it.

The day after the new year, Raimon raged, beating his head with his fists. Now it was he who berated the Flame for not doing something, anything, that would have saved those who had sacrificed so much for it already. He couldn't bear to be still, yet he could only shuffle around their pen in shackles like a tethered tiger, pulling Yolanda with him. She longed to tell him that Aimery wouldn't carry out the executions, that perhaps Hugh might intervene, but what use was false hope? Neither Aimery nor Hugh would give any quarter if they felt that no quarter was deserved. So she was forced to shuffle after Raimon, becoming as bruised and battered as if she were his enemy. Brees followed too, unable to comprehend this new state of affairs. He had a growl permanently lodged in his throat that Yolanda, fearful for his safety, was hard put to keep in check.

They traveled in great zigzags through the thickest part of the forest until one afternoon, with a storm threatening, they came quite by chance to an abandoned abbey that had clearly been too remote for even the most austere of monastics. They broke through the gate and discovered that although the forest had begun to absorb bits of the building, there were still fine stone cloisters, a chapter house in which the monks had once gathered daily to discuss monastic business, a dozen monks' cells, and an abbey church with a bell tower attached. It was a perfect place to hide out.

At once Sir Faidit had the precious basket placed on the altar at the top of the church. The church also boasted two thick doors, one on the outside wall and one leading into the complex. Raimon and Yolanda were to be kept there until more appropriate provision could be made. The horses were corralled below the bell tower, which stuck out behind the cloisters, forming part of the back wall.

The two prisoners were unshackled and reshackled separately and not left alone. A guard stood by the altar and when he complained of the gloom, was given a small stub of candle. Raimon and Yolanda were to be allowed nowhere near the basket, he was told, and Yolanda was to keep Brees right at her side.

Raimon stood by what had been the abbot's chair and gazed at his feet, his head full of Parsifal and Cador. Yolanda crouched, her eyes fixed firmly on the altar. After some time she rose and nudged Raimon. "It doesn't look quite right," she whispered.

"What doesn't?"

"The Flame. It's in the draught but it doesn't flicker properly."

"It must. You can't really see anything through the basket."

"No. It really doesn't flicker properly, or at least not how it did."

Raimon looked up. "I don't know, Yolanda. With the basket and the box, how can you tell?"

"I'm telling you."

He shook his head. "You're seeing things."

She pinched him as her pulse quickened. "I'm not."

Raimon peered. "It's the right basket."

"Yes, but it's not the right flame." She brought her lips to his ear and swung her hair, grown past her shoulders again, so that it formed a curtain. "It's in a different box and it's something else."

"What?"

"Shh. Just listen. The night before we were married, Sir Hugh gave me a present, a glass flame. I wanted to leave it in Paris when I came home but Laila must have taken it because she thought it was valuable. She's somehow got that one into the basket and given it to Sir Faidit."

"How could she?"

"You may not like her, but she's clever. You've seen her pull things out of people's ears. Perhaps she switched them when nobody was paying attention. Or perhaps when she first galloped off on Bors. What does it matter? That's what she's done, I'm sure of it. There's a flame underneath the glass, but it's not the Blue Flame."

Raimon was now scrutinizing the basket. It did seem to be true that the breeze now chilling his hands and feet and causing the stubby candle to gutter left the "Flame" oddly unmoved. "My God," he said and stood up.

They both stared at the altar. Raimon turned his lips to Yolanda's ear. "You know her best. What will she have done with the real Flame? Will she have taken it to the king?"

"I don't know. She could have done anything. She could have taken it to the king. She could have sold it to the first person she met. She could have used it in a fire-eating trick. There's one thing, though. She won't have thrown it into the river. She knows the price of everything."

"What price will she set on saving Cador and Parsifal?"

Yolanda was silent.

Moments later they were removed from the church, piled through the kitchens, past the dormitory and the chapter house, and pitched into what had been one of the monk's cells. It was bare of everything except a straw pallet and a slit for a window. Their feet were reshackled with thick rope. Brees sniffed about. The cell was so narrow that when he wagged his tail, it beat from one wall to another.

Raimon was fired up with nerves and anxieties. He could hardly wait for the bandits' footsteps to fade before he burst out, "Why doesn't Faidit realize his flame's a fake?"

"Well, you didn't and he's never seen the real one. He hasn't really looked at it much either because he's so frightened of it going out." Yolanda also found it difficult to be calm. She began to braid Brees's fur to keep herself occupied. "What will happen to us when he decides to look harder?"

"I don't know. But what will have happened to Cador and Sir Parsifal? I just can't think of anything else." It was unbearable, intolerable, not to know. He couldn't stay still, not for a second. The visions in his head were making him mad.

Yolanda stopped braiding. She could see where the monk had gouged crosses into the wall, counting his paternosters. "I'm going to pray," she said.

He heard in his head his last conversation with Parsifal but old furies bubbled over. "You pray if you want to. God's given us nothing."

"He's given us each other," Yolanda said.

Raimon dragged his shackles through the straw. His face was leaner and more sculpted—a man's face now, with nothing of the boy left in it—and his body, still whip thin, was like iron. He wrenched her hand from her braiding and pointed to Hugh's ring. "He hasn't really, though, has he," he said. He knew it was cruel but suddenly he couldn't bear to pretend. Yolanda took back her hand and did not reply.

A day passed, and then a week. Sir Faidit did not open the basket for he was busy making the place secure. Nor did he starve his prisoners. Food and water were thrown in, and they were taken out individually to the latrine ditch. Sir Faidit did not like to think himself inhumane. It became clear to Raimon that they might well spend the rest of the winter here. The thought nearly broke him.

Relief came with no warning. Raimon only knew that one evening, when dusk was already closing in, the rustle of winter leaves suddenly turned into a great beating of drums, blowing of bugles, and baying of hounds. Yolanda leaped up and Brees opened his mouth and sang out. All three clung together.

In minutes they heard the fumble of keys. Sir Faidit was panting in the doorway, two of his men behind him. "Get them—get them—" His head moved from side to side, nearly catching his hair in the flambeau he carried. "Get them into the bell tower and keep them up there. Who has led these people here? It cannot be an accident. Who is it? When I find him, I'll skin him alive and feed him to the crows. To arms! To arms!" He disappeared.

It was impossible for Raimon and Yolanda to move in their shackles, so these were undone and they were prodded out of the cell, outside for a moment, and then forced to wind up the bell tower's oak staircase with the bell ropes, stinking of the urine in which they had been soaked as a safeguard against fire, gently swaying behind them and the hollow dome of the bell itself directly above. The stairwell was pitch dark and the guards stopped to light one of the flambeaux that rested in iron holders at regular intervals. They could move much more quickly now and by the time they reached the top they were all breathless. Brees followed behind, with Yolanda calling his name, although his devotion was challenged by older, less tender instincts woken once again by the sounds of war. Those drums, the scrape of steel, the grinding of wheels, and above all the baying had his neck bristling. He longed to disobey.

A wooden platform, nearly nine feet square and with two

holes for the bell ropes, had been built under the open gable, and the bell itself was suspended not from a hook in the stone but from a thick iron ring plunged deep into a vast and solid beam. This rested on two equally solid wooden pillars that, in their turn, rested on immovable stones sticking out from the tower walls themselves. The bell, to which the sulphurous whiff of the furnace still clung, hung like a fat bronze pear roughly five feet above the platform, its cloudy surface and cavernous hollow casting a velvety shadow over the clutter still lying about: coils of different materials, ordinary ropes of varying thicknesses, and a small barrel of oil with a cloth draped over the side. The bell was a valuable thing. The monks surely intended to come back for it. But the noise below was clearly not monks.

The brighter of the two guards edged Yolanda around the lip of the bell to the very edge of the platform and held her tightly. Small bits of garbage, dislodged by her feet, bounced and skittered over the edge. "If you resist, I'll push her over too," the guard said to Raimon. "And hold that dog." Raimon did not dare disobey.

Gushing through the trees below like the splash of a stream, Yolanda could see the tops of helmets rising and falling and the odd flash as a steel plate protecting a horse's face caught the last rays of the sun. The horses stretched their necks as their riders unsheathed their swords and couched their lances. This was no haphazard company of soldiers, this was an experienced, disciplined troop. Behind the horses, an enormous protuberance thrust out. A thick tree trunk had been hewn. Sixteen men carried it and they were running.

"Who is it?" Raimon cried out. He didn't know what he

hoped. "Is it the king? Is it Raymond of Toulouse?" He echoed Sir Faidit. "How did they find us?" The bell seemed to absorb his words, making a faint vibration.

The guards didn't care who it was. They were just enemies. They collared Brees and attached him to one of the pulley rings hammered low into the timber strut in the far corner and then, with the dog now straining and snapping, took Raimon, ripped up his tunic, and gagged him, then reshackled his feet and shoved him to the far side of the platform, away from the stairwell. Then they took a rope, made a noose, and threw it up over the horizontal beam, caught it and passed the loose end through, pulling down to secure the noose around the beam. With the other end, they tied Raimon's hands behind his back. They gagged Yolanda and tied her in the same way, fumbling the knots in their hurry to finish the job and be gone. If the bell swung, the lip would hit both the prisoners and pitch them over the edge of the tower, yanking their arms up behind them and wrenching them out of their sockets. The timber creaked as the men fled back down the stairs and joined the general melee. Only then did Brees stop his racket and Yolanda, shaking from top to toe, answer Raimon's question.

"It's Hugh," she said.

Hugh raced off hotfoot from Carcassonne moments after Laila had fought her way into his presence. It was not wise to abandon his duties there. The king would disapprove. But he couldn't help himself. He felt a fury against Raimon for not protecting Yolanda properly and then a much greater fury against himself for imagining that such a boy could ever have done so. He cursed the guards he had sent with them, particularly after Laila had finished embroidering and embellishing their cowardice, and then cursed himself that the silly notions and vain hopes of love had gotten in the way of the hard business of living. He praised only Laila. That girl was sharper than any of his household knights, even Amalric and Henri. She had no idea of maps or place, no notion of being guided by the stars, but she had brought back not only the Flame but a means of finding the outlaws again.

"Ugly will show you," she had said in that lofty, supercilious way she had. Hugh's knights had scoffed but she was right. After Laila had got them to the bandits' original camp, the dog had quite naturally followed the trail left by Brees, whose rank smell was a godsend now. Hugh swore he would never part Yolanda from her pet again.

His men had barely been allowed to rest on the journey. Now that they had arrived at this place, although Hugh should have ordered camp to be pitched to reconnoiter overnight, he galloped straight to the tower and issued his challenge. He didn't wish to desecrate the church, he yelled, but since Sir Faidit was already using a place of worship as an armed camp, he would raze it to the ground if Yolanda was not released, unharmed, at once. If Sir Faidit refused, he would not be killed, at least not right away—not until he had been turned into an example of what happened to kidnappers who fell foul of Sir Hugh des Arcis. His voice boomed out, rising like the wrath of God. "I am the keeper of the king's oriflamme and I will have my way." He did not mention Raimon or the Flame.

There was no reply and, indeed, Hugh hardly gave time for one. Almost before he'd finished, he raised his hand and the sixteen men, still panting from their run, gathered themselves together and swung the tree trunk three times against the church door. It groaned at the first onslaught, bent at the second, and splintered at the third. A dozen mounted knights, Hugh at their head, poured into the nave, making a strange percussive symphony on the uneven flags.

Even in the blackness, they could feel that the church was empty, so abandoning their horses, they poured through the side door and into the cloisters, leaving the door swinging. Nobody. The knights peered into the gloom, their swords slicing at nothing. Hugh's heart beat with sickening intensity. The painted girl had fooled them. The dog was an idiot.

But then, from the storerooms, Sir Faidit's men erupted and in moments the place was filled with the clash of battle. Hugh saw the bandits' horses, Galahad among them, and dodged and buffeted his way through to cut them loose. "Go, Galahad, go!" he cried as they piled out. But somebody was clinging to Galahad, lying flat on his back in an effort not to be seen. When Hugh grabbed, the man slid off the other side and began to run. Hugh could see from his shadow that he was clutching something under one arm. The man ran to the bottom of the bell tower, threw open the door, and began to mount the steps. Hugh pursued him, yanked him around, and found himself face-to-face with Sir Faidit. Above, he heard Brees's rolling bark. "Yolanda!" he cried.

Standing above Hugh, Sir Faidit had the advantage but he also had the basket containing the "Flame" and dared not put it down.

Hugh threw his helmet off and charged. Despite his deft sword work, Sir Faidit found himself forced upward and soon both men were on the steps. Hugh seized the flambeau lit by the guards. Jabbing and thrusting, occasionally almost wrestling, they climbed up, both hampered by the narrow space, until they reached the platform. Now Sir Faidit was at a disadvantage, for he had to look behind him or risk either crashing into the bell or tripping over something. Hugh pushed after him. Neither saw Raimon and Yolanda at first for the light had almost vanished up there. Sir Faidit, grasping the basket more firmly and feeling the lip of the bell at his back, chopped again and again at Hugh's neck, so vulnerable without even a mail coif, but he was unlucky. Hugh kept himself just too far away and stopped trying for the killer blow, preferring to seek the weak points in Faidit's chain mail. He cut, Faidit parried, and Hugh's sword slid away from Faidit's body and caught the basket. He pulled backward and the basket fell to the ground.

Faidit yelled as it bounced away into a corner and quickly sidled around the bell to catch it. Hugh followed him, the flambeau held high. Both he and Sir Faidit saw Raimon and Yolanda at the same time. Hugh raised his sword again but before he could bring it down, the bandit yelled, "Do that and they'll die." It was then that Hugh saw the ropes and Sir Faidit poised to kick the bell. Panting, he lowered his sword.

Sir Faidit, panting too, leaned on the bell just enough to make the clapper shiver. He leaned a little harder. The bell shifted and Yolanda gave a muffled cry. She could feel the air behind her and imagined the rope tightening. "Now," said Sir Faidit, catching his breath, "this is an interesting situation. Step back and drop your sword."

At once, Hugh dropped his sword. But instead of stepping back, he dived into the corner and swept up the basket. Faidit lurched. "Give me that," he hissed.

"This is far more valuable than Yolanda." Hugh tried but failed to keep his voice steady.

"It's only of value if it's still lit," Faidit replied. He couldn't take his eyes off it.

"It's the Blue Flame of the Occitan," said Hugh. "But perhaps you're right. Well, I'll just take the risk. If it is still lit, I'm sure I'll get a good price for it." He turned, as if he was going to descend the steps.

"No!" cried Faidit.

Hugh waited.

"You can have the girl. But I want to see the Flame. I want to see that it's alight. I want to see it face-to-face. Open the basket. Show me."

Hugh could not refuse. Faidit was so near the bell and could push it at any time. Very slowly, he opened the basket and took out the box. "There," he said. "I can see it flickering."

"I can't see anything," said Faidit. "Open the box. Bring the Flame out. Do it." He flexed his arms and touched the bell again. "Do it. Do it now."

As slowly as he could, Hugh opened the box.

"Hold the flambeau to it."

Hugh held the flambeau underneath it. Faidit gasped. The "Flame" was shattered into a thousand tiny pieces. It did not shine so much as twinkle like a broken necklace. Underneath was a tiny wick, now extinguished. At first he did not seem to understand. There was still so much blue. Perhaps there were many flames. He peered. Raimon and Yolanda were silent shadows.

"What's this?" he asked stupidly, his shoulder still too close to the bell. Then he began to realize. "My God, it's glass! You scoundrels! That girl! That witch! I'll have her hunted down and roasted. I'll have you all roasted."

"It *is* the Flame," insisted Hugh in a desperate play for time. "Take the flambeau and look properly. See." He held out the torch. The blue pieces flashed again. Sir Faidit hesitated, then snatched the flambeau and at once moved around the bell, away from Hugh. "It *is* glass!" he shouted. "You can't fool me! I see now! The wick is a kitchen wick covered by some kind of vase or something. That was *never* the Blue Flame, not for a moment." Then he hunched up. He would not just nudge the bell, he would shove it as hard as he could. Raimon and Yolanda would not just drop, they would swing right out and then drop like stones. "Glass!" he repeated, again and again, louder and louder. "Glass and kitchen wick!" And to gather more weight for his great effort, he leaned back just far enough to put himself within Brees's reach.

The dog, already at fever pitch, didn't hesitate, but stretching every muscle in his body he sank his jaws into Sir Faidit's hauberk. He did not pierce the skin but caught his teeth in the steel mesh and pulled the knight off balance. Faidit dropped both sword and flambeau. The torch rolled and the spilling flames caught the rag draped over the oil barrel. The rag smoked for a moment then lit like kindling. Faidit kicked the barrel toward Hugh and burning oil flowed over the platform in a fiery tide, dripping through the rope holes before sweeping over Hugh's sword and down the stairs.

Sir Faidit was lurching back and forth, trying to extricate himself from Brees. He could barely reach the bell, only occasionally slapping at it with the flat of his hand. But he could get no purchase and the bell didn't move. If only he could reach the bell ropes! But he couldn't. Hugh ignored Faidit, seized the flambeau, and rushed to Yolanda, burning through the rope around her wrists and then kneeling to burn the loops of her shackles as she yanked away her gag. He groaned. Once his men saw the smoke, they might take it into their heads to ring the bell as a warning of the fire. "Get out of here right now, Yolanda! Get down the stairs," he ordered as he frantically pulled the last of the blackened threads. "Don't wait, not even for a second."

"But Raimon! Brees!" She kicked away the rope and pulled off Raimon's gag.

Hugh pushed her around the bell. "I'll free them. Just go!"

Raimon added his pleas to Hugh's. "Go, Yolanda! For God's sake!"

They could hear Faidit screaming. Brees had him on the floor and burning oil had seeped between the chinks in his armor. Hugh rushed around the bell, seized the outlaw knight's own sword, and plunged it straight into his neck. The blood hosed out, adding its red to the flames as Faidit gurgled in disbelief. Giving a last lurch, he rolled off the platform and crashed into the trees below. Cursing the loss of the sword, for his own was too hot to pick up, Hugh burned through Brees's ropes. The dog rushed to Yolanda, who was still on the platform, pulling at the ropes on Raimon's arms.

"I'll do this. Go on! You must!" Hugh pulled at her. "Go down and stop anybody who tries to ring the bell. If you really want to save Raimon, you must stop them!"

"Oh God! I didn't think!" Yanking Brees after her, Yolanda finally ran to the stairs, pulling off her skirt to wind it around Brees's head and her own. Some of the steps were already ashes.

She was shouting "don't ring the bell, don't ring the bell" but the fire had caught in the stairwell and was beginning to roar. Brees was terrified. He couldn't go into that furnace. He whipped around and fled upward again. Yolanda sobbed but she had to go on. She had to stop anybody from pulling on those ropes.

The fire's spread was making things difficult for Hugh. Their urine bath was protecting the bell ropes very well but the platform under his feet was beginning to disintegrate and the heat came at him in great gusts. The bell shuddered as it warmed. Flames were licking the wooden pillars. The flambeau melted, so Hugh threw it down and seized a smoldering plank, sawing it against Raimon's restraints. Raimon did what he could to help, working his hands up and down. Hugh pressed the plank closer. Everything else was burning! Why were these damned things so stubborn? Hugh sawed and sawed until, just as the rope finally snapped, the horizontal beam above the bell cracked and the bell tilted slowly and stopped for a second before, with infinite weight and heaviness, it began to toll.

Raimon, his feet still bound, dropped onto the platform and flattened himself, his face and hair singeing in the oil. The bell swung harmlessly over his head. Hugh was not so lucky. His armor hampered his fall and as the clapper hit the side of the bell, the bell's lip hit his forehead. A cry jerked out of him as the force knocked him backward.

Raimon saw Hugh crash to the floor just as Brees reappeared. The dog was almost blind with fear and pain but he wagged his blistered tail at Raimon. Raimon freed his feet. The beam above him cracked a little more and the bell sagged. Too tilted now to toll, it began to melt. Raimon scrambled around for a coil of uncharred rope, found one, and slung the most makeshift of slings under Brees's shoulders. Batting out the flames as best he could, he pulled the dog back to the stairwell. The steps had completely vanished but he pushed the rope through one of the pulley rings and lowered the sling at breakneck speed. It was like lowering Brees into a furnace, but what else could he do? When the rope went slack, he let go. He had done his best. He could see the bell ropes themselves now beginning to fray as the urine finally dried. Any moment now that last escape route would vanish.

Hugh was lying with his head to one side and a gash as long as a dagger opening up his forehead. Raimon lunged for the nearest bell rope, already bracing himself to jump. He looked back at Hugh. There lay his enemy in war, his rival in love. There lay Yolanda's unwanted husband. There lay a Frenchman, a follower of the king, and not just any follower, but the upholder of the oriflamme. It wasn't wrong to leave him. It wasn't. Hugh was unconscious. He would die without suffering. Surely this was God or the Flame, or even God and the Flame giving Raimon and the Occitan their chance. *Take the chance,* a cold voice told him. *Take it. Take it. It won't come again.* The flames were everywhere now, turning from red to blue. The bell rope was shredding. The very tower was shaking. "Oh, God help me!" Raimon cried, and turning, he reached out his arms.

15

Chalus

They sat at dawn amid the smoldering ruins. The last thing to fall had been the bell itself. It had hung on, long after gravity should have done its work, as if in blind hope that all might yet be well. It was not well, however, and as the last of the staircase, the timber struts, the immense horizontal beam, and the platform were finally reduced to nothing, it crashed sonorously to the ground, a swift and inelegant descent followed by a small bounce that grooved the earth and another that didn't before finally coming to rest, the clapper crumpled into the crown. It was astounding, so everybody said, that apart from a few dents in the lip and some fire staining, it was essentially undamaged. Yolanda was leaning against it as the heat drained slowly out. "I must stay," she said. "Don't you see? I must."

Both she and Raimon were filthy, their hair clumped and their clothes in tatters. Beside them lay Brees, nose on paws. He had no fur now, his tail and legs were bare and the rest of him tufted, like half-mown grass, but he was alive and Ugly was licking his wounds.

Raimon could see Yolanda only dimly through the spreading

light of campfires in a clearing that Hugh's men had hewn and in which they were now milling about in some dismay. Raimon kicked at a charred lump of something no longer recognizable. "I should have left him up there."

"Of course you shouldn't."

"Don't you understand, Yolanda? I want him dead." He didn't ask her why she didn't too. He did not want to hear her reply.

"You may want him dead, but not dead at your hand," Yolanda told him, as she had been telling him for hours.

"I'd have left him there if I'd known it would turn out like this."

"No you wouldn't," said Yolanda gently. "Now I must go and see if there is any change."

She got up and Raimon followed her.

Hugh was corpse white, his arms stiffly at his sides and a cloth bound around his head. Amalric and Henri were with him. It was those two who had relieved Raimon of his human burden, a burden he had managed, with a mixture of luck, brute strength, sheer adrenaline, and desperation, to balance on his back as he slithered down the bell rope moments before everything collapsed. They had taken off Hugh's armor and tried to rouse him without success. Yolanda had bound his wound as best she could and when Henri had announced that he would be taken back to Carcassonne, Yolanda had at once said that she was going with him. This was what Raimon refused to countenance and what Yolanda was now trying to force him to accept. "If Hugh dies," she said steadfastly, "I'll be by his side. It's what I have to do." There was silence. Raimon turned his back. She pulled his arm to make him look at her again and touched her hand to her breast where the leather ring still hung. "Faith in each other. That's what we agreed. I have to be with him. Don't you see?"

He touched his own ring, now black and greasy. "I don't see at all. He won't even know whether you're there or not. You can't bring him around. You don't know how. I doubt anybody does." He gave Hugh a cursory glance and then walked away.

Yolanda caught up with him. "I know I can't cure him but I can't just abandon him. I can't." She spoke quickly. "He came to save us, Raimon. We owe him something."

"He came for you because he loves you."

"He could have left you but he didn't."

"He only saved me because he thought that if he didn't, you might never forgive him."

She stopped. "That's unworthy of you, Raimon," she said quietly. They walked on. She began to speak again, trying to bridge the distance she felt growing between them. "Amalric says that the king has lost patience. He's been waiting for the Flame too long and now he's decided that Hugh didn't really care whether it was ever delivered to him or not because when Laila brought it to him, he let her take it back to Castelneuf."

"That girl, at least, seems to have behaved better than I thought she might." Raimon heard the sourness in his voice but was too tired and dispirited to make it sweeter. Yet Laila had saved Cador and Parsifal. Laila and Aimery. According to Amalric, on New Year's Day, Aimery had blustered and threatened and even had his sword specially sharpened. But when the two hostages were dragged into the courtyard ready to die, both had refused the blindfold. In the end, according to Amalric, Aimery told everybody that the old knight was too sick and that the execution would wait a fortnight. It was in that fortnight that Laila came. This too should have made Raimon rejoice but it made him feel sourer still. Of course he was boundlessly happy that the Flame was safe and Parsifal and Cador were alive. But that he should find himself in debt to Laila and Aimery stuck in his gullet. He struck out again. "Are you sure Amalric's telling you the truth?"

Yolanda pondered, then shrugged. "I think so. Why wouldn't he?" She stopped walking and leaned against him.

"I don't want to let you go," he said, and his fingers sought hers.

She sighed very deeply. "I know." She turned to him. "Oh, Raimon. Wouldn't everything be so much easier if Hugh was a monster? But he isn't. You know that as well as I do." She could see Raimon's face hardening. "If we didn't live in these awful times we might all have been friends."

"Knights don't make friends with weavers' sons."

"That's because some weavers' sons are too proud to accept their friendship. Too proud and perhaps too needlessly jealous. Yet you saved his life too."

He couldn't bear to hear her say these things. He let go of her hands and moved away. "He's still the enemy, Yolanda. Even now, he'd kill me for the king."

"And you'd kill him for the Occitan." But she didn't want to argue. Instead, she stood in front of him. "I'm going back to Carcassonne with Hugh. He needs me now just as he needed you in the bell tower. You didn't let him down and I don't think I can either." He tried to turn away from her but she drew his face to hers so that their noses were almost touching and she could see all the crooked furrows in his brow, could see where the bone in his nose bent slightly to the left and where ash lodged in the dimple in his right cheek. "All will be well, Raimon."

He was aware of every inch of her and scrunched great handfuls of her hair into his fists, as much as he could hold. He hurt her, but though she blinked, she didn't complain. She could feel more through his fingers than through his words.

"How can you believe that?" he whispered.

"I believe it because I want to believe it, and my father used to say that I always got what I wanted," she replied, and his fingers tightened so hard that she thought her hair might come out.

His hands dropped to his sides. "I'll go back to the Amouroix alone then," he said to her, "back to Castelneuf. Parsifal and Cador will be expecting me. And the Flame."

She could hardly forbid him. "Will you wait with me here until first light?" she asked. Both of them could feel that cold wall rising up again between them.

He replied at once. He couldn't help himself. "No," he said. "I'll not wait with you in this place." He looked over at Hugh and then back at her. "But I will wait for you, Yolanda, I'll wait for you for as long as it takes." He paused. "But I hope it's not long."

She watched him walk off and take a sword from the pile of armor belonging to the dead bandits. Then he bridled Galahad and picked up a saddle only to discard it. He would ride bareback, as he had always preferred. He found a cloak and wrapped it around his shoulders. She held her breath, wondering if he would come to her again before he left. She covered her face when she thought he was leaving without another word. Then he was beside her, already mounted, with Galahad snorting, still nervous from the fire.

She put her hand on the rein. With his legs swinging down and his hair tousled, he looked so much as he used to. If she shut out everything else, they might have been back at Castelneuf, just the two of them, exulting in their own resplendent world. All she had to do was raise her arm and he would swing her up behind him. She knew that was what he was waiting for. Her heart shivered, her arm rose, and then it sank as her legs dissolved beneath her. With a tiny exclamation, he twitched the rein.

She fell to her knees as he disappeared. Had he returned at that moment she would have abandoned Hugh and flung out not just one arm but two. Hugh would find somebody else. What was his need compared to her love? But Raimon did not return and she was left on her knees alone.

Nor did Raimon go straight back to Castelneuf as he should have. Though the Flame called to him and though he was desperate to see that Parsifal and Cador were well, he rode like a madman not noting his direction at all. How he reviled himself for his impulse in the bell tower. He could have left Hugh. He should have. It hurt him almost physically that had he done so, Yolanda would have been behind him now, her arms around his waist, her body molded into his back. He ached for her as others ached for a missing limb. Though King Louis threatened, though the inquisitors were casting their nets, and though the Cathar heresy was still haunting the Occitan, they would have been together, properly together, and that would have been more than enough to soothe all his other pains. He filled his lungs as he hurtled away, yelling at himself, punching his head, and berating the horse when he stumbled at the lunatic pace, forcing him to go faster. It took nearly an hour for this anguish to spend itself, and longer still before the horse's sobbing breath had Raimon slipping off, apologizing and stroking, stroking and apologizing, praising the gallantry and obedience of the dumb animal he had so fearfully abused. It was midmorning when, after dunking his head in a stream, he made a decision and vaulted on again. Galahad braced and his haunches tensed. "No, that's over, my friend," Raimon murmured, and the old horse, willing but relieved, mustered himself and set off at a steady canter into the spangled trees.

Much to her surprise, Yolanda slept and was woken by anxious hands at her shoulder. Her eyes flew open in hope of Raimon, then fell. Henri didn't notice. "Sir Hugh—," he said.

Yolanda struggled up, falling over her skirts in her hurry. "Is he dead?" She didn't know if the flutter in her heart was hope or dread.

"Is that what you'd like?" Henri didn't hide the fact that he neither liked nor trusted her.

She didn't answer. She ran to Hugh. His skin had turned the color of buttermilk and the bandage around his head was soaked in blood. Rapid and shallow, it seemed his breathing might stop at any moment. He looked like a hermit Yolanda had once seen: suffering, mortally tired, far older than his twenty-six years. She stared down for some time. Even if it would please Raimon, how could she hate this man, unwanted husband and enemy that he was? How could she wish him dead? In another time, or if she'd been born in Paris, or if she'd never met Raimon, perhaps she really could have been the wife that he wanted.

She was beside him when he opened his eyes and they regarded each other carefully. Hugh's eyes swam for some minutes before they finally focused. She could not tell if he recognized her. "Are you in pain?" she asked.

Hugh frowned. It was a huge effort. "Pain?" he said, as if he didn't understand the word. "I'm not sure." He tried to move his arms and then his legs. "Am I—Have I—"

"No, no," she tried to reassure him. "You took a blow to the head. Do you remember?"

He waited. There seemed to be a blank where his memory used to be. "I remember fire," he said at last.

"Do you know who I am?"

There was an even longer pause. "Yes." Slowly the jigsaw of pictures in his mind slotted back together. He closed his eyes several times. "Yes, I know who you are, Yolanda. I know exactly."

It was then that she began to cry. She had no idea if they were tears of relief or tears of disappointment. All she knew was that she could not stop them because she was here and Raimon was not. She cried for a long time and with such ferocity that when, eventually, Hugh did manage to lift his arms and put them around her, she did not have the strength to pull away.

Raimon reached the château of Chalus Chabrol in three days. He would have reached it earlier had he not been misdirected and followed the wrong river. He traveled fast and though his head and heart were so full, he couldn't help marveling at the richness of the Limousin land. Even in the dead months the hills rolled and swelled and the air smelled so sweet and fecund you could believe that just breathing it would make you fatter. It was good, in its way, to think of Parsifal here.

When Chalus's round keep rose before him, he pictured the old knight at the same age as Cador, firing off the crossbow bolt that had killed King Richard the Lionheart over forty years before. What a scene that must have been. He scanned the keep and the ground beneath trying to work out where Parsifal had burrowed up into the light, clutching the Flame that had first destroyed then enhanced his life. He rode closer. Now he could see where Richard must have pitched his besieging camp, for the land had not changed its shape although the place did have an odd air about it, as if the crossbow bolt that had killed Richard had also killed time. A few people gathered to stare at him. When they saw he was alone, unarmed except for a crude sword, and that his horse didn't even have a saddle, they ignored him.

On the right of the keep was a square hill, man-made by the look of it, and on it four stumps, rotting and green, poked out. He slid to the ground, knotting his reins. Leaving Galahad to graze, he climbed up. This must have been the place of execution. Tentatively, he touched one of the poles, sticky with winter grease and scabrous weathering. Yes, this was where Sir Parsifal's father and his fourteen knights had met their end. He had never really thought of Sir Parsifal's father before, but he thought of him now. It was a magnificent thing he had done, taking the blame for Richard's death himself and sacrificing his life for his son and for the Flame. And the sacrifice had not ended with Sir Bertrand. Sir Parsifal would do the same for

Raimon. Raimon knew that without a shadow of a doubt. That's what made finding Unbent so important.

He put his hands on his hips and his heart sank. There was no reason to believe that the armor of the executed knights would still be here. Indeed, there was every reason to think that it wouldn't, since it would have been greedily pounced on by those who made a living out of stripping the dead. Much more likely that Unbent was hanging by the side of some Norman or English knight, with the de Maurand coat of arms painted over and a new one imposed. That certainly would have happened had the knights been killed in battle. Yet it was possible, Raimon supposed, that somebody might have ordered that the armor of these rebels and king killers should be tossed into the pit along with their bodies, as if it too were tainted, thus heaping disgrace onto disgrace.

It was not hard to see where the corpses had been buried. At the bottom of the square hill a green circle marked the spot. Raimon saw the luxuriant growth and felt slightly sick. Nevertheless, he walked quickly back to Galahad and rode into the village to borrow a wooden spade. He did not say for what.

Four hours later, with curious and silent children gathered about, Raimon uncovered one skull and then another. The children screamed and ran away, which delayed things, since Raimon had to stop digging and keep watch in case they returned with an armed gang. He feared for Galahad. But nobody came. The villagers believed the green circle to be cursed, so they pulled their screaming children inside and bolted their doors. "The devil has come," they told each other.

After the skulls, with every thrust of the spade, Raimon found bones, many, many bones, and bits of clothing, mainly rags now, but recognizable as the shirts the condemned knights must have worn at their end. Raimon's arms ached and his stomach revolted. Bones and the foul detritus that clings to bones, but no armor. He should give up. This felt like desecration. Then he saw a ring still attached to a knuckle. Trying not to gag, he picked it up and wiped off the mud. It was a signet ring. He laid it down. The corpses had not been stripped of their valuables. Perhaps the armor was still here. He dug wildly now, without reverence or respect, just wanting to find what he had come for and get out. He shoveled deep into the loam again and again, finding nothing until, with a dull thump, he hit something hard. At once he threw the spade down. Sweat blinded him. He steadied himself, forcing himself to breathe more deeply and trying to slow his heart. When he felt ready, he knelt in this charnel pit, the mud oozing into his knees and through his fingers.

The shape of the first piece he pulled out puzzled him. Though broken up, it had clearly been long and curved into scales. He knocked off great clods of earth. Then he started. It was a crinet, the piece of armor that covered the top of a horse's neck. Good God. Had the Lionheart's men executed the horses too? Fearfully, he began to scrape away the earth again, more carefully now. He found no more horse armor. The crinet must have been lying around and just got tipped in with everything else. It was a small relief. Soon, however, he had a good collection of chain mail: an odd number of gauntlets, nine hauberks, several sets of greaves and sabatons, and four helmets.

He found the swords all together. Fifteen blunted but faithful companions, one for each of the knights at that fatal siege.

Slowly, and with no sense of relief—that would come later—he laid them out on the grass, some more badly rusted than others but each as individual as the men who had wielded them. One had a brazil-nut pommel, another a mushroom, a third a five-petaled flower. Some were jammed in their scabbards. Others had no scabbards at all.

It was not immediately obvious which was Unbent. He had to examine them all, spitting on the hilts to see if anything was inscribed. His prize was the sixth of the fifteen. A huge, two-handed affair, Unbent's name was engraved in flowing writing that neither age nor rust had destroyed. He raised it high and bowed his head in a sudden, unbidden urge to pray as Sir Parsifal's father would have done when he received this sword from his own father, as Sir Parsifal should have done but had never had the chance. He closed his eyes and the words that came to him were Parsifal's. "Keep faith with God and the Flame and love." Raimon felt the crusted blade above him. The sword was still straight and true, still—Raimon gave a small, aching smile—Unbent. "So help me but I'm trying," he whispered, feeling all its great weight in his shoulders, "I'm trying."

When he could hold the sword up no longer, he laid it back on the grass and began to place the bones back into their grave, not higgledy-piggledy but in ordered lines, the skulls neatly together. The other fourteen swords he rested over the bones. He would take only Unbent. The armor he buried in as tidy a pile as he could make and when he had finished, he made the sign of the cross and walked with Galahad back to the village. Nobody unbarred their door and he propped the spade against the well. Then he carried Unbent down to the river and spent a long time scrubbing and washing it. A smith would have to beat off the rust and resharpen the blade but when Raimon had finished, Unbent was recognizably itself again and Raimon had discovered something else. Its pommel too sported a decoration: a single flame, a brave and tiny curl atop this great instrument of war. He fashioned a baldric from his belt and swung it over his back. The sword bumped against his spine. It was a good feeling. "Come," he said to Galahad, "no more detours," and hitching his leg over the horse's withers, he at last turned for home.

16

At Castelneuf

Why cannot life be simple? Certainly, Count Aimery tried to make it so. He had agreed to hand me, the Amouroix, over to the French in order to save himself and those who looked to him for protection. It was his opinion, and who is to say he was wrong, that it matters less what a place is called or by whom it is ruled than that its people should be fed and secure. After all, what is a name and an overlord compared to a peaceful life? Whether I, the Amouroix, was part of France or part of the Occitan, I would still be as I had always been. The French could dig up my vines and denigrate my language but they could not flatten my mountains or deaden my air or cut out the heart that beats below the stone. That was Aimery's simple belief and it was armed with this belief that he waited for the king's message of praise and thanks for his foresight and cooperation. Except, life not being simple, when the message did come, it was not quite as Aimery expected.

King Louis did not, of course, bring the message himself. He did not feel that necessary. Count Aimery of Amouroix was small fry to him. Aimery forgave that and did not hesitate to open the gates to two of Louis's senior officials, an earl and an archbishop—I purposefully forget the rest of their titles. When the king heard that Hugh had allowed the Flame to return to Castelneuf he had dispatched these two to collect it, and though they had come to the château alone, they had taken the precaution of bringing along a whole battalion of the king's men, who were even now hanging about on my borders.

"I'm not clinging on to it, I assure you," Aimery told the two men, after they had accused him of doing just that. He noted that the archbishop as well as the earl was fully armed. "I'm not clinging on to anything." They were in the great hall and the visitors wouldn't sit or take refreshment, preferring to stand together as if warding off an infectious disease.

"Don't play with words, Count Aimery. You still have it." The earl stood, his feet apart, as though he were a disappointed father and Aimery a son sent for punishment.

The stance was deliberately insulting and Aimery was duly insulted, but he knew better than to show it. "Yes," he said crisply, "but that's because it has only just returned here and in these troubled times, I can't leave at a moment's notice. I'm fully intending to take it to the king. How can he possibly doubt that?"

The two men looked completely disbelieving. Aimery gestured. "Sit, eat. You must be tired." Jean appeared with wine and pieces of roasted pig.

The archbishop hesitated. Aimery pressed him. He sat and the earl, annoyed, nevertheless perched on the edge of a bench.

From their places by the fire and listening to every word, Gui and Guerau picked up their instruments. They sang gently at first, just background music, but then, gripping their instruments more tightly, began to sing a new song, one Gui had just finished, a song of arrogance brought low and the conqueror being trampled by the conquered. They sang in Occitan and then in French, enunciating each word clearly so the visitors could not mistake their meaning. When Aimery fully took in what they were doing, he silenced them, but they carried on singing as they gave two mock bows and stalked out of the room with their heads high.

The earl and the archbishop were on their feet. It was they who were insulted now.

"Tomorrow those two will get the lash," Aimery declared. "Now, more meat?"

Unfortunately for Aimery, Laila chose this moment to prance in, her hair blue to remind people how she had saved the Flame. She saw the visitors, noted their expensive garb and, guessing who had sent them, at once began to tell of how she had outwitted the bandits. She insisted that the king owed her a large annuity.

The earl tapped a steel-capped foot. "Who is this creature? Why does she speak of the king? I'm telling you, Count Aimery, King Louis will not wait for the Flame any longer. Give it to us at once. We wish to be gone."

"I understand the king's impatience." Aimery was violently gesturing for Laila to leave but she remained, dangerously hovering. He took a deep breath, sat again, and took another slab of pork, hoping that his visitors would do the same and the atmosphere would defuse. "But I shall take it to him personally. You see," he wiped his chin, "I have other things to bring to him too: a perfectus called the White Wolf and a heretic who won't recant." He smiled and stretched out, a picture, he hoped, of relaxed confidence.

The earl never moved. "He'll leave the heretics to the inquisitors. They'll be here any day now. He just wants the Flame. Come now. Where is it?"

"I tell you, I'm going to bring the Flame myself." Aimery put down his slab of pork. "Please go and convey that message."

The earl glowered and placed his feet far apart in a manner of extreme belligerence. "I'm asking you again," he said, as if Aimery were an idiot. "Give the Flame to us." He and the archbishop exchanged a glance. "You may come with us, if that's what you want."

Aimery saw the exchanged glance and also saw just what it meant. He stood himself now and his voice was smooth. "No," he said, "I can't do that. If I come with you, it will look as though the Flame was taken from me by force. No. I shall take it by myself and then King Louis will know for certain that I hand it over perfectly willingly."

The earl threw back his head. "Fine words, Count, but we know what you're really up to. Admit it. You're really waiting for Count Raymond of Toulouse. Once his army gets here, you'll hand over the Flame to him."

"Count Raymond?" Aimery gave a belly laugh. "Oh no. I don't expect Count Raymond. He's the king's man already, is he not?"

"Count Raymond's a nuisance," said the archbishop with feeling.

"He's signed a peace treaty, I hear." Aimery tried to engage the archbishop in conversation. That might calm things.

"You know as well as we do that Count Raymond's peace treaties are worthless," said the earl, and it was clear that his temper was about to explode. "Worthless!"

"Look," Aimery said. Perhaps the earl would appreciate conciliatory frankness. "I've no intention of being a nuisance, but I shan't hand the Flame over to you. I repeat, I shall come, with my own men, and hand it over to the king myself. I've sent a message saying as much to Sir Hugh des Arcis, the man to whom the king entrusted the sign of the oriflamme. As you know, Hugh's also my brother-in-law, and you won't have forgotten that it was he who sent the Flame back here when he went to rescue his wife, my sister. The king knows all this. He will wait for me."

He found himself grasped by the neck by the archbishop. "Wait? The king will wait? What mighty notions of yourselves you southerners have. What do we care for your brother-in-law? The king knows all about him. We come with the authority of King Louis himself. Look!" He pulled out the royal seal.

As soon as she saw it, Laila rushed over and burst between them, breaking the archbishop's grasp. Aimery tried to kick her away but she dodged him. "The king's seal! I've never seen one of those before! Take *me* to him, sir," she cried. "I'll tell him all about the Flame." She pulled the archbishop's surcoat. He brushed her off but she persisted. "No, I'll not be silent. You listen to me. My name is Laila Hajar Mais Bilqis Shehan and my father is a man of magic and my mother the daughter of a queen. I want to come back with you. I deserve at least to meet the king. It's my right."

"You deserve nothing," said the earl, raising his hand at her, "and you have no rights. You're a heathen."

She gave a small, lizardlike shimmy and her blue hair danced. "I was born in Paris," she declared.

"In the gutter." He leered.

She stood completely still and put her hand over her mouth. Then she skipped over to a sconce, plucked it out, and appeared to swallow the flame before running at the Frenchmen full tilt. She looked so odd that they backed away from her. She pursued them, her hair spiraling around her face, waiting until their backs were against the wall before shooting flames from her mouth, not blue flames, but white flames that singed the earl's beard and blistered the end of the archbishop's nose.

"My God!" they cried in unison, crossing themselves madly. "Witches and heretics! This place is an affront not just to the king but to the church."

Aimery was trying to grab hold of Laila. "There are no witches here," he retorted vehemently, "and the heretics are in the cellars awaiting the pope's inquisitors. As for this girl, why, can't you see? She's just a trickster and a French trickster at that," he added pointedly.

"And exactly how many heretics have you actually burned here, Count Aimery?" The archbishop's nose was agonizing.

Aimery refused to cower. "Is our loyalty to merciful King Louis to be measured by the number of pyres, my lords?" he asked.

Laila wriggled, stuck up her arm, and removed a frog from the archbishop's ear. He gasped. Aimery let go and at last she galloped away, flashing bare legs.

"Enough of this place!" The archbishop spun around and the earl quickly followed. At the door, the earl turned. "Count Aimery of Amouroix, you have treated the king's emissaries with deliberate contempt. I ask you once again. Give us the Flame."

"I shall take the Flame to King Louis myself," Aimery

repeated obstinately. He refused to give up his dream. Why should he? "And in the meantime," he added, still making a bid for the tiniest spark of goodwill, "he should be in no doubt as to my loyalty."

"Would that be Occitanian loyalty, the kind that changes with the wind?"

All hope of goodwill vanished. "It's the kind of loyalty that keeps people alive," Aimery said coldly. "Isn't that the only kind?"

As they mounted their horses, the earl and the archbishop conferred. Both agreed that despite all his protestations, Aimery was untrustworthy and rude. He had insulted them and thus insulted the king. He had not given up the Blue Flame and they could not return to the king without it. He would have to be punished. A messenger was sent to Hugh at Carcassonne. The archbishop and the earl rode swiftly back to their troops where, with the archbishop dangling the royal seal above his head, the earl gave his orders.

In his bed of sickness, for he could not yet stand without dizziness, Hugh received the earl's message. Grim-faced, he passed it to Yolanda. She read it. "It's not true," she said hoarsely. "The king would never sanction such a thing."

He pointed to the stamp in the wax.

Then she exploded. "You can't," she cried. "You can't do this, Hugh. For God's sake and for mine! You can't burn the Amouroix! That was the contract! That was what you promised! Oh God, Hugh! Castelneuf!"

He quieted her with difficulty and pulled himself up. "Get our swiftest messenger," he said.

The man came at once. "Send to the earl that I cannot

mount a horse and am reluctant to send men for such a task without leading them myself," he said, all the time looking at Yolanda. The messenger made to leave. "No. Wait. Get parchment and a quill." Hugh knew he must write, so the message would not be twisted. He tried to grapple with the paper. "I can't see. You write, Yolanda." She seized the quill. He tried to concentrate. "Write what I just said, that I can't go to the Amouroix but that I am the king's loyal seneschal."

She wrote. It seemed woefully inadequate. "Tell him it's against every law!" she said, her hand shaking so hard that drops of ink splattered across the page.

"He makes the law."

"Tell him he just can't, then! Remind him of his promise."

"You can't tell a king anything. You can only suggest."

"Suggest then. Oh God, Hugh." Terrible images flashed before her.

"Send Henri and Amalric to me." She ran out and dragged them in. "Now leave us."

"I want to—"

"Leave us. Go. This is wasting time."

She left. A longer letter was written and Henri, offering her a shrug that was a mixture of sympathy and triumph, left to deliver it.

Just over my borders but still thirty miles from Castelneuf, Raimon saw the first plumes of smoke. At first he thought it was chimneys catching from overstoked hearth fires. Yet the smoke kept pouring over the horizon. With increasing alarm, he spurred Galahad on, repeating to himself that there must be some mistake. After all, wasn't my safety part of Aimery's devil's bargain?

But my villages told a different story. In those singled out by the earl and archbishop for punishment, no barn, workshop, cellar, or mill was spared. And I, the Amouroix, could do nothing except bear these fires and listen to the people's cries. For two days, his rage as hot as the flames, Raimon tried to pull out villagers from under burning roofs and to rescue stored grain, without which there would be starvation this winter. But the fire-raisers did their work well. Using oil and tar, they ensured that once things were alight, even the heaviest rain couldn't quench the flames. It was a bitter irony that only now did Catholic priest and Cathar perfectus, finding no difference made between them in this holocaust, cry out together, "What have we done to deserve this?"

In the ceaseless heaving of water from rivers and wells and in the hopelessness of human chains and human tragedies, Raimon lost track of everything: time, place, even himself. As day piled on day, so fire piled on fire. But after nearly a week of racing from one ruined village to another, some familiar faces appeared on the road. At first, he refused to believe he knew them. That wild, hopping creature could not be the farrier. That fat man rolling and sweating with a bundle on his head could not be the shoemaker. That one-legged crone hobbling on a stick could not be the same Nan Roquefort who coyly told fortunes and made charms that people wore in secret. Those three crying children could not be Beatrice's sisters.

He hunched over Galahad's withers. No. Not Castelneuf. It was high up, well defended. It at least must be safe. But he changed course, filled with dread. After two hours' hard riding, he was at the river. In three, he was less than a mile away and now his fear was raw.

Just before the road twisted and Castelneuf came into view,

two loose packponies rattled around a corner and tried to push past him, their ears flat and their bundles askew. Raimon had no interest in them until he saw their blankets, then he grabbed the bridle of the nearest pony and forced it to stop. The blanket was so crumpled, he couldn't be sure. He leaned over and pulled at it and his heart began to pound. He stretched it out. Oh! At last! At last! Hope poured through his veins like brandy. It was unmistakeable, that star and crescent moon. "Count Raymond," he breathed. "Finally!" He let go of the pony. "Come on, Galahad! Come *on!*" The old horse flew.

Now Raimon rode with fierce joy. All the rumors about Raymond were false. He had seen the plight of the Amouroix and he had come to her aid. Though he had been slow and though he had been unsure, in the end he could not stand by and watch as Occitanians were systematically slaughtered. He knew all about Aimery's disloyalty but still, at Castelneuf's time of need, Raymond had brought his rebellion here and Raimon would rush to his side. "Faster, faster," he cried, as Unbent thudded rhythmically against his back.

To save time, he left the road and forced Galahad up a goatpath through the trees. The old horse never faltered, winding up the track like a plume of smoke himself, the dead leaves crackling and squelching under his iron shoes. They breasted the rise and Raimon gasped. The château stood black against a red horizon, flames licking around it as if it were a cauldron set to boil. Galahad catapulted down toward the graveyards near the river bridge and there Raimon saw Count Raymond's men gathered in force. He could make out little in the town except screaming.

It only struck him when he was almost upon them how

quiet Count Raymond's men looked, how calm, how *unconcerned*. All around, people were howling and begging for help and yet they appeared to be doing nothing. He saw one mounted soldier shake off a girl who was holding up her baby, clearly pleading with him to hold it while she went back into the town to rescue other children. High anxiety turned to horror. Indeed, even after it was obvious what was happening, he could not quite grasp it because he wouldn't believe it was true. How could it be? It was not possible. Yet there, right in front of his eyes, Raymond's men were not putting out fires, they were lighting them. He did not know when he began to yell, only that he was still doing it when he pulled Galahad to a halt.

The men at the bridge waited for him to finish yelling before one removed a straw from his mouth. "What are you so upset about, son? They're heretics. Town's full of them. They'll be no loss."

"But this is an Occitanian town! Count Raymond can't—"

The man put the straw back in his mouth. "Count Raymond can. He's on God's side, or haven't you heard? God's and the king's. He's signed a piece of paper." The man spat the straw out and replaced it with another. "We're all Frenchmen now."

Raimon sat quite still. "What did you say?"

"I said we're all Frenchmen now."

"No," Raimon began quietly, not meaning to yell again, but the words just rolled out like thunder. "No. Not me. Never. Never." He expected the man to try and seize him and was already pulling at Unbent but the man seemed uninterested although he did spit the straw out of his mouth again. "Oh, for goodness' sake. Take it easy. Do you know that the Blue Flame's up there? That's what all this is about. French soldiers have gone in to get it. Once the king's got his hands on that, well, the Occitan—" He sliced a finger over his throat.

"And don't you care?" Raimon could still not quite comprehend the full enormity.

The man shrugged. "I'm Count Raymond's man. Where he goes, I go."

"But you're an Occitanian."

"As I say, we're all Frenchmen now." He came nearer to Raimon. "Look, son, off you go before you get into trouble."

Raimon wheeled around. Abandoning Galahad, he threw himself into the river, beating his way through molten colored water. As he neared the Castelneuf riverbank, he had to fight through a scrum of people, half drowning, half setting themselves afloat on anything they could find. He scrambled out and ran upward, past the French soldiers still tossing firebrands and past the horse troughs into which people were leaping. He could barely see, barely breathe, and barely run through the piles of ash, the last remnants of everything the fire had so far swallowed and spat out. A flock of chickens tumbled out of a coop like feathery fireballs. Raimon choked. At the château gate he found a crowd. The gate was shut against the French soldiers and the people were beating their fists against it. "Let us in," they were imploring, "let us in. For pity's sake, Count Aimery. We're your people."

Raimon pushed his way back and made for the hole in the wall that he and Yolanda had often used as children. Here, here. It should be here. But Aimery's renovations had stopped it up. The château wall was, for the first time in its life, impregnable. Raimon ran back to the gate. Aimery was a devil. But somebody in the château had some humanity left. The gate was swinging open.

Raimon pushed through with the crowd and the fire, unstoppable, followed in their wake, snaking up the gateposts and sending gossamer embers to catch at the straw stacked in the courtyard. Above the stables, the pigeons had abandoned the new loft and were circling higher. They would have made easy prey for hawks except that no hawk dared come near. The enemy soldiers hung back. The château looked like a deathtrap.

Aimery was in the great hall, pulling his beard and shouting. Laila was tying Ugly to her with a leather thong so that they would not be separated. Everybody else was running this way and that, screaming as the fire roared at the windows, gorging itself on a surfeit of fuel. The tapestry hangings were already shivering in anticipation of their fate. Raimon ran to Aimery. "Parsifal and Cador?" Aimery didn't answer. Raimon caught Laila by her hair.

"Ouch! They're in the chamber where you left them. Parsifal's very sick. Cador won't leave him."

"And the Flame?" He tugged. "The Flame, Laila."

"In the chapel. Simon Crampcross is supposed to be guarding it but he fled hours ago. Gui and Guerau are with it now."

Raimon let go and then found his own hair seized. "Count Aimery's been keeping the White Wolf in a cage in the small hall," Laila told him. Raimon's lips tightened. "Your father and sister are in there too."

"Oh God in heaven. I thought they would have starved by now."

"No. The perfectus gave them permission to eat bread. I think he thought they might give in to Aimery if they got too weak, especially your father, so they've had a fistful of crumbs a day. He's a fool, that White Wolf. Adela would never give in. Not to anybody. But he ordered her to eat, so she did."

"I can't get to them. I must get to Parsifal's chamber and the chapel."

She let go of his hair. "You can't get to both. You haven't the time. Parsifal and Cador or the Flame?" She did not seem troubled by his cruel dilemma.

"Can't you—" He had her by the shoulders.

"I'm going to save the falcons," she said, and flashing her teeth, she ran off.

Aimery had vanished. Raimon guessed he had gone for the Flame and began to run after him, then faltered and made for the stairs.

Ironically, all the sconces had gone out and Raimon stumbled up in the pitch black, almost sobbing as he missed his footing and wasted precious seconds. He fell through the door and blinked.

The scene before him was one of perfect light and almost preternatural calm. Parsifal was lying in bed, his face sunken flat with the pillow. Only his feet and knees were prominent under the blankets and his hands, still their curious shade of white, were unchanged. The rest of him appeared to have vanished. Cador was standing at his side, his cheeks twitching, praying for courage. With an inarticulate cry, he flung himself at Raimon. "I knew you'd come back for us! I knew it. You'd never have let us burn."

Parsifal could hardly speak. "Raimon!"

"Sir Parsifal!"

"Just Parsifal, please."

Raimon fell to his knees. "What have they done to you?"

"They? Oh, nothing. They've looked after me very well. This sickness comes from the inside, not the outside." His hands clutched Raimon's sleeve. "But never mind that. Take the boy and get out of here. Even without the fire, I shan't last the night."

"We're not leaving without you."

Parsifal tried and failed to pull himself up. "I'm not begging you, Raimon, I'm ordering you. Don't you see? I'm truly finished and I'm happy. But the boy, this marvelous, loyal boy, he's not finished and he won't go without you. It's a miracle that you're here! A last miracle in the miracle that has been my life since I met you. But you can't save me now, not even if you were to carry me out shoulder high. Take the boy and go."

"But the Flame! I must get the Flame!"

Parsifal gave a strange smile. "The Flame will survive, of that I'm quite sure, because it's not the Flame of Death, Raimon, it's the Flame of Life."

"How can you know?"

"I trust in God. He didn't light the Flame for you to die here and be forgotten."

Cador was crying gently, not for himself, Raimon realized, but for the old man. Though he was terrified, the boy could not bear to leave him.

Parsifal caught Raimon's eye and then Raimon stood and motioned to Cador to prop Parsifal up. The old man grimaced with pain but Raimon could not mind about that now. Reverently, he drew Unbent over his head. Parsifal's eyes took a moment to understand and then his words were only a whisper. "Unbent?"

Raimon laid the heavy blade, blackened from the fires,

across those white palms, where it imprinted its form in grimy powder. Raimon spat on his finger and cleaned the engraving, but Parsifal had no need for such proof. He took hold of the hilt as best he could, to catch the last warmth of his father's grasp. "Come closer," he said to Raimon.

Raimon knelt.

Parsifal's breath was hollow and smelled of nothing. "As my father's son I gift you this sword," he said, "and with it my father's title, a title that I have carried with little distinction but which is still my right to pass on. You are now Sir Raimon de Maurand." He paused to gather the last of his strength. "But though you are like a son to me, promise that you'll never forget that you are truly the son of a weaver as I, for so many years, forgot that I was the son of a knight. A man should remember these things. They are important." His hands were stroking the sword, stroking away the dirt and the disgrace and the rusty years. "You're a knight by disposition, my dear boy, as I, at your age, was not."

There was no time for false protestations of unworthiness. They could all see the flickers at the window and hear people piling up the stairs, making for the roof. Raymond's soldiers and those of the king were long fled, leaving the Flame to its fate.

Raimon gently took Parsifal's fingers and slid them along Unbent's engraved flame. Then, when Parsifal let go, he took the sword, maneuvered it back into the baldric, and kissed the old knight's wrinkled forehead. There was a long moment between them, which Raimon had to force himself to break. "Good-bye, Sir Parsifal de Maurand," he said. "You were born a Knight of the Blue Flame and you die a Knight of the Blue

Flame. I shall carry Unbent in your name for the Flame, for the Amouroix, and for the Occitan."

The old knight sighed. "For the Flame, the Amouroix, the Occitan, and for love," he murmured. "And tell me, dear Raimon, which is the most important?"

Raimon bent close. "Love, Sir Parsifal."

Parsifal crossed his hands back over his chest and smiled.

It was a terrible moment, the final departure, but it was done and when the latch clicked Raimon hurried Cador down the stairs, the little boy sobbing and protesting until Raimon had to pin him against the wall. "Stop it, Cador! Stop it!"

"But Sir Parsifal! He's all alone."

"He's given us a chance. We've got to take it. Now you go on. Get out of the gate."

"Where are you going?"

"I'm going to the chapel. I want to get the Flame if I can."

"I'm coming with you."

"No."

"I am!"

There was no time to argue. They ran together.

The chapel was already engulfed and burning, and outside what had been the door, they met Aimery. He had the Flame and Raimon fought the impulse to kill him there and then with his bare hands. Aimery lay at the heart of this. It was his doing. He had gambled and lost and brought the whole place down with him. He deserved to die. But all he said was, "Gui and Guerau?"

"I've sent them onto the roof." Aimery didn't seem surprised that Raimon had returned. He was shifty and shaking.

Raimon was appalled. "They'll die up there."

"No," Aimery said, "there are ropes. Remember the spare stores we keep in case of siege? The roof's the best chance. Are you coming?"

Raimon shook his head. "The small hall, Aimery."

"You don't care about the White Wolf, surely?"

"My father and sister are in there too."

A spasm crossed Aimery's face. "They're heretics and anyway it's too late. I'm sure it's too late."

"Give me the keys to the cage."

"I—"

"Give me the keys! You can't just leave them."

"I'm going to the roof and I suggest you do too." He pushed past. Raimon was torn between fighting for the keys or getting to the hall. He pushed Cador upward but the little boy shook his head. "Come on then. Pull off your shirt and tie it around your head."

They descended. The château's timbers were putting up a good fight although the great hall was now roofless. Rain was beginning to fall, the drops evaporating with faint hisses. Raimon kept Cador very close as they fought their way through the debris, taking shallow breaths and dousing themselves liberally from a water barrel that mercifully had not been overturned. The small hall was smoldering and the ceiling rumbling where the flames were beginning to break out. Smoke billowed down. They could see almost nothing but they could hear coughing. "Father! Adela!"

"Raimon," his father's voice croaked back. "Is that really you?"

"You must help me. Kick the bars."

A cool voice emerged. "It's no good doing that." The White

Wolf's face appeared, very close to Raimon's. It was as cadaverous as Parsifal's. "There's no way out."

Raimon shook the cage door. "I don't care about you. I've come for my father and sister."

"Perhaps, but even if you manage to kick the door in, I don't think they'll come."

"Raimon." Sicart put his hands out through the bars. Raimon had to take them. "Don't waste your life here."

"Is Adela there?"

Sicart pulled her forward.

Starvation had rendered her hideous, parching her lips and thinning her hair until her scalp shone through. She didn't speak and Raimon could see she was frightened. Laila was wrong. Bread had not been quite enough to stiffen her resolve beyond cracking.

"Get back," Raimon urged, and he pulled out not Unbent but the rough sword in his belt. Leveling it between the bars he began to saw. He made very little progress and Cador was soon scurrying about trying to find something, anything, to help. He brought a pricket candlestick and an iron shovel but they were useless. Aimery's chair was now burning merrily and the roof cladding was falling in great clouds of powder, adding to the smoke.

Sicart was spluttering. "Save yourself! I beg in your mother's name, Raimon."

"There must be a way!" Raimon would not give up. "There must be a way."

"Here, catch." The voice was so unexpected that Raimon thought he had mistaken it. He turned and caught what was thrown.

Aimery was standing there. "Oh for God's sake, don't look at me like that," he said. "Unlock the cage!" He held the Flame's box close to his chest. The White Wolf stepped out first, but Adela seemed paralyzed. Raimon dropped his sword and stretched his arms to help her.

When he turned around, the White Wolf had both the sword and Cador. "The Flame for the boy," he said. The ceiling was well alight now. "Quick quick. The Flame for the boy."

"You can't kill. It's against everything you believe in," Raimon cried.

"God will grant me dispensation at such a moment." He twisted the sword.

"Give him the Flame," Raimon shouted. "Give it to him, Aimery."

"You don't mean it," Aimery said. "The Flame's everything to you."

"Not everything. Give him the Flame. Do you want more blood on your hands?"

Aimery held the box closer.

"You're not going to give it to King Louis," Raimon was beside himself, "and you're not going to give it to Raymond of Toulouse. Not now." A small shudder passed through Aimery. "So give it to the White Wolf," Raimon begged. He wanted to leap at the Flame, but he did not dare in case Aimery ran away again.

The perfectus held the sword closer to Cador's throat and the little boy's eyes, peering through his shirt, were black pools. *Dear God,* thought Raimon, *he's going to be executed after all.* "Give it to him!" he yelled. There was no time left. He had to get it. He lunged. Aimery remained still. With a low growl,

Raimon ripped the box away from him and in a moment had handed it over. Cador was released and the White Wolf fled as the ceiling crashed down.

Stumbling, and with Sicart carrying Adela, Aimery, Raimon, and Cador made it out into the courtyard. The rain was now falling in torrents and under the deluge, the ordinary fires at least were beginning to lose impetus. There was not a soldier to be seen. "I'm going to see if I can save my pigeons," Aimery said, and vanished. Raimon and Cador, panting, sank down by the wall. They could hear Laila urging the falcons away before she too sank down beside them, for once in silence.

In the following hours, as the town cooled, people crept back to salvage what remained of their belongings. There was little looting. Nobody had the heart. Neighbor wept with neighbor as the dead, some recognizable and some beyond recognition, were buried. The rain continued to pour. Sicart and Adela sat propped against heaps of rubble as Raimon and Cador went up the stairs, back to the chamber where Parsifal lay.

This room was undamaged by the fire, perhaps the only room to be so, but the old knight was quite dead, his face tranquil. They carried him out, through the château gate and down the hill. There was no wood for coffins and barely any cloth left for a shroud so they buried him just as he was, with his hands over his heart. It was Cador who led the prayers, his words and tears falling as quickly as the raindrops, and after a few moments, fumbling, Raimon joined in. Was God listening? Who could tell?

Afterward, Raimon returned to the château and found Aimery standing silently where the herb garden had once been. He was holding the charred remains of a bird and when he saw

Raimon, he put the remains down, as if caught holding something shameful. "My best pigeon stayed too long," he said.

Raimon gave a hollow laugh. "Safety and security," he said bitterly. "That's why you sold Yolanda to Hugh des Arcis and the Amouroix to the king. For God's sake, Aimery! How can you live when all these people are dead?"

Aimery swallowed. "Because I'm still alive," was all he could offer.

"That's a stupid answer."

"It's the only answer there is." He shook his head slowly. "I never thought it would come to this. I never thought the king"—he raised his hands helplessly at the devastation—"or Count Raymond . . . How could he? But then, Raimon, if you'd delivered the Flame to Louis as you were supposed to do—"

"Do you imagine we didn't try?"

The rain was streaming down both their faces.

Aimery kicked away the pigeon's remains. "I don't know." He seemed utterly at a loss. "What on earth do we do now?"

Raimon regarded him closely and then marched him down into the courtyard and picked up a piece of plank. "We keep going."

"Why?" Aimery shrugged. "It's all over."

Raimon dropped the plank and grasped Aimery's shoulders. "How dare you shrug! Of course it's not over. Nothing's over yet. For a start, King Louis can never be forgiven for this, nor Count Raymond, especially not Count Raymond, who's not an Occitanian anymore but a devil. And if I find out that Sir Hugh des Arcis had any part in this, any part at all, I'll murder him myself and be happy to hang for it. It's us against them, all of us against all of them, as it never was before."

"But the White Wolf has the Flame. He'll be even stronger now." Aimery was like a rag doll, all the bravado drained out of him.

Raimon stood square. He could hear Parsifal's voice, calling him Sir Raimon de Maurand. He could feel Yolanda's hands in his hair. The leather ring, forged in the Flame, was still on his finger. He touched Unbent and felt a surge. "Don't imagine I've forgotten that," he said, "but the Flame's still the Flame of the Occitan. And look about you."

Aimery did. "Castelneuf's destroyed."

"No," Raimon said, "that's not what I see. It's half destroyed but it's still standing."

Aimery looked at the ground. "Barely."

"Are you or are you not the count of Amouroix?" Raimon demanded.

"Why?" Aimery looked up with some of his old derision. "Do you want to take my place?"

"I'll take it if you give up."

Aimery roused himself. "I've always disliked you," he said.

"And I you," replied Raimon. "More than disliked. I've hated you, Aimery, and part of me still does, perhaps more than ever. But you didn't execute Parsifal or Cador." He paused. "And you came down with the key. Why did you do that? And why did you let me take the Flame from you?"

"I came down because I was too late to escape from the roof," Aimery said. "As for the Flame"—he gave a small shake of his head—"well, why should the White Wolf get to execute that boy when I didn't?"

They stood in silence as puddles formed at their feet.

At last Aimery took a deep breath and stood a little taller.

"War makes for strange bedfellows, Raimon. Look at Raymond of Toulouse and King Louis." He shuddered. "I shall never like you and, as you say, you certainly don't like me, but it seems we've ended up on the same side after all." He shivered. The wind was arctic. "I can't believe that I'd like to light a fire." He began looking about for suitable kindling.

Raimon picked up the plank he had dropped. He could have hit Aimery on the head with it there and then and been avenged of all manner of wrongs, but that would not bring Yolanda back to him, or Parsifal or the Flame. And it was strange. Though Yolanda was at Carcassonne with Hugh and Parsifal was gone forever, the sense of bleak foreboding and bitterness he had been carrying with him since the troubles had begun the previous spring was dissolving. In its place he felt something he could describe only as being like the blue the Flame had offered him at his moment of greatest despair, when everything he had ever hoped for seemed lost. Now he felt the color burn deep inside him, not with the roaring heat of a firebrand but with a steady pulsing warmth that both comforted and thrilled. It was ironic, Raimon thought, that he felt closer to the Flame having lost it than when, last June, he had first held it up as a beacon on that high, disastrous hill.

And there was something else, something quite immediate. Though Castelneuf was no longer a proud silhouette against the sky, its mess of collapsed masonry and crumpled ironwork seemed to him purer and cleaner than all Aimery's renovations. When it was rebuilt, it would find new dignity.

On impulse, he called out to Aimery. "What happens when we get the Flame back? Who will keep it?"

"Whoever deserves it," Aimery called back and gave Raimon a sideways look that could have meant anything.

Raimon walked away, out of the gate and down the hill. The rain began to ease and a cockerel suddenly emerged from a bush. Four of Aimery's pigeons flew overhead, returning home. He saw somebody driving a muddy cow into a pen. Perhaps tomorrow there would be milk.

Galahad was still standing just where he had been left on the other side of the river. The bridge had been destroyed, so Raimon stripped and swam over to get him, swimming back with the horse, and then walking him into the town and making a stable amid the wreckage of the old weaving shed.

After that, he found a farrier's toolbox and an anvil. If, as Parsifal hoped, he was to be the Flame's true champion, Unbent must be restored and refashioned. He didn't heat the forge and scrape the rust. That would have been the right thing to do but he wouldn't wait. Instead, Raimon just rolled up his sleeves, and there, as the sun set over my blighted countryside, he took the hammer and beat out the song of our future.

Author's Note

I n the author's note for *Blue Flame*, I explained briefly the history of the religious and territorial conflict between Occitania and France in which Raimon and Yolanda's story is set. However, whereas Amouroix is a fictitious county within Occitania, the Paris to which Yolanda is taken at the beginning of *White Heat* is, I hope, more or less accurately described.

We tend to think of medieval towns and cities as being ready built. In reality, of course, they were permanent building sites, so researching Paris involved less looking things up in books and more wandering about the place itself, blotting out the present to see with ancient eyes, smell with an ancient nose, and listen with ancient ears. For pictures and interesting bits of information, not necessarily medieval, about Notre Dame Cathedral, there is *The Horizon Book of Great Cathedrals*, compiled by the editors of *Horizon* magazine, published in the US in 1968 by American Heritage Publishers and in the UK in 1969 by Hamish Hamilton, London. Be warned: it is one of those books you pick up for one thing and end up, an hour later, engrossed in something entirely different. The Web site of Notre Dame Cathedral itself, www.notredamedeparis.fr, is full of useful stuff too.

For information about Saint-Denis, the abbey four miles from central Paris to which Yolanda pays a memorable visit, I am indebted to the pamphlet published by the Centre des Monuments Nationaux, picked up on a visit there myself.

A little more about Saint-Denis. Once the richest and most powerful abbey in all France, it now stands a lonely restored medieval beacon in a concrete jungle, its fame unjustly diminished. Its aura remains, however, because for over a thousand years it was the royal necropolis. Forty-six kings, thirty-two queens, sixty-three princes and princesses were buried in Saint-Denis until their tombs were destroyed during the French revolution and the royal bones scattered. In 1429, Joan of Arc hung up her armor here. The oriflamme—not a fiction of the Perfect Fire trilogy but the real banner of the French kings, whose last outing was at the battle of Agincourt in 1415—was originally the banner of this abbey. Although there are many versions of the oriflamme, I have adopted the one drawn around 1250 by the English chronicler Matthew Paris.

For the Occitanian action of *White Heat*, yet again I acknowledge my debt to Zoé Oldenbourg's book *Massacre at Montségur*, also to the book of photographs taken by Gerard Sioen and published in *Cathare: The Soul of a Land*. I bought that book on a research trip to the Ariège—on whose landscape Amouroix is loosely based—undertaken with my sister Alice. In crisp autumnal weather we flew to Carcassonne, hired a car, then traveled as we pleased, spoke when we pleased, stayed silent when we pleased. We picnicked at lunchtimes, utterly seduced by the glories of the mountains and the charms of the valleys and astounded at the ingenuity of medieval man, building amid the clouds. Memories of that trip through "Cathar country," with the Pyrenees glowing and glowering in turn, will sustain me all my life. Gerard Sioen really has captured "the soul of a land," and when I open his book, I am transported back. No wonder Raimon and Yolanda loved this place.

I finish with a quotation from the troubadour Cercamon. Written in the early twelfth century, so slightly before Raimon and Yolanda's time, it nevertheless echoed in my mind as the last words of *White Heat* spun themselves out and I moved on to *Paradise Red*, the book with which the Perfect Fire trilogy ends.

> *It's high time for me to sing*
> *I have been slumbering so long*
> *That my music wasn't heard far away anymore,*
> *But now I am waking up,*
> *And I will keep retrieving my joy*
> *Against the winter and the cold north wind.*

Cercamon, whose name means "word-searcher" in medieval Occitan, is a fitting muse for a writer of historical novels, and if the story of Raimon and Yolanda helps readers hear the singing of magical Occitania, I shall be very pleased.

Some Key Dates for the Historical Placing of *White Heat*

1002   Executions of first Cathars in France
1163   Construction of Notre Dame Cathedral, Paris, begins
1180   Papal legate preaches crusade against Cathars
1199   Richard the Lionheart killed at Chalus Chabrol

1200   Work on western facade of Notre Dame begins
1208   Papal legate murdered
1209   Towns in Languedoc (another name for Occitania)
        captured and burned
      Heretics captured and burned—as happens almost
        every year
1221   Death of Saint Dominic (founder of the Dominicans,
        from whose ranks many inquisitors were selected)
1226   King Louis IX succeeds King Louis VIII
      Death of Saint Francis of Assisi
1241   Count Raymond VII of Toulouse promises King Louis
        IX to destroy fortress of Montségur
1242   Count Raymond's rebellion
      Massacre of inquisitors at Avignonet (see *Blue Flame*)
1243   Opening of the siege of Montségur
1244   Montségur capitulates on March 14
      Massacre of Montségur on March 16
1250   Notre Dame's western towers completed
1345   Notre Dame fully completed

For a quick overview of the Cathars' activities and beliefs during the 1240s, there is a good booklet, text written in association with Michèle Aué and translated into English by Alison Hebborn and Juliette Freyche, published by MSM, a small French publisher, ISBN number 2-911515-41-2.